In 1981 Molly Keane rea[...] with the publication of G[...] (short-listed for the Booker Prize and filmed for television). She had written other novels during the twenties and thirties, and several successful plays, but under the name of M. J. Farrell because in the Irish country houses of her youth young men would not have wanted to dance with a girl known to be 'brainy'.

TIME AFTER TIME (also filmed for television) followed in 1983 and in addition almost all of M. J. Farrell's books have now been reissued in paperback by Virago under the author's real name. The opinion expressed many years ago by Compton Mackenzie that M. J. Farrell was an 'infernally good' writer has been widely and enthusiastically accepted. It would hardly have been surprising if a writer in her eighties had decided to rest on laurels such as these – but no. In spite of having to contend with illness during the time when she was writing LOVING AND GIVING, Molly Keane brought the book to its conclusion early in 1988. Her readers will see for themselves that her powers are undiminished

Also by Molly Keane in Abacus:

GOOD BEHAVIOUR
TIME AFTER TIME

MOLLY KEANE

Loving
and
Giving

ABACUS

AN ABACUS BOOK

First published in Great Britain by André Deutsch Ltd 1988
Published by Sphere Books Ltd in Abacus 1989

Printed and bound in Great Britain by
Cox & Wyman Ltd, Reading

ISBN 0 3491 0088 8

Sphere Books Ltd
A Division of
Macdonald & Co (Publishers) Ltd
66/73 Shoe Lane, London EC4P 4AB
A member of Maxwell Pergamon Publishing Corporation plc

~ Part One ~

*I*t was first love – there had been no time for earlier romance because Nicandra was only eight on April 8th, 1914. She had been christened Nicandra on the insistence of her father who, in his luckier years, had bred and trained and ridden an outstanding winner of that name. He very much objected to the inevitable contraction of Nicandra to Nico, which seemed to him common. Perpetually subdued by the rigours of behaviour, and almost unable to express himself outside the vernaculars of Hunting, Racing, Shooting, Fishing and Cricket, he had never been able to make his case against Nico: "Awful, *awful*" was the best he could do.

It was to her mother that Nicandra clung spellbound in loving (she was born to trouble) since life began. Love had found its proper expression when she became old enough to repeat little verses her governess taught her, mostly in French, or to stumble ludicrously through songs her mother sang. She almost knew her performance was good for a laugh, sometimes a kiss. She was pretty sure of the places to make her baby mistakes. Few things earned more pleasant congratulation than abstinence: "No thank you," to a second chocolate, and Maman's face lighted gently as she snapped the lid back on the choc box before Nicandra could change her mind.

Her mother's hands were very important – a distant importance for they scarcely ever touched her (old Nan still did up her buttons), or she them; but she felt a longing to

3

kiss their faintly pink thumbs – bite them perhaps, not to hurt, of course. She enjoyed the faint intoxication in the scent of violet soap or handcream when Maman pulled her gardening gloves off her warm, dry hands – the gloves were gauntlet-cuffed, the right gloves for a very small armoured knight – smaller than the suit of armour in the hall, a baby knight.

Love encapsuled every minute they spent together – not many minutes as there was a lot for Maman to do in the day, hours of grown-up stuff which ate up her time. When she was absent, the shadow of her presence was the assurance of a world of love. To earn her displeasure was to forgo all delight; through the days Nicandra devised love tokens, as much to stimulate interest towards herself as to express her deep affection.

Nicandra came every morning to her mother's room, accompanying the early morning tea. Punctually at eight o'clock Lizzie the housemaid, apron fresh and cap on head, carried the tray, large enough to hold two cups, a charming pattern of violets scattered over them, matched by a teapot, also wreathed in violets, and a plate of bread and butter, slices cut as thin as veils, up three flights of stairs. She knocked quietly, as good discreet housemaids do, on Maman's door.

Nicandra waited breathless for "Come in" to sound, before running to Maman's bed for the first kiss of the day. Her father would groan sleepily as she hurried her kiss to him through the smell of cigars on his night's breath. His morning kiss was always rather a trial. Apart from the smell, there was his gritty chin and his sweeping moustache to repel affection. Neither could she approve his striped pyjamas, coarse and unpleasing in contrast to Maman's ribboned cambric nightdress.

After kisses, Prayers: God bless Nicandra and kind Maman and Dada, and Aunt Tossie and all of us. . . . As she prayed, Nicandra squinted through her fingers to watch the

4

exquisite bread and butter swallowed and followed by gentle sips of tea on her mother's part and grosser gulps from her father's side of the bed.

There was a silver hand-candlestick on each side of the big bed. Among the stacks of pillows there was not one without its goffered frill. Nicandra tried to think of something pleasing to say: "Maman, do you think the Little Lord Jesus heard me?" she came out with at last. "Of course he did darling." "He's always on the look-out, watching the corner of some covert," her father sounded a bit impatient. "Oh give her a lump of sugar," he said; she might have been one of his least favourite horses. "It's so bad for her teeth," Maman wailed. Much as she disliked her pony, Nicandra was undefeatable in her wish to please: "I'll keep it for Ducky," she promised. She dragged her way slowly towards the door, waiting for Maman to call her back. Before she had quite shut the door she heard Maman give a tiny laugh, and her voice say "Oh darling, *no*, not now. . . ." She trotted off, content that Dada too had been deprived of something or other.

$$\sim\!/\!\sim$$

Good morning with Aunt Tossie was a more comfortable, if a more pedestrian affair. Before knocking on her door Nicandra had quite a way to go. Turning her back on Maman's room, and Dada's dressing room, she crossed the pavilion-like hallway – useful only to light the double staircase through its long floor-to-ceiling window. Passing the proper guest room and its dressing room (where Aunt Tossie did not sleep) Nicandra went halfway down her favourite side of the stair flights to the landing space from which both stairs ascended and descended like swooping birds. Here a door opened into the older and more modest side of the house, the side where, in stages of inferiority, less important guests, children and, in a still more distant wing, servants slept. There was only one bathroom in the wing, the bath in it a classic example of early plumbing furniture. It was made – built rather, for its size was mammoth – of some kind of fortified china, cold as iced marble. Its great plug was lifted up or dropped down through a tubular cage of brass, and its brass taps gaped wide as the mouths of sea lions. On either side of the taps, two shells, nearly the size of soup plates, were sunk – the largest cake of brown Windsor soap seemed a wafer in their generous spaces. The bath was widely rimmed by mahogany, its noble proportions rightly left naked, to descend with dignity into brass claw feet of a proper size. The hand basin, blue and white china, patterned in a Venetian design, was surrounded by, and supported on, legs of wrought iron with a motif of lilies.

Nicandra thought it might be a good idea to go to the lavatory, next door to the bathroom, rather an adventure as this lavatory was sacred to Dada. There, sitting on comforting mahogany, she ate both the sugar lumps. On a plate beside the water plug (a hand-lifted device) Bromo paper was arranged in a semi-circular pattern, kept in place by a white stone. Lizzie liked perfecting this pretty piece of domestic felicity. "There's always time to make things nice," she would say with precise pleasure in her voice. When Nicandra had refastened all three buttons on the placket back of her white drawers, she felt ready to pay her morning visit to Aunt Tossie.

Aunt Tossie, Mrs Florence Fox-Collier, was Maman's (Lady Forester's) elder and widowed sister – widowed for two years but still wearing full mourning regalia. She knew it became her. She enjoyed nearly everything, even widow's weeds . . . perhaps most of all widow's weeds, as her married life had not been as exciting as she might have wished, and besides, they were so graceful and pretty. She ironed their tiny strips of white embroidered cuffs and collars herself,

6

and sewed them on fresh nearly every day. Now she could fabricate for herself rich and happy memories. She liked to do that. She now lived permanently at Deer Forest, family home of the Forester family, fulfilling many useful functions in the household; nothing came amiss to her. Oddly enough, for one in pseudo-authority, all servants loved her and she liked them and made allowances for their faults and failings. She enjoyed dispensing their weekly portions from the store room on Monday mornings: a quarter-pound of tea for each – that made one and a half pounds and quite enough too; half a pound of butter; one pound of sugar for each and a small tin of Epps cocoa between them all.

Her duties were many, and none of them seemed onerous to her. She kept her eye on things generally, such as: tactfully suggesting to an under-housemaid (caught out bypassing Lizzie's careful instructions) that pos were meant to be scrubbed till their inner china gleamed, as well as being emptied every morning. She knew the long list of silver almost by heart and counted it monthly that nothing might go astray. No dishonesty was suspected, only carelessness. Brass rods, tethering the red carpet to the flights of the staircase, were importances she never saw neglected. She loved their pale shining; clean brass was a pleasure, its proper maintenance a pleasure to herself as well as to Lizzie.

Another pleasure was "doing the flowers", their arrangement in the drawing room, in the morning room, on the dining room table. She absorbed praise with delight and laughed off criticism with good humour. She had a plot of ground in the kitchen garden where no ignorant person could tamper with her treasures. As well as that, she had a private, unheated, frame for her cuttings. What more could she want? The constant diligence she gave was given ungrudgingly. She never questioned or regretted her position. She was part of the family.

She had, of course, her private life to maintain. Some part of her energy was spent inventing her own luxuries –

luxuries that preserved a precious self-importance such as: the photograph of herself wearing a train and with presentation feathers in her hair, and the one of Hubert Fox-Collier in full dress uniform, with decorations. She had fits of putting things back in their exactly proper places, thus leading to the postponed satisfaction of finding them again, laying a hand on them without thought. At those times night-dresses were folded and piled, sachets between each; camisoles threaded anew with narrow ribbon after washing – all glimmered secretly in a deep drawer. Gloves were important – always made of chamois leather, white with black stitching, or faintly primrose coloured, soft as kid from careful washing. They were soaped and stretched on hands and ivory glove-stretchers while drying. Shoes were kept on wooden trees, never to lose their shape, or seam across with age. Shoes should be ageless. Good shoes, made by the right house, were beyond any whim of fashion – a mellowing lifetime lent them extreme quality.

Hair combings from her brush went at once into hiding – a small stoup, designed for Holy Water, concealed their rather sordid twirls – in accordance with the unspoken law that anything ugly should be put out of sight, which applied to more things than hair combings.

One of Aunt Tossie's luxuries was an early breakfast in bed – later she came down to the dining room where she ate a second. Ignoring the existence of six servants she organized this breakfast herself. There was a tiny kettle in her room. Ignorant of the fact that it was Battersea enamel she lit the wick beneath it, well soaked in methylated spirits. While she waited for the water to come to the boil she put on her boudoir cap to conceal the steel haircurlers (dragon's teeth through the night but never mind that), and her Jaeger dressing-gown (which cost the awful sum of £5), and set forth for her regular deliverance on the lavatory. This was every morning's adventure, because the idea of meeting her brother-in-law, or any gentleman, on her way to or from her goal was an excruciating though exciting embarrassment to be avoided at any cost.

Back in bed, breakfast tray on her knees, slowly and attentively she poured out a cup of tea, the cuffs of her nightdress drooping over her hands. With a gesture almost roguish, as if she slapped a hand away, she tossed the frills back before lifting the lid off the biscuit box (velvet-covered and braided) that stood on her bedside table, to choose from its varied collection the biscuits most suitable for breakfast – two crackers and two water biscuits. She enjoyed the discipline of eating them without butter – the idea of keeping pats of butter overnight in a bedroom was abhorrent to her, incompatible with her picture of herself, swansdown on her bedjacket, broderie anglaise at her wrists, nibbling away in a leisured manner, her widow's weeds for the moment forgotten.

On this and every morning Aunt Tossie greeted Nicandra most agreeably. "How's my little lamb today? Done anything naughty yet?" She gobbled and gabbled in the mornings – that was to do with her teeth, not very pretty either. But her warm pleasure in Nicandra's arrival was evident. She was drinking her tea, making a comfortable watery chirrup as her long upper lip drew the tea into her mouth. Her nightdress was nothing like as pretty as Maman's, no lace, only broderie anglaise the same as edged Nicandra's drawers ("knickers" was a common word, not to be used. For the same reason, if you had a pain it was in "your little inside", not in your stomach – and there were no words beyond "down there" to describe any itch or ailment in the lower parts of your body).

Nicandra felt flattered and amused at the joke about being naughty, but did not comment on it.

"I'm very well, Aunt Tossie, how are you?"

"Only so-so. Never mind. Could be worse. Be a love and take the cover off Gigi. Open up. Let her out. She's longing for a chat. Aren't you? Bless you. Dear one. Yes."

The parrot crawled, more an animal than a bird, out of her cage and, helped along by her powerful beak, climbed the various terraces of Aunt Tossie's bed until she reached her pillow where she crept along by shoulder to neck. There they made love together. "How's my darling? Slept well? Warm enough? Quite sure? You *are* a happy bird. Aren't you a happy bird? Promise?" Each enquiry was answered by a smothered croak of love.

"You do think she loves me, don't you?" Aunt Tossie asked anxiously.

"Yes, Aunt Tossie, of course." Nicandra's answer was inattentive. During the parrot's walkabout her eyes had been focused on the chocolate biscuit in silver paper protruding slightly from under Aunt Tossie's third and last pillow. "Oh I see – the chocky bic. Do have it. Please. You know how I need a bit of comfort in the night. And bring me my mouth-organ, if you would. Over there – on the dressing-table."

Aunt Tossie's dressing-table was a picture of proper arrangement, quite unlike her tumbled bed, or the pink satin corset playing fast and loose with the long slit drawers thrown together on a tapestry chair – a chair covered in great beaded roses, laughing at the fun, over one arm black lace stockings trailed negligent as if there was no tomorrow. In marked contrast, on the white embroidered cloth of the dressing-table lay an ivory family: a hair brush, a hand mirror, two clothes brushes, one soft, one hard. In the centre of each was a monogram in gold, the lettering shaped like a small shy coronet. The mouth-organ, big and bright, seemed rather out of place in this quiet company. Somehow it was more in keeping with all the rather dirty diamond rings, hooked on to and falling around a ring stand in pink china, matched by its china tray, candlesticks, and small boxes for goodness knew what trivial uses.

Nicandra picked a ring from the china tree, a dark blue stone surrounded by diamonds. The setting that clawed them was as dirty as old teeth. "Oo, Aunt Tossie," Nicandra felt very adult pointing out the dirt with disgust and pleasure. "Yes my darling, aren't they filthy? They'll be yours some day unless Mummie hurries up with a little brother. Come along with my organ – Gigi loves a tune."

While she ate her chocolate biscuit Nicandra shared Gigi's enjoyment of the familiar air: Yip-I-Addy-I-Ay, I-Ay, Yip-I-Addy, I-Ay. . . . Aunt Tossie just failed to reach her top note on her mouth-organ. She put it down and sang . . .

> *"I don't care what becomes of me,*
> *So long as they sing me that sweet melody,*
> *Yip-I-Addy, I-Ay, I-Ay,*
> *Yip-I-Addy, I-Ay, I-Ay."*

The parrot joined in with a screech of pleasure. "Hear that? Clever girl, aren't you? Isn't she?" – "Yes isn't she, Aunt Tossie," Nicandra agreed. She was never enthusiastic about successful performances other than her own. She wandered back to the dressing-table and stood fiddling and picking over every little object on it. A diamond ring on almost every finger, she approached Aunt Tossie again. "They are dirty aren't they? Not like Maman's, are they?" "Much better actually – I must put them away in my jewel case, mustn't I?"

Aunt Tossie paused – in the pause she saw the fat unfriendly child she loved, only approachable when disconsolate. Once more her eyes consumed the beauty of that sad face – she saw its fruit-like quality (Aunt Tossie loved nectarines) but it was an unripe fruit she saw, greenish in its pallor. The blonde hair, blonde as barley, streaked its growth into points and levels of untidiness –

no coquetry: no curls. And no touch of tease or laughter in the long grey eyes, eyes set so far apart that they belonged more to the temples than to the full face. Under the dark blue pleated skirt and the white drawers, brown woollen stockings were anchored to a liberty bodice; under the bodice and the Jaeger combinations, long-sleeved, Aunt Tossie could see the hairless breastless body of a child. The thought of it filled her with an immense regret because a child could not stay a child – there would be men (*a* man she hoped) in Nicandra's life, Aunt Tossie thought with pity and some disgust – her mind scampered hurriedly from the contemplation of a subject not forbidden so much as not existing for her. She spoke again, unaware of the change in her mind: ". . . And you'll help me clean up my jewellery, won't you? I don't quite trust anyone with that job, and they must go back into their box. Run along to the kitchen and ask Mrs Geary if she has some bread-soda with a bit of fizz in it – we shall have fun, shan't we? Bread-soda is magical. We'll see these dirty diamonds shine."

Nicandra pounded down the second flight of the back staircase leading to the ground floor – here one imposing door marked the entrance to the hall, another was the service door into the dining room. Leaving this area of the house behind her, she ran down the passage as far as the open pantry door. Here she stopped to watch old Twomey the butler shaving himself with a cut-throat razor. It did not strike Nicandra as odd that last night's dinner dishes were still lying under the water into which flakes of soapsuds and hair were falling. She watched the rhythmic strokes of the razor for a moment, then turned her attention to Twomey's own cat which was miaowing and writhing uncomfortably in the wooden wine case which was her quiet bed.

"What's wrong with Patsy-Pudding, Twomey?" she asked. "I think she has a nasty pain in her little inside." She peered closer. "Oh, Twomey, Twomey, she has a kitten in her box."

"Out now, out, Miss Nicandra," Twomey turned on her, not surprisingly, for they were not always the best of friends. He looked very unlike his usual tidy self, his collarless shirt changed him completely, so did the ruffling lather on his chin. She knew he was hiding something from her about the cat, something nasty, that should not be spoken of, she was sure. She slunk out of his pantry backwards. She was on the edge of some nasty secret. "I won't tell on you if you don't tell on me," Twomey called after her.

What about? What about? Her mind raced round forgotten slips into wrongdoing of her own. For Twomey to have erred in any way was unthinkable.

The end of the passage brought her to the head of the kitchen stairs – the head of a mine-shaft. Here stone steps, with narrow iron rails, plunged downwards to the basement, a great world of industries and mysteries, a dark place where windows peered up the sides of a steep area. It was in this dusk, prevailing even on a summer morning, that the throes of cooking came to their birth. Agnes Geary, something between a witch and a midwife, was the cook. She was often fierce and always strange, but she was kind and big-hearted in her way.

"Bread-soda?" Mrs Geary made it sound a quite unorthodox request. "Haven't you a great cheek to go looking for bread-soda at this hour of the day? In the name of God who wants it?" She was breaking an egg into a curl of boiling, salty water – the top of the big coal range glowed under a copper saucepan. Pieces of buttered toast were arranged in a regular pattern on a silver dish – four slices awaiting their crowning with four perfect eggs.

"Aunt Tossie wants it – she wants it now."

"Don't annoy me, child. I have my breakfast to cook and today's the day of the Two Thousand Guineas, I can't keep my mind on everything at the one time."

Well as she knew Mrs Geary's concentration on the main events of the flat racing season, Nicandra persisted: "It's to clean her diamonds."

"Jesus, Mary and Joseph, pity her simplicity, she'll only turn them jewels green – tell her I said so, tell her that's what I said – and say Mr Twomey and myself have a fancy for the Aga Khan's in the 3 o'clock."

"Oh please, Mrs Geary – I'm going to help her, it would be such fun."

Mrs Geary paused, as a musician might pause for a climax, while the water in her saucepan regained its just heat. She cracked an egg, exact as a pistol shot, and watched its white fold inwards to cover the yolk preciously again. Then she looked up: "There's not a grain of soda in this kitchen. It'll be here some time all right, it's on Hanlon's list and today's their day to deliver if the old horse is able, tell her."

"Oh well, thank you. I'll tell her."

After she left the kitchen, Nicandra delayed her disappointing return to Aunt Tossie by a wander in the lower regions where the doors to other domestic businesses opened out of the kitchen passages. She could hear Breda, the under-housemaid, Lizzie's supplementary, and Peggy, Mrs Geary's slave, murmuring and giggling in the laundry – their jokes were beyond her. As well as that, the laundry was a steamy, rather smelly place where sheets were stewed in the boiler and then hand-scrubbed on a ridged board and further rinsed and processed before they progressed in a wooden tub, a girl at each handle, to hang under the sun or the rain in their private drying ground, screened by laurel and flowering currant from the sensitive eyes of the gentry.

The dark passage-ways of the basement had other doors with interests behind them. The boot-and-brushing room, where Twomey did the hunting clothes and Dada's clothes and boots and shoes; a lesser room for lamps and other people's boots and shoes. In the game larder, pheasants and duck and partridge hung by their necks in winter time, and bunches of snipe waited, pin-eyes closed, to be plucked – once Nicandra picked up a little bird, too mangled to hang in the bunch and faced him with a fellow. She walked them towards each other, their clawed feet bent stiffly inwards, on the cold slate shelf: "How did you get shot, little brother?" each asked the other in a high child's squeak of imitation. No dead birds in the larder in springtime. Possibly a salmon. Nicandra looked in. No salmon. Why not? Dada was on the river yesterday.

The dairy, when you could have it to yourself, was a far more entertaining place than the laundry, and less lonely and special than the game larder. The game larder was a man's place; it had an affiliation with the billiard room, certainly with the gun and rod room – both on the upper floor. An altogether lighter atmosphere pervaded the dairy. For a start, there was the fountain, about the height of a squat sundial, and crowned by a lily; you turned on a tap, pumped energetically on a foot pedal for a minute or two, and water gushed pleasingly from the lily's gaping mouth. The fountain was the centre-piece of the dairy, circled by a grey marble basin into which the water splashed with a mild exactitude, never exceeding the allowed space for its reception. Heavy slate slabs ran round the walls – on some pans of milk were set and left to stand until cream rose to the surface, on others there were pounds of butter, ridged by wooden "butter-hands" and stamped with swans, which sweated cold salt like beads or tears to their surfaces. A wooden churn, big as a barrel, tipped empty on its trestle. It stood, open and scoured, to breathe the air that purified it from any hint of sour milk. Eggs were stored here too. One basket was for the house; a different basket held larger eggs, chosen to be set for hatching. For winter time, when hens were cold and idle, great crocks of waterglass stood, massive, under the lower shelves to receive and preserve eggs for cooking – scrambling, perhaps, never poaching or boiling.

Nicandra looked forward to Sunday mornings when she had a soft-boiled egg for breakfast – on weekdays it was porridge and milk, take it or leave it, sometimes fried bread, the fat not always bacon. Breakfasts in the holidays, when Mademoiselle had gone back to France and Nicandra to old Nannie in the nursery, were of even poorer quality. Mrs Geary had a low opinion of Nannie – a spy and reporter when she wasn't mending the sheets and darning the stockings, and at all times a pensioner to be despised and deprived whenever possible.

Back with her bad news for Aunt Tossie, Nicandra found an empty room and a cold bed with its sheets and blankets turned over its brass footrail and Gigi sulking in her cage. Aunt Tossie must have gone to the Place, or the bathroom. In either case she would take her time. Aunt Tossie never hurried. To hurry was to dispel any feeling of luxury. She pondered kindly over all her actions.

Nicandra, on the contrary, hurried from one kind act to the next with undivided concentration and energy. Now she would feed her pigeons, the fantails whose cote was in the stableyard. Her special pigeon was a hen, one of a pair. It had been a birthday present from Anderson, the land steward from Scotland, whom she dearly loved and hoped to marry – if he was still single when she was sixteen. Anderson was not like the other men on the place. He was in authority over them and in a class above them. He dressed differently too – he wore a collar and tie while their shirts were collarless. He was tall and thick as a tree. Under the peak of a cap his green eyes shot long glances – aware of any trouble or any fun that was going. He kept

16

the cock pigeon for himself. Their shared ownership of the pigeon family and its brood gave Nicandra a happy importance, lending strength to her in her prolonged controversy with Fagan. Fagan was the gloomy little stud-groom who objected strongly to the pigeons' custom of sitting on his horses' sheeted backs, balancing and cooing, and doing other things as well.

Fagan was standing at the door of the feedhouse when Nicandra approached him, as saucily as she was able, to demand handfuls of grain for her birds.

"I have the whole damn lot of them fed."

"Oh Fagan, why?"

"To keep them off my horses' backs and their dirty droppings out of my horses' feed."

"They won't want to talk to me now."

"It's a pity about you, Miss Nicandra." Fagan turned away.

It was in vain that Nicandra cooed and called. The pigeons, puffed, sullen, full of oats and spring thoughts, kept their distance. When they needed her there was no familiarity too close for them to keep as they brushed their feathers against her cheek and went toppling along her arms to eat out of her hands – then she could feel they loved her. Today they cared only about themselves. She would insist. She would bribe them with love: "Just a handful, a small handful, Fagan," she pleaded.

"They have too much already." He was not to be persuaded. Fagan was a bleak and determined little man, tidy and forbidding as only an ex-steeplechase jockey can be. There was melancholy in all his remembrances, hardly a gleam of satisfaction, even though he had ridden a few unexpected winners in his time. He wore a neat thread of a handkerchief round his neck which somehow conveyed the idea of important days behind him, but nothing was left from those days except arthritic hips and old concussions, their reminders of sensational falls ever-present. Now that he had only hunters to school and exercise and Mrs Geary

17

(who loved the lads) to feed him well, no question about his weight, life was kind and easier; but he was the last to admit it and showed sympathy to nobody, least of all to Nicandra.

"What about my poor old Ducky," she changed her demands from the pigeons to her pony. "Just a spoonful for her. Oh, please, she's always hungry."

"If you give that little rat so much as a teaspoonful you're the one who'll know all about it when she soars into the air with buck, lep and kick. Who's going to hit the ground then? Tell me that."

Nicandra turned her back on Fagan, and on two kind deeds frustrated. The morning was growing, lengthening into a day, a long day to be filled with acts of kindness.

> "*Little acts of kindness,*
> *Little deeds of love,*
> *Make the world around us*
> *Like the Heaven above.*"

Nannie had taught her that one, and she felt it was very true. On this bright morning she was especially inspired to follow any clue leading to almost any little act of kindness or deed of love. She thought of the dark corner in the kitchen garden where discarded violets grew, pallid, but obstinately scented as strongly as their pampered descendants, grown in glassed-over frames and raised on beds of leaf-mould. Here, near the two fig trees, she would pick a little bunch, and Maman would sniff at it while she was eating her breakfast.

At one end of the stableyard the walls of the kitchen garden joined the backs of the loose boxes – an archway crowned by a belfry was built across the carriage-way leading out of the yard to the great swirl of gravel in front of the house, and onwards down the avenue. Before the archway came the garden gate – a modest green door. Close beside it steps ran up to the door of Fagan's flat, which formed a part of the hay and straw loft. There was no water in the flat, no lavatory, no bath or sink. None of these lacks had any significance for Fagan. Fagan "managed" tidily.

The garden ran uphill. On one side a stream, full of watercress, hurried down to pursue its tunnelled course through and beyond the stableyard. The half-acre of kitchen garden was as full of lilacs and wild raspberry canes, unpruned morello cherries and azaleas reverting easily to their ancestry, as it was of vegetables. Asparagus, ignoring the growth of weeds, sank its serpentine roots far down to where bones, once carrying flesh for foxhounds, now formed the foundation for the greatest asparagus beds in the county; its spears were famed for their luscious, indecent appearance, when served at Sunday luncheon parties from early May to the end of June. Peonies and the smaller varieties of shrubs grew in a long border, stuffed with other treasures and backed by apple trees, grown espalier.

Carefully grasping a fat little bunch of violets, Nicandra left the heavy dusk of the fig trees behind her and walked in sunlight along the length of the flower borders. As she went she arranged her violets: "Put their feet together, dear, and the flowers will fall into a pretty natural shape," she had been told; not so easy to achieve when neglected violets had such short legs. She did her best, and bound the stems tightly together with a thread split from a New Zealand flax – nothing must delay her now, or breakfast in the dining room would be over. But something did delay her; she stopped and stood to stare at a marvel of nature, so strange as to suspend belief. Admittedly, it was a rather small marvel, but one of such grotesque rarity as to excite the deepest interest, and to earn the highest possible commendation for its discoverer. The marvel sat, in its quiet perfection, on the scented, firmly rounded flowerhead of a white viburnum, its four upfolded wings trembling a little under the early sun: it was a *double* butterfly.

Quietly as a cat stalking a bird, Nicandra approached the heavily blossoming viburnum (first, of course, disposing of the violets; luckily there was a pocket in her pinafore); she very much doubted the possibility of picking the viburnum without disturbing its phenomenal occupant. Holding her breath, she forced her nails through the softer stem below its blossom – she held it with delight and relief at the sight of the still clinging butterfly. She covered it with her other hand, then, fearing that a hot hand might be enervating, she opened her fingers just wide enough to let in a little air and light. When she peered through her fingers it seemed to her that the butterfly was quite happy in its warm cage: not a flutter from its four wings as she proceeded carefully along the box-edged paths that led back to the green garden door. She crossed the stableyard and went into the house, hurrying down the long passage until she arrived, flushed high in expectation, at the service door to the dining room, where Maman and Dada and Aunt Tossie were eating breakfast.

Nicandra opened the door wide and stood a moment, attentive to the breakfast silence into which she was about to break. Maman sat, her back to the light, lovely as usual with the morning sun in her piled-up yellow hair. Impossible to connect such beauty as hers with the enjoyment of food. Aunt Tossie, now in the full regalia of her widow's weeds, was eating heartily but in a subdued way. Her usual chuckle, hoarse as a nesting pheasant, was silent. She lifted her enormous Spode coffee-cup with both hands. She sighed when she set it back in its saucer – and sighed again with pleasure as she bent over her poached egg. Dada, small and unapproachable in the breakfast silence, gave his absolute attention to the kedgeree that he was pushing tidily under his great moustache – little did they suspect the surprise in store for them as Nicandra advanced, speechless, down the length of the white-clothed table, solemn in her pinafore, carrying her now quivering treasure. She herself was taut and quivering too – awaiting the cries of amazement, curiosity and wonder that she was about to release. The big moment came: she opened her hand and laid down the burdened flower by Maman's plate. "Look! Look what I found for you!" Maman looked, but did not speak. Dada and Aunt Tossie looked, and were silent too – quite naturally, they were all too stunned to utter a word. Nicandra waited. At last: "A freak, I suppose," Maman spoke without interest, but somehow conveying distaste – she put down her coffee-cup and looked across the table. Complying with her appeal, Dada abandoned his kedgeree and, sucking his moustache inwards – always with him a sign of annoyance – he picked up the viburnum, still with its precious burden, opened the bottom sash of a long window, and flung out the double butterfly as viciously as if it had been a slug in the salad. When he sat down again to finish his kedgeree Aunt Tossie gave him quite a funny look, and burst out laughing.

"Shut up, you prurient old thing," he said shovelling in his kedgeree – salmon kedgeree, Nicandra noticed. There followed a silence that Nicandra could neither interrupt nor question – they were the Grown-Ups. Somehow she had erred in deed or manners. Maman spoke at last: "Have you fed your bantams yet? Take them this nice scone – and hurry, dear," she added as Nicandra lingered.

Bewildered and cast down as she was, Nicandra managed a few skipping steps – this jolly movement her evidence that she was not in a state of unattractive sulks. Out through the service door again, she skipped her way along till she reached the narrow vestibule at the foot of the double stairway and from there proceeded through the entrance hall, where her skipping lapsed.

The hall was not the place for little pounding feet. It was large, cold, uninhabited – a place as set for arrivals or departures as any railway station. This relationship with steam trains was scarcely lessened by the portraits of lesser ancestry on the walls, the mahogany chairs with crested backs, the fireless marble chimney-piece, and all the shining brasses. For the family it was a place to traverse when coming in or going out: familiar, unnoticeable.

Once through the hall door, massive under its fanlight and fitted with a brass lock as big as a bible, and down the steps on to the gravel, Nicandra changed back into whatever sort of purposeful animal all the long-sustained acts of kindness and thoughts for the happiness of others had left in her. She ran, sharp and sly as any fox, round the corner of the house and on, beneath the three windows of the drawing room and two of the morning room, until she stopped, chilled in anxiety, under the open window of the dining room, through which her marvel had been cast out.

Flaccid and vacant on the gravel lay the viburnum flower; its double burden had flown. Parting the thorny pyracantha which spread an orderly growth, regular in its production of white flowers and orange berries, to this level of the window-sills, she searched, meticulously and in vain. Voices from the breakfast table came to her through the open window.

"Should we have said something?"

"You missed quite an opportunity." That was Aunt Tossie.

"Oh not at breakfast. Too nasty."

"Rather interesting I thought." That was Dada. "Obviously the bitch had turned. She can be quite tiresome at times."

"Beautiful as well." That was Aunt Tossie.

"Not even pretty."

"And never will be." That was Aunt Tossie again. "Plain beautiful; that's all."

"Oh steady on!. . . . If she was a horse I wouldn't buy her . . . not on looks . . . have to be performance."

No point in listening. Not one word about the butterfly, or her cleverness – only grown-up talk. Even to the clear hearing of childhood Dada's language was difficult – this time the word "bitch", a forbidden word, stood out like a sore thumb. Although it could not, in any way, be connected with

22

her butterfly, its force lingered, linking up with the rejection of her act of love.

∽∾

At the age of eight, through an incorporate resilience, slighted confidence restores itself. The life of a day is full of chance and sudden changes. The hours of liberty are long, full of wonder and narrow escapes, precautions, hidden devices and daring. There was the bull in the river field to be avoided, the idiot boy in the Gate Lodge to tease until his frenzies frightened her and she had to run.

Now there was her bantam hen to visit – that tame favourite who sat on her head when she walked into the drawing room, the admiration of all, whose food she sometimes nibbled at. Only yesterday Nicandra had found the nine white eggs, distanced from the ordinary into magic by the wild nest her bantam had chosen to build in a broken flowerpot beneath a Ponticum rhododendron, well away from a wire compound, the night-time enclosure of the bantam flock.

Carefully and with love the nest full of eggs and the dozy hen sitting on them had been removed from the wild to a neat little coop in civilization and safety, every convenience for the hatching mother attended to with particular care.

Cheered and keyed up in expectation of the pleasant story-book sight in prospect, her hot hand squeezing the scone in her pocket, she followed the path as it passed under the line of windows, before it skirted the domed conservatory where flowers were grown for the house: cactus, geraniums, gloxinia, palms, bird of paradise, passion-flower, maidenhair fern, all throve here in damp and forceful luxury. Best of all, her own and the gardener's favourite, calceolaria, puff-jawed, tiger-striped and spotted, flowered each year more grossly perfect.

After its dignified circling of the house and the conservatory followed by a dive into a tunnel of laburnum and lilac, the path became meaner, more secret. Taking its way along the high sad wall confining the stableyard, it crossed, by a minute stone-walled bridge (gateposts in exact relation to its height and arch were built into the walls tight as ingrowing toe-nails), the same stream that hurried down the garden hill. With lavish indiscretion the stream was at one point crossed by the baby bridge and, fifty yards further, went underground on its way to feed the sliver of still water called "The Lake".

Nicandra took the path leading away from pleasure-garden policies, through heavy laurels and on into a grove of hazels patched with sunlight. Here dear Anderson had built a retreat for her bantams – there was no man kinder or more trustworthy. The bantams were waiting for her to let them out of their safe house. They were in her power and at her discretion in all ways – how she loved them. She could deny them nothing – they sometimes died from overfeeding. Today they scattered out, bright as Mandarins, then came running back to her, importunate for food.

She turned from them: "Just a minute, chicks," her voice was warmly imperative, its tone taken from Aunt Tossie at the store room door, before, after a suitable delay, she dealt out a rock of coffee sugar to a waiting child. Using the same pace and gestures, and wearing something of Aunt Tossie's expression, she scattered measured handfuls of grain before bringing a special handful, with all her warm and kindly thoughts, to the mother bird in her secluded nesting-place, so comfortable, so well-arranged. DO NOT DISTURB was in her attitude as she squatted down in front of the coop and bent to peer in, navy-blue skirt rising above white cotton knickers .... She fell forwards in dismay – no bird sat there, hot feathered breast spread low over her clutch. The deserted nest, neat as a pin, had a forlorn accusing air. The small eggs, when she held them, one by one, in her hand

and against her cheek were as chill as glass. A deep sense of another's ingratitude invaded her – she found this foolish light-minded bird quite detestable in her desertion, in her stupidity and folly, in her lack of recognition of the comfort and safety arranged for her own good, contrived and given with heartfelt care and love.

Tears running down her face, she put the eggs back in their nest – a false picture of natural felicity. They could never hatch now – or, could they? Anderson would know. Perhaps, if there was a common broody hen in the yard, she might be a steady foster-mother. There would be no wild charm in the situation – with her own thought and skill to tame the dangers – but a possible way out of the present disaster. Anderson, kind and dear, would have an answer. Her eggs might still be hatched.

On her way to the consultation she hesitated and turned off the path into the hazel thicket where yesterday the treasure had quietly nested. Sitting on stones under the same rhododendron a small bird spread her wings and dozed. "You fool, you fool!" Nicandra screamed at her, while some mortal sympathy forbade her to hunt the bird from her barren nest. Renewed tears flowing, dirty hands in dirty pockets, she ran from that terrible, disloyal little hen – ran as fast as she could to find Anderson, with his promise of comfort and sound advice.

Back down the changing pathway, hazel to laurel, laurel to laburnum, laburnum to high walls, then the bright conservatory and all the long windows of the house; past the terraces falling leisurely on her right hand, then along the back avenue she was still running and crying. The back avenue was a secondary way from the house, only as wide as a street, it ran between a shrubbery and a park-like field until it reached the farmyard wall. The wall's length was broken by a green wooden doorway, for the house to use, beyond which, gates admitted carts and horses, cattle, sheep and such stuff from the fields. Nicandra had to jump her

25

best to reach the latch on the friendly green door. When it lifted, the door, with her weight against it, swung wide open . . . .

Anderson, half turned from her, was standing across the way. On the ground a sheep lay, its four feet tied together, its head flat on the stones, held down between Anderson's boots – its white, frightened eyes were turning upwards – Anderson stood above it. His raised hands were somehow triumphant. He was edging a knife on a scythe-stone. His green eyes gleamed with pleasure as they started towards her. He didn't have to tell her to go, she ran away so fast.

She knew she would never be able to love or trust again – she would always remember the wild pleasure in Anderson's bright, expectant eyes. What she had seen was indecent and terrifying, and she could tell her fear to nobody. It was a secret as dark as that couplet (written in pencil on the back page of "First Lessons in English Grammar") read over and over and never to be spoken aloud: "Pee-Po-Bum-Shit-Piddle-Bugger-Damn . . . . " Keep out of the farmyard was all the grown-ups would say if she told, it's not the place for little girls. . . . They needn't say that again. The placid green door was the way into Bluebeard's cupboard.

∾∾

She was enclosed in a darkness where ignorance had no answers and she had no questions ready to ask – wandering back up the empty driveway, kicking a loose stone for company, on this bright and gloomy morning. She included in her discontent each miscarriage of her own generosity, but nothing was so bad as what she had seen in the farmyard. It was not so much the death of a sheep that had shocked her. It was Anderson's wild pleasure in what

26

he had to do. She was alone with her shaken heart and her rejected gifts.

Then, as light follows darkness, she saw Maman coming down the drive. She wore her lilac coat and skirt, braided with deeper lilac; the skirt widened at the hem and floated out over thin boots, the tidy laces criss-crossing on shadowy ankles – there was something playful in Maman's way of walking, something jaunty that swayed her hips, and made her straw hat tilt up on her frizzed curls . . . . From the shrubbery side of the avenue fresh wet heads of lilac bowed over her, heavy in their prime flowering. She lifted her arm to catch at a branch and, as she held it down, rainwater fell on her face – her eyes were shut; it was as if she was drinking the scent of lilac.

Nicandra ran towards all that beauty – although she could not tell her trouble nor make any mention of the displeasing butterfly, she could be close in the adored distance.

"Where are you going? Can I come too?"

"Oh, darling, perhaps not just now," Maman parted a sticky strand of Nicandra's green-blonde hair and looked at it sadly for a moment. "Maman has to talk to Anderson – a boring old business talk – no fun for little girls."

"Don't go now – wait – don't go yet," Nicandra took a handful of lilac skirt and pulled it backwards. She could not find words to convey what she had seen, any more than she could say aloud "Pee-Po . . ." and the rest.

Maman retrieved her skirt sharply: "*Please*, Nicandra, don't be tiresome. Run along to your banties – go and play." She took her by the shoulders and turned her round to face the house. She gave her a tiny push. "Off you go! Keep running," she laughed. "I'm watching you," she promised.

But when Nicandra looked over her shoulder Maman was not watching her. She was running, running towards the green door. Something white flew out of her swirling skirt as she ran, fluttered its way, unnoticed, to the ground. A handkerchief? An envelope? It didn't really matter much – it was an opportunity to seize on, to keep and cultivate for its potential usefulness: what a useful child ... thank you, darling .... It was an envelope.

Next: here comes Dada, neat little Dada, small as a doll on one of his big horses, coming nearer down the drive, stopping his horse gently, quietly turning in his saddle towards her, easy and rather grand, as he never looked on his feet. As usual, he had nothing much to say, but he was always agreeable.

"What are you doing?" he asked.

"Playing," she answered sadly, fiddling with the envelope in her hand.

"Posting letters?" he laughed.

"No. Maman lost it – oh go and get her Dada, she's in the yard and Anderson – I don't know what Anderson's going to *do* to her."

She was crying and jumping up and down. The young horse took a horrified plunge away from the crazy little object. Dada swore at him as he pulled the bit through his teeth before he could get his head up. He bent towards Nicandra. "Give me the letter." His words were rough as when he swore at his horse. Nicandra shrank away – she was not at all courageous about horses, especially when they were fidgeting threateningly and blowing out through their noses at the same time. "I'll keep it safe, Dada."

"You heard what I said." He got off his horse and took the letter gently out of her hand. She knew he despised her. Not a word as he put his foot back in the stirrup iron (only stable boys and jockeys jump up from the ground) a hand across the saddle-tree, and he was up, quick and certain as a fly landing. She watched him ride on, past the lilacs, past the green door and on towards the main gate to the farmyard.

She was more than dispirited now, grudging the loss of that letter. No stamp on it. No address, so Maman would have been delighted to recover it – all thanks to her observant little girl. There would have been a grateful kiss, kisses, perhaps. Now the cumulative effects of her morning's efforts turned sour on Nicandra. Disappointment surged through her. She had done everything to please her loved ones: violets laboriously gathered – she squeezed their overheated remains in her pocket: the double butterfly, so unkindly rejected and expelled; the pigeons, sated and uncaring before her own hands could minister to their hunger and earn their cooing gratitude. No gratitude came from feathered friends. Shock and disapppointment joined in the recollection of a nest of cold deserted eggs. Surely such a sensible little bird, a bantam so civilized as to sit gently and happily on the head of a human child, should have known that her removal from an ill-chosen resting place, in the wilds of hazel and rhododendron, was for her own good and safety? She ought to have known. She should have accepted a comfortable change for the better. At the same time, a nasty backward glance, a creeping suspicion suggested a consultation with Anderson might have been a wise idea before taking the practical action that had ended in such discouraging disaster. . . . But now the very thought of Anderson was abhorrent. She had seen what she had seen – she would always see it, and could never tell it.

What now? She knew a miserable distaste for the day that loomed ahead. Nicandra could not name Depression, but she had a cure for it: teasing Silly-Willie at the West Gate Lodge. Any social contact with Silly-Willie was strictly forbidden. He was six years old, but had no more sense than a child of three. He was her perfect victim. The West Gate Lodge was quite a distance from the farm avenue, where now Nicandra stood maturing a change of direction in her assaults on love and popularity. Now she was going to be nasty. The idea warmed her through and through.

Mrs Kelleher, Willie's mother, was keeper of the gate and lived in its lodge – so far as Nicandra knew Silly-Willie had no father. But that was neither here nor there. He had a mother and she had been, since an early age, housemaid in Nicandra's house. Since Silly-Willie's birth she had lived far away at the grand end of the West Avenue, in the Gate Lodge, which she kept as spruce as any bedroom in the Big House. Few people went in or out to gossip with her. She was on call to open and shut the gates at any hour, in any weather. She raked and kept the gravel sweep as meticulously as she kept her house – a convenient house, its well of water only a field distant. It was a pretty house too; being built beside beautiful entrance gates, gates hinged to cut stone posts, dignified as pillars in a temple, gate lodges were designed with appropriate distinction.

The West Gate Lodge was one-storeyed, as was usual. It had deep eaves and little stone eyebrows above each lead-paned window. An architrave, of the exact proportion to become this perfect dolls' house, was over the door. The door was permitted to be of the cottage order, double, the bottom half, lower than that of a stable door, was designed to keep children in and chickens out – not that chickens were approved, their appearance was not conducive to the small dignity of the Gate Lodge. Children, too, were rather expected to play, and to play quietly, behind the house – no balls or tin trumpets were ever to be left on the gravel sweep.

Silly-Willie spent most of his days shut in a back room. Well as she cared for him, he was quite an embarrassment to his mother, and the less he was evident in her life the better. Nicandra knew her way through the tiny, bright garden to the leaded window of that back room. There were bars across it, behind which Silly-Willie whiled away the time. In the late evenings his mother would take him by the hand for walks, and would play the concertina to him when they got home. But the walks were never long enough to please him. Mrs Kelleher had her duty to the Entrance Gates to put before the exercise or the amusements of poor little Willie, as she called him kindly in her thoughts.

This morning she was on the farther side of the gates raking the gravel into a pattern exact as a piece of embroidery, when Nicandra came tittupping along, her hat hanging by its elastic on the back of her head. She was in a rakish mood now, looking forward to her games with Silly-Willie – games that she knew Mrs Kelleher discouraged as too exciting. This morning, inattentive to everything except the rhythmic ruffle of her rake in the fine gravel, and to the notes of the song she was la-la-ing quietly to herself as she worked, she did not notice Nicandra's arrival, nor see her as she slipped round the corner of the house and pushed her way through the low branches of the Portugal laurels that screened Silly-Willie's window from inquisitive visitors.

Nicandra knocked and tapped against the bars for quite a minute before Silly-Willie's white face, like an oversized moon, filled the small window. Nicandra jumped up and down in front of him, appearing from and disappearing into, the laurel leaves. Each time she appeared she made a different face – sometimes a monkey face, sometimes a crying baby. Now and then she put out her tongue. "Pee-Po-Bum-Shit-Piddle-Bugger-Damn," she yelled. Soon Silly-Willie was yelling too. "Shit-shit-shit," he cried, and jumped up and down in unison with Nicandra's unrestrained antics. The nastier the faces she made, the dirtier the words she chose, the happier she grew.

Long before the fun was over Mrs Kelleher heard the noise. Poor little Willie was fairly screaming the place down and banging on the barred window that separated him so carefully from the world. She laid down her rake and ran in to administer a good belt of a stick to whoever might be making little of her darling.

31

The affair took on quite a different aspect when Mrs Kelleher saw that it was only Miss Nicandra having a bit of fun for herself – nothing but smiles now and urgent invitations to a cup of tea. Tea was very bad for children, Nicandra knew, but in her exhilarated state she accepted it happily, and hoped for a slice of soda-bread to go with it.

". . . And *another* little slice," Mrs Kelleher offered ten minutes later as they sat, Silly-Willie sprawled like a baby on his mother's lap, and Nicandra, remote and sedate, quite Miss-of-the-Manor now, sitting on a stool under a picture of the Pope. "Please play a tune on your concertina for me, Mrs Kelleher," she invited, the ascendancy in her giving kind encouragement to the Peasant.

Mrs Kelleher put poor little Willie off her lap and took her instrument down from its high shelf (roses and blonde ladies were intertwined on its end-boards), spread her knees apart as though to nestle Willie again, then, stretching out the pleats of her concertina, sent it screeching into a wild tune for dancing. Silly-Willie danced to his mother's playing, his feet flashing and tapping and glancing, his ugly body quiet and still above them as a little gravestone.

Nicandra watched, moved, almost frightened, as the music entered her. Then she got up, took off her hat and danced too, her dancing awkward as a buffoon's compared to Silly-Willie's complicated steps. His silly face, so meaningless and without awareness of danger, seemed translated into sense through his return to music, and his entire concentration on the rhythms of the jig – Nicandra felt exhausted and exasperated by the realization that it was not in her power to be either kind or cruel to Silly-Willie. Fool that he was, he escaped her – his dancing was so much superior to her own that she could not even praise it. She only wanted him to go on dancing till he dropped.

Mrs Kelleher looked up to the yellow face of the kitchen clock. She knew the timetable of the Big House.

"Lunch time, Miss Nicandra," she said, shutting her still breathing concertina decisively. "Say 'Goodbye' nicely to Miss Nicandra and thank her for coming to pay you a little visit."

Silly-Willie mouthed some sort of goodbye. Nicandra responded in a stately manner, at variance with the wild exuberance of the dance, the rude faces, and the exchanges of dirty talk: "Very nice, little boy," she intoned, "very good indeed. You'll be a great dancer some day if you practise." She was back in the proper life. Magic had fallen from the air.

Running back down the avenue, daffodil leaves yellowing on its verges, young beech leaves playing with the light overhead, Nicandra felt purged of the morning's unfortunate happenings: of all of them except the thrust of horror that had pierced her before the death of a lamb. She thought now that it must have been a lamb, because of Sunday luncheon. No doubt that was why Maman had insisted so rashly on seeing Anderson. Nicandra dreaded ever having to see him again – this embarrassment and fear engrossed her more fully than her love had ever done.

When the dark blue sidecar, a red coat-of-arms on its tailboard and a grey horse between its shafts, came swirling towards her, iron-tyred wheels crunching merrily along, with the noble sound of a horse's well-shod feet, the very last person she expected to see was Anderson. But there he was, sitting in a dégagé manner on the left-hand seat of the sidecar, which Fagan was driving. Anderson was wearing his Sunday suit; not dark blue serge, like the other men, but grey, with a black over-check – a dash of a white line through it – a narrow tie, dark and clearly spotted, and a hard black hat, cheekily tilted.

Whatever the occasion, Fagan had not dressed up for it. He wore breeches – the same in which he mucked out his horses – stockings and short laced boots, a neat covert coat and, like Anderson, a hard black hat. He drove from the side of the car, not from the box seat, where he sat when he drove the family. Seeing Nicandra flinching on the cut grass verge of the avenue, he took the long, supple driving whip out of its case and flicked his horse into a more dashing trot. Apart from that gesture of hastening away, neither man took the smallest notice of her. Before the side-car receded from her along the straight avenue, she observed a gun case (sometimes Anderson shot the bogs with Dada), a rod case, and a bulging Gladstone bag tied together in the space (called the well) situated between the opposite wings of the sidecar.

At half-past one she was sitting beside Maman at the dining room table: Maman who spoke not a word, who ate nothing – Twomey looked quite concerned as she waved away his offerings. Nicandra was pleased with her own plateful of roast chicken, helped by Twomey at the side table – pleased with everything except the spinach. Twomey knew she hated spinach; there had been previous arguments about its consumption, so why had an extra-large portion, fainting into the mashed potato and infiltrating the bread sauce, been dealt to her? Simply Twomey's injurious spite. She ate a little of it, smothered in bread sauce and leavened by chicken, and through both its heavy bitterness persisted. The brown-green mountain on her plate loured at her. She flattened it out with her fork, and hoped for mercy: the mercy of no notice taken.

Dada and Aunt Tossie talked to each other with scarcely a pause, showing a concern for Maman's silence as though to be silent was to be sick. The form for the Two Thousand Guineas kept them going. Dada contradicted everything Aunt Tossie said, so they stayed at Newmarket until Twomey brought in the pudding. When he took Nicandra's plate away he held it for Maman to see, hoping perhaps that a little annoyance might irritate her back to liveliness. He was right. She spoke for the first time since luncheon began: "Darling, your spinach, *please*." She said "please" in a way that made it a special request of her own.

Moved by love, Nicandra tried. The spinach was in her mouth when a terrible sound came from her throat – the gaping croak of nausea. She rolled the liquefying spinach into her cheek – she could not spit it out. She could not swallow it.

Dada and Aunt Tossie stopped their talk about racing. They sat in embarrassed silence. Talk ought to go on, even if murder went on at the same time; at the sideboard Twomey turned his back before he smiled.

Maman spoke again: "Just for Maman." She offered a small forkful as coaxingly as to a baby. Nicandra burst into tears and, as she opened her mouth for a bellow, the stored spinach and saliva shot out, into her plate, on to the tablecloth, a horrid defilement. Maman put down the loaded fork with a sigh and turned to Twomey at the sideboard: "Please give Miss Nicandra a clean plate and help her to some spinach." Her voice was gentle and emphatic, as if nothing had happened.

Twomey took away one plate and laid the next, in the centre of which a neat pile of spinach kept its cool shape immaculate. He slipped a clean fork quietly on Nicandra's right hand and moved back to the sideboard, the rhubarb fool and the junket, in his perfect colourless way.

"Now, Poppet, no more nonsense." Maman's voice changed from a coaxing note to one of authority.

Aunt Tossie put her elbows on the table in a rude way and, with her chin in her hands, stared at Maman through the epergne of silver and little vases that came between them. "Please, why?" was all she said.

"Because spinach happens to be good for her – and because I say so."

35

"Steady up, Violet, steady yourself, old girl." Dada bit heavily into his moustache as he filled a glass with wine and pushed it gently towards her. He might have been giving an apple to a horse. "Can't you see she's stopped with you – poor little brute."

"Would you mind," Maman shoved the glass of wine away. "I don't want it," she said. It could have been spinach she was refusing. The glass rocked and wavered for an instant before it fell and a dark pool of wine spread over the tablecloth between them.

Tears rolling along her cheeks, Nicandra felt that Maman was now far more angry with Dada and Aunt Tossie than with her. If only they hadn't interfered she might have been let off – minute by minute her situation worsened.

"And another thing – I mean her to eat it if she sits there till her bedtime."

". . . et les pantalons peut-être mouillé," Aunt Tossie's French was her own invention: "Ou plus pierre," she added thoughtfully.

"Good God – yes – anything could happen," Dada said anxiously.

Maman paid no attention to them. She whisked Nicandra's large linen napkin off her knees and tied it round her waist, then joined her own to it and knotted it securely to the back of Nicandra's chair.

"There you are, darling, and when you've eaten up your nice spinach, Maman will undo you and give you a chocky." Authoritative mother, gracious mistress of this house, she rose, gathering the eyes of non-existent guests (for she would not look near Dada or Aunt Tossie), indicating that luncheon was over and coffee would be in the drawing room.

Alone in the dining room – for Twomey had stopped softly jangling spoons and forks and fitting plates each to each, and gone, quietly as his shadow – Nicandra's mind became a perfect blank. She did not feel injury, only a sustained sense of misfortune. Tears dried on her cheeks as time went by and she still stared, impotent, at the unforgiving spinach. Nothing could induce her to take even a morsel into her mouth – the imperious strength of a child's sense of taste forbade it utterly. In a secondary sort of way she knew that, beyond the opportunity to please and placate Maman, there was more for her to give if she should eat the horrible spinach. The other two grown-ups would see that Maman had been right in her judgement. It would be a kind of "sucks to them". It was all to do with the silence, and the wine stain – turning now from red to black as it spread and seeped.

The terrible boredom of her isolation was relieved by the mental exercise in which she told and re-told herself how, in five minutes exactly, she would eat the spinach as a loving sacrifice to Maman, then sick it up, so that her own martyrdom should be apparent. The green marble clock on the grey marble chimney-piece ticked the minutes away on its golden face. Next time. Next time, it ticked, wait till next time. It was like waiting to jump off a cliff – and then, not jumping. Twice she was in the very act, loaded fork in her hand, when her breathing quickened, her mouth drew into a forbidding shiver of disgust, and she waited for the next signal to come round.

The dining room door opened – she did not look up, for how could she face Maman? She truly felt she had sinned and failed. It was not Maman. It was Aunt Tossie, leaning over her, picking up the plate and fork and then shovelling the spinach into her own mouth, aborting the sacrifice Nicandra knew she was just about to make.

"Too ghastly, I quite agree," Aunt Tossie put the empty plate back in front of Nicandra and moved towards the sideboard in a predestined kind of way. She poured a little whisky into a glass, put the stopper back in the decanter, thought for a moment, then took it out and helped herself to a more sensible amount. "And I need it," she swallowed a mouthful slowly. "All between our two selves, all between you and me – isn't that it, old pal? Now I think a little lie-down perhaps would be rather lovely." Glass in hand, she bundled herself out of the room.

A double load was on Nicandra now. She hadn't eaten the spinach, and in doing so created a martyrdom; now she must restrain herself from the agonizing satisfaction of telling Maman all the truth, thus getting Aunt Tossie into dreadful trouble. She was near to wishing the spinach back on her plate when Maman came in to bend over her – in her nearness so hot and sweet, her precious body smelling faintly true behind the Rimmel's Toilet Vinegar and Violette de Parme.

"My precious one," she said, "and I almost forgot her." She put down her leather dressing-case – the dark green one with a strap across the lid – that went with her on train journeys, and began to untie the knotted napkins. She hardly glanced at the plate and didn't ask about the spinach. So, when Nicandra, freed, threw herself uninvited into the depths of an embrace, she took from it no true satisfaction, Aunt Tossie had deprived her of her martyrdom and its crown as well.

Maman put her away, laughingly, and straightened her hat, pulled down her veil, and between finger and thumb, twisted its little knot neatly beneath her chin.

"Where are you going?" Always that was the vital question. It was the veil that told it was not the garden, then the hat that went to race-meetings and the dressing-case made up the rest of the story: Maman was going away.

"Don't delay me, darling. Fagan's waiting to take me to the station."

"How long for? When will you be back? ... When will you be back?"

Maman smiled brightly. She swung her heavily stuffed silver-mesh purse on its long chain and made something like a little skipping step towards the door – Nicandra thought she had never looked prettier.

"Don't worry, pet. Just be Dada's little girl. Promise?"

"I'll try – I really will try – only wait a minute, Maman, I've got to tell you – I must say it before you go."

"Look darling, it's the 4.30, you know it doesn't wait a moment. . . ."

Maman was gone. Only a drift of her stayed on the solemn air of the dining room – a drift of Parma violet and a heavy load on Nicandra's mind. When Maman came back, even if it was tomorrow, the telling would no longer match the moment.

What next? Who to love? She decided it had to be Aunt Tossie. Aunt Tossie wanted help in cleaning her diamonds. So: the bread-soda – the bread-soda was on the list for Hanlon's – Hanlon's pony cart delivered in the morning, bringing the groceries. She would be Little-Miss-Never-Forgets, obtain the promised bread-soda from Mrs Geary and carry it to Aunt Tossie's bedroom. A trip to the kitchen first: a reminder to Mrs Geary. And she was set on her mission of kindness.

In the kitchen there was no sign of Mrs Geary, only a floured pastry-board, covered in tiny circlets of dough, and a rich smell from the oven telling she had been there lately. It was in the boot-and-brushing room that Nicandra found her at last – after a search through the larders, the dairy, and the empty laundry, its warm steam now subsided into a vaporous chill. She pushed gently on the closed door of the boot-and-brushing room. It was Twomey's province, a dark, three-cornered place with a sink, where he cleaned Dada's hunting clothes, scrubbing boots and breeches in winter time, and boned his shoes and brushed his clothes all the year round.

Here she found Mrs Geary, kindly smoothing Twomey's hair with her hand, while he boned away at an elegant shoe.

"Will you meet me, Tom?" she was saying as she bent over him, "when I'll have my scones out for the tea."

Twomey muttered something. He seemed nervous and displeased.

"Ah, the ice-house is nice and quiet," she said, dividing his hair between her fingers. "Isn't that a fact – you and I know that." She laughed. The sound of her laugh was rich and free as the smell of hot bread on the kitchen air.

It was only then that she was aware of Nicandra standing silent in the doorway, unwilling to interrupt a conversation. Mrs Geary turned, quick and venomous, before a certain yielding to obsequious kindness displaced the threat in her previous movement. "Were you looking for me, Miss Nicandra?" she cooed. "Did you want something, dear? Any little thing at all, only say."

"I'm very sorry to interrupt," Nicandra felt that she had indeed erred, in some way, against the conventions.

"Ah, what interruption? I was just having a little word with Mr Twomey about his silver for the dinner. The salmon won't hold a minute more for me and fish takes two forks and he's a busy man. . . ." While she talked she manoeuvred Nicandra unhurriedly out of the brushing room and towards the kitchen, "What is it you're after?" she asked again.

"I only want bread-soda for Mrs Fox-Collier's diamonds."

"Come on till we see did it come – you couldn't trust Hanlon's man – late today again – and left half the stuff after him I wouldn't wonder. . . ."

A great cornucopia from Hanlon's tumbled its fruits on the kitchen table. Every item in it was parcelled separately, most of them tied with string. . . . "Ah, here we are," Mrs Geary pounced on a stout little package, a thick blue paper bag, its mouth folded as securely as a glued envelope. "Take the lot up to Mrs Fox-Collier with the cook's compliments – wait," she said, as Nicandra turned to leave, "there could be a scone ready for yourself." She lifted the heavy latch-like fastening of the oven door and took one tiny, golden scone from a shelf-full before she shut the door again, her hand as quiet as a cat's footfall.

Up the long stone stairs from the kitchen, into the green enclosed light of the pantry passage, then on up the next staircase, its turns mean and sudden compared with the twin sweeps of the main stairs, Nicandra plodded her careful way to Aunt Tossie's bedroom door. There was no answer to her knocking, so, when she had balanced the buttered scone on the parcel of bread-soda, she opened the door and put her head round the jamb. Aunt Tossie was there. Still wearing her full widow's weeds, she was lying on her bed. She was not asleep for her eyes were staring contentedly about her. An empty glass lay on the eiderdown.

"And how's my little lamb tonight?" she asked in her pleasant drowsy way.

"I hope I didn't wake you up, Aunt Tossie – I brought you *these*," she proffered the scone because she had decided that Aunt Tossie really merited some small recognition for her mistaken act of kindness over the spinach. Somehow, a silence about that was inviolable.

"Oo, darlin', Oo, Bless-oo, oo, I couldn't – thank oo *so* much."

"And the bread-soda – shall we clean the diamonds now?"

Aunt Tossie stared. She had no words in which to express her present distaste for the idea.

"Tell you what, lambkin pudding, pie, I mean," she stirred and shifted about among her pillows. "Just nip down to the dining room and put the tiniest whisky, only up to *here*," she held three of Nicandra's fingers against the glass, rolling empty on the eiderdown – "very nice, too. I'll keep it for breakfast," she pointed to the scone which Nicandra had laid on top of the po cupboard, "I love them . . . scones."

"Shall I put soda-water in the whisky?" Nicandra asked, willing to please in any way she could.

"No darlin', please, no. There's oceans of water over there," she waved towards the marble-topped wash-hand stand. The wash-hand stand was very fully equipped. A large jug and basin, charmingly ornamented with a design of blue ribbon, was its centre-piece. Surrounding it were a little hand-basin, a sponge dish with a perforated movable top, a lidded soap dish, a slender jar holding toothbrushes, and a cut-glass watercroft, crowned by its tooth-glass. Each china object was ribboned like the jug and basin, in appropriately lesser proportions. Towels hung neatly on a mahogany towel-rail, hinged in two parts like a screen, behind which stood a slop-pail and a deep foot bath.

Hurrying away on her next mission, Nicandra felt quietly elated because the little act of kindness in donating her scone had been accepted with so much pleasure and a thoughtful reservation for breakfast.

On a small landing at the turn of the back staircase there was the lavatory reserved for gentlemen only – neither Maman, Aunt Tossie nor any visiting lady ever used it; and, of course, the servants had their own "outdoor" in the cobbled courtyard beyond the gun room. Dada was coming out of this, his special lavatory, as Nicandra, on her return from the dining room, arrived at the landing. She was going very slowly and breathing heavily in her resolve that not a drop of whisky should be spilled. Dada was overcome by natural embarrassment on meeting his daughter at that moment. He would have been happy if he might have affected not to see her. But, now, as part of the outcome of this very unfortunate day, he felt a new responsibility towards "that funny little thing", his daughter. He noticed that she was puffing along with a glass held before her in both hands – he could smell whisky.

"Did Twomey give you this?" he asked.

"No, I got it by my own self."

"I didn't know you touched the stuff."

"It's for Aunt Tossie. She's not feeling up to much." That was a useful phrase of Nannie's.

"Oh hell," he said, "not again? I'll have to speak to Twomey."

"He's gone to the ice-house with Mrs Geary."

"Nicandra, are you sure?"

"Yes. When I went for the bread-soda she was patting his headache away, and the scones must be cooked by now."

"Twomey .... Oh, I give up. All right. Run along and play."

"I'm too busy, Dada. Please may I have my glass of whisky?"

"Yes. All right. I don't know what I'm supposed to do about it. Don't do it again. That's all."

"Not if Aunt Tossie needs a little bit of a refreshment?"

"Actually, specially not then."

Condemnation and worry were joined in his voice – unhappiness consumed the distance between them. "Shall I come to the drawing room after tea?" she asked. Perhaps she could be a help and comfort to him. That would be nice.

"Yes, of course," he spoke as if answering a very silly question. "Why not?" he added as he opened the door between the two staircases, "Put lots of water in it." She heard him running down the stairs, problems at his heels.

❧

"Not asleep. Just having a think," Aunt Tossie said when Nicandra roused her with a gentle nudge.

"This is the whisky and here's the water," Nicandra poised the watercroft over the tooth-glass. She had thought of everything. "Shall I pour it out?"

"All right, darling, if you must – don't drown it. Stop STOP!"

"Dada said to put in lots of water."

"Oh." Aunt Tossie never seemed worried – but she looked surprised. "Poor little chap, he's had an ugly day," she said.

Yes, Nicandra thought, it had been a difficult day, what with everything. "And now, shall we clean the diamonds?" She felt she had earned this amount of entertainment.

"Certainly," Aunt Tossie sat up and took a sip from her glass. "First: go to the bathroom and fill the soap dish with warm water, not too hot. . . ." The process went on step by interesting step. Bread-soda fizzed pleasurably in the soap dish of warm water, softening the rigours of Aunt Tossie's toothbrush. "Seen worse, this won't hurt it," Aunt Tossie said. She never made difficulties about little things. "Now, my jewel-case – no – the second shelf. I put them in before luncheon I know I did. Ah, *there* we are! And the key – in the onyx snuff-box – now we'll get to work. Give it to me and I'll hand out the stuff. You do the hard work – I'll look on."

She fiddled a tiny key into an infinitesimal lock and turned back the lid of her jewel-case. A tray, divided into small partitions, lined in blue velvet, lay empty. She lifted it out and peered further in. She took out little leather boxes and opened them one by one.

Nicandra felt a growing impatience. "Can't I start?" she asked. "The water's getting cold."

Aunt Tossie took a long pull at her drink. Then she shut the jewel-case and took out the key. "You haven't locked it," Nicandra said helpfully.

"Not much use now . . . look, darling, let's do this job tomorrow, shall we?" She wavered a little in her words. "Aunt Tossie really is rather tired, silly old thing I know – Done in, actually. . . . Have to think things out. . . ." She fell back among her pillows, her widow's veil a curling black crown behind her head; one narrowly white-cuffed hand still held the glass of whisky erect – there was a magnificence in her yielding.

Whatever it was that had come over her family today, Nicandra could not guess at. She had done her utmost to excite, please, soothe, serve; yet everything had gone awry. Pigeons, butterfly, bantams, Maman, Aunt Tossie – she had given her all to each, only Dada was left. Little Dada, poor soul (as Nannie would say), he does seem upset. She was hopeful that he would enjoy reading *Dora's Dolls' House* to her after tea, when she came downstairs from the nursery. They had just got to the part about Dora's Naughty Friend.

Tea, like breakfast, was taken with Nannie when Mademoiselle was on holiday – Nannie was not really Nannie for a great big girl of eight. Now she was more Maman's maid, and mender of everything in the house in which she could discern a wear or a tear. If there was nothing wrong with a sheet or a pillow-case or a chair cover she might take it apart, so that her skill was needed to put it together again. Quite often she went on visits with Maman – shoots, race meetings, perhaps a ball or two, that kind of thing. On this evening, Nannie, like everyone else in the house, seemed to be in trouble. "Come on, *eat-up*. Drink your milk. Time to go down. *Stand still* till I do you up."

Nannie was a tiny little woman. When she sat in a chair her feet didn't meet the ground; they swung about, kicking under her long grey skirt. Tonight her eyes were red as two fire holes in her face.

"Have you got a headache like Twomey?" Nicandra asked, hopeful that Nannie would observe her kindly anxiety.

45

"I have nothing like Mr Twomey, I'm glad to say." There was an acid note in Nannie's reply. "Only my stomach is cramped up under my arms with pain. Run along now and don't ask questions – and don't worry your father with silly questions either."

For Nannie to use the word "stomach" instead of "little inside" was an infringement of the rules for polite talk. If she told Dada about Nannie's complaints, she herself would certainly say "inside", perhaps "little inside", as Nannie was smaller than any grown-up person she knew.

When she came down to the drawing room, Dada was looking particularly small, too. He was sitting behind the tea tray, with its vast load of silver, reading *Horse and Hound* – Twomey came in to take the tea tray away, and with it the smaller table which held the dish of scones, the plate of sandwiches (Gentleman's Relish), the fruit cake and the plain sponge. This table was made like a tray; when lifted, its legs could be snapped up or snapped down – a solemn sort of conjuring trick which Twomey performed with quiet authority.

"How is your headache?" Nicandra asked him.

"It's all right, I expect," Dada answered for him. "Bring your book here, old girl. It's time for the reading session." He sighed rather when he opened *Dora's Dolls' House*. "Couldn't we give old Kipling a run? This one looks a bit above my handicap."

"It's much more exciting than Mowgli, Dada. Really – Dora has this Naughty Friend and they're just going to – I won't tell you, it's awful."

"I don't want to read about Naughty Friends, not tonight." Dada sounded quite decided. "What about the photograph book?"

"I do wish I had a Naughty Friend," Nicandra spoke from the bottom of her heart as she lagged her way back to Dada and the sofa, bringing the red leather-bound book that had lain on top of other red leather-bound books piled one

46

above the other on the lower shelf of a mahogany whatnot. Dada took the book from her and looked at the first page. "Good. Kenya mostly – sit down and I'll tell you about them." Nicandra fidgeted in the crook of his arm while he turned the thick cardboard pages and gave a commentary on their contents.

"That's a field full of vultures . . . That's my lion . . . That's my lion again . . . That's my loader and my lion . . . Half an hour after that was taken, that cheetah bit me through the calf . . . That was a very nice bull I shot, but I lost his head . . . That's a bitch I once had . . . That's another bitch . . . I wish I had that bitch now . . . That's my sister and Kill and attendant . . . That's the layout of the Terraces at Government House. . ."

"No, black wives are rather taboo," he answered her only question. It concerned a picture of a native Princeling in full regalia. "That's the ceremony of Crossing the Line . . . Aha! here we are . . . ." At the reappearance of Twomey with the evening drinks tray, he shut the book.

It was quite a performance that Twomey gave every evening. The ceremony of the drinks tray had a little something sacred in its enactment. Square-faced decanters of Scotch and Irish whisky flashed the many facets of their globular stoppers. Sherries showed, primrose or gold, through their elegant bubble-shaped decanters; enamelled labels chained to their stork-like necks declared them dry or medium. Long, very long, tumblers were for whisky-and-sodas; slender, flower-like glasses for sherry.

"Thank you for listening. Bedtime now, I suppose." Dada got off the sofa, pulling her on to reluctant feet. It was too early for bed, but she wouldn't say so. Not tonight. She watched him as, like a boy let out of school, he hurried across the room to the tray of drinks. There was none of the carelessness with which he usually waited for Twomey to bring him his glass.

"Good-night, Dada."

"Good-night, Nicandra."

"Shall I come and say my prayers in the morning?"

"No. I'll let you off prayers tomorrow."

"Till Maman gets back?"

"Yes," he shouted the word as he missed the whisky in his glass with the soda-water syphon. Quite enough to annoy anybody, Nicandra thought. She went on her way to bed without pausing for the goodnight kiss that he had forgotten.

From the drawing room door she turned to her right into the small vestibule at the stair foot. The flight flared upwards to its useless and beautiful division. Standing for a moment on the linking landing between the two worlds, Nicandra felt the blessed evening sun slanting benignly towards her. She opened the door into the other life where there was only Nannie to be pleased, if not actively loved.

Nannie seemed to have got over her cramped inside. "Sit down till I unlace your boots." Someone who knew about these things had told Maman how the perpetual wearing of boots might encourage the proper shape of a girl's ankles. So Nicandra wore white kid boots for after-tea sessions, dancing class and parties; brown laced boots for all lesser occasions.

Nannie was now in a caring mood. She sat Nicandra down on her own chair, the chair that always smelt, in a hesitating way, of Nannie's bottom, and knelt to take off the laced boots – Maman held to a rather Chinese theory on the suppression of growth; the white kid boots were on the small side and not often replaced because they were French, very expensive, and not obtainable from Start-rite. There was a minute comforting sound in the soft clack as Nannie worried the laces apart like a gentle dog. She drew off the boots and put them, lolling side by side, as it were breathing together, before she stuffed them full of tissue-paper to keep their shape. Next it was the tussore silk smock (Liberty), rather a babyish garment; Nannie had let it down and let it out since Nicandra was six. Now she was eight and four months, quite old enough to undress herself without Nannie hovering and undoing everything. At last she stood naked, her long legs like a jointed wooden doll's, ready for her bath.

"We'll excuse you your bath tonight – I'll just sponge your face and hands." Nannie sighed as she dropped the Viyella nightdress over Nicandra's head. Groping her way into the sleeves, Nicandra wondered uneasily what these unusual indulgences portended. Dada had excused her morning prayers; now, Nannie her evening bath. What was wrong with them? Or with herself? Suddenly frightened, she wondered if she was going to have an operation and they wouldn't say – never would she forget her tonsils. She had come back to the nursery ready to sympathize with Nannie about the underarm cramp caused by her inside. Now she found that, on the contrary, it was Nannie who was offering love and comfort to her. It was the reverse of what she needed. She felt especially depleted by the No Bath indulgence, and even more uneasy when she saw the delightful supper prepared for her; honey sandwiches and cocoa with cream floating on its surface. She felt a change, felt it as though she overheard a secret, and now, sipping at her delicious cocoa, she could only suspect that something really nasty was coming next. She must beware.

It was when she was in bed, sleepless in her anxiety, that the true malevolence of the past day became plain to her. The lamb turned up its white, despairing eyes. Anderson towered above it, carefully sharpening his knife. She was glad to think of him being driven away. The sound of wheels tearing through gravel engrossed her memory. The sound of wheels turned in her ears again as she thought of Maman driving off to the railway station as if on some brisk pursuit. It would be a dinner party, most likely. She often went by train to some distant party beyond the reach of horses. Tomorrow she would be back again. She

49

knew that Nicandra could not do without her. She must come back at once. The Forsaken Merman came to mind: Come, dear children, let us away, he advised his sad family. The unresolved problem of the spinach still confronted her. She saw it, glued to its plate, a terrible love token, hers to give or to withhold. Of course, she would have eaten it if her resolution had not been broken and nullified through a gross and mistaken act of kindness. There was embarrassment and resentment for this act of a grown-up, taking her part, playing down at equality. Grown-up people should not make extravagant advances. Better to be like Dada. She did not love him, but he knew his place. He kept his distance. He was nobody. She fidgeted between her sheets at the thought of those photograph books, so stupefyingly dull, when *Dora's Dolls' House*, or a game of Happy Families might have cheered him up. His evasion of her sensible scheme for his comfort had been another repulse.

On this day, when they had all sinned against her in their separate failings, only Silly-Willie, while of no positive comfort, had been devoid of malice. With him she was free of any binding love or duty. He was not entirely harmless either, not when she thought of him spread on his mother's lap. Then an obscene rootless jealousy came over her, although, of course, she herself would never allow or enjoy such an unseemly embrace.

They had all sinned against her, and in some way rejected her advances. Not one among them was worthy of trust. The terrible kindnesses of the evening roused her worst suspicions. No prayers. No bath. It must mean another operation. She saw a knife, smaller than Anderson's. She saw her own blood spurting as the lamb's must have spurted out. Before that you choked and struggled into a sudden darkness of chloroform, then woke to pain that no ice-cream could mediate. They were going to do this to her again. . . .

Aunt Tossie was bending over her, one hand on the bedrail.

"I heard you shouting," she said.

"Not me. It wasn't me," Nicandra denied the idea of such unrestrained behaviour.

Aunt Tossie was leaning closer. Nicandra heaved on her mattress. Aunt Tossie's body, inside the floating black clothes, filled her with a sad disgust. It was not the body she needed for her comfort.

"You do know Aunt Tossie loves little Nicandra," Aunt Tossie said. As she stooped lower her breath, caught in all the black veils, smelled terrible. Nicandra threw an arm out over the bedclothes and turned her cheek fiercely into the pillow.

~ Part Two ~

*n*icandra and her naughty girlfriend, Lalage, were dressing for the Hunt Ball.

"You have first bath," Nicandra implored her friend – she was justly nervous as to the extent of the hot water, and, in every way, she put her friend's comfort before her own. Apart from her proper feelings as hostess, with Lal's heroic behaviour on the day before fresh in her mind, Nicandra felt her friend deserved every loving consideration.

The girls shared the night nursery, and the day nursery adjoining. Aunt Tossie, for eleven years mistress of Deer Forest, understood very well how girls must have their chatter after a ball. So, ignoring the many bedrooms in which a guest might have slept, poor old Nannie's bed was aired and made up. Two hot-water bottles slumped against each other in the crevasse that Nannie had left in her mattress.

Nicandra regretted that her friend was not sleeping in the largest guest room, with the biggest possible fire taking the edge off its disused chill; for not many visitors slept at Deer Forest. The brisk frills that Maman had once draped and ribboned and bowed on dressing-tables, hung now, limp and faintly discoloured by sunlight dwelling quietly in empty rooms. No one drew the curtains on moonlight either; dead and dormant butterflies clung undisturbed in their folds. Altogether it was much jollier in the nurseries with their rose-bud patterned wallpapers, and high wire brass-bound fenders guarding fires that never sulked and chimneys that never smoked.

All a bit mingy for such a big house, was Lalage's inward comment. She was a girl who took everything as it came her way and never felt slighted or rebuffed. Lalage Lawless was her name. Her father was a rich and respected solicitor – not quite the right breeding, socially speaking, in County Westcommon, but Lalage's charm and silly looks guaranteed her welcome in many houses to which her mother had never been invited: she and Nicandra had been "best friends" at their English school.

"All right," she accepted the first bath without hesitation, "shall I leave the water in for you?"

The idea was slightly repellent to Nicandra. Hot or cold, her bath water was her own. But to reject the offer was beyond her. Refusal might seem ungrateful or unkind: "Oh please do," she said. When Lalage, neat as a Nannie's child in her blue Viyella dressing-gown, had darted off to the bathroom, Nicandra, for the present absolved from her duties as friend and hostess, wound up her gramophone and, as she undressed, surged and swooned pleasantly to the heart-breaking cadences of the *Caprice Viennois*. She grudged the muffling of the violin as she dragged her Fair Isle jersey over her head. A childish shirt with a round Peter Pan collar she unbuttoned slowly, breathing her way along with the music. Her grey flannel skirt, hooked, not zipped, at the placket opening, fell round her feet. She leaned over the high nursery fireguard when she unleashed her paltry breasts from the needless support of that new invention, the Kestos brassière. The slight indecency of nakedness, emphasized by her stockings, four times suspended to an elastic girdle, bothered her. She hurried them away from their anchorage and stripped them down her thin legs. Anxious that Lally should not return to find her naked, she huddled into a blue satin kimono that had been one of Aunt Tossie's many over-grand presents. Such presents marked the passing from girlhood to accessible maidenhood; this state was made manifest on the day when Nicandra's striking blonde hair was pinned, a pale hillock, low on the back of her neck.

Properly speaking, Aunt Tossie should have presented Nicandra at Court, which she would have greatly enjoyed doing. Dada, however, raised every obstacle and objection he could think of to baulk this plan because, as he put it (only to himself), the dear old girl might feel her oats and something unfortunate could happen.

Apart from the happy circumstance of the Dear Old Place staying precariously solvent owing to Aunt Tossie's money, he was quietly and constantly fond of his sister-in-law. He considered her sound as a bell in most ways, apart from this mad preoccupation with Nicandra's social life. That his daughter should need any brighter prospects than the established background of her name, and her eventual inheritance of the Dear Old Place, was beyond him; while, for the present, two good reliable hunters surely provided all the enjoyment and exercise any girl could ask.

Much as he wished that Aunt Tossie might keep her mind on the Form Book, where their interests in beating the Handicapper ran together, he had nevertheless acceded to her insistence on a party, a small house party, for Nicandra's first real ball. Who to invite had been a difficult point. "Where have all the young men gone? I'm always asking myself." Aunt Tossie asked Dada too. "And a damn sad answer you'll get. There's been a war remember . . . Charlie Fortescue's two boys . . . Humphrey Bird's little Dickie . . . that ass Eustace Browning. . . ." The list of sons of the right sort, still available in this country, was miserably short in comparison with that of the golden lads who had come to dust in Flanders and other places. The only certainty was Robert Lester, son of the Bishop of Aherloe, dull but acceptable, although he didn't hunt and was a poor shot; still, he had been to Winchester (on a scholarship). Miraculously, when invited for the Hunt Ball, he had asked if he might bring an old school friend who was staying with him, hiring horses for a few days' hunting.

～～

As she waited for Lally's return from the bathroom, Nicandra sat on the thick rag hearthrug that Nannie had made. She pulled the cold embroidered spaces of satin kimono closer to her and pressed her back into the wire of the fender before she drew the basket, full of wounded dog, nearer to herself and to the heat – the little bitch trembled amongst all her luxuries. But for Lally's courage and abandon, Nicandra thought, she might not be alive and trembling now. Again she heard the boys' warm approving voices, voices that left her outside the heat of that dangerous moment.

The heat, the danger, the moment were unforeseeable when she and Lally, arm in arm in giggling familiarity, watched from the nursery window for the boys' arrival. Robert they knew, and all his limitations. The unknown friend was meat for their curious excitement. At the window they laughed together and bit a knuckle, like children or housemaids – watching avidly, they saw the two boys get out of a car that could not be Robert's.

Robert's friend stooped over the boot, pulling out suitcases. He put back a saddle, shut the boot, and stood up. He was tall. He was mystery. He ignored Twomey, fussing over the luggage: a rather yellow suitcase, that would be Robert's, and dark leather for everything else. The friend's name was Andrew Bland. Aunt Tossie said she had danced with his father.

Dada stood on the steps in the cold, shaking hands, saying something pleasant through clenched teeth. He was a child's height compared to Robert's steady bulk. Robert knew nothing about horses and cared less, unfortunately.

But he had been in the Winchester XI – not quite the same thing, of course. They watched them turn towards the house. Andrew was asking Dada something. He stooped gracefully towards the little man and laughed loud and shyly. Robert took his suitcase out of Twomey's over-burdened hands and followed the other two. Twomey showed neither gratitude nor approval for Robert's kind act, only a cold embarrassment. He liked gentlemen to behave as he expected them to behave.

They were gone. The window was lifeless. "Let's go down and get it over, shall we?" Lalage suppressed any hint of eagerness.

"I expect Dada will send someone to tell us."

Unwilling to make an unheralded entrance, Nicandra quivered in a distance of expectancy. She was right. Twomey sent old Lizzie with the summons: "Mr Twomey says, Sir Dermot says, for ye to come down to the morning room – the young gentlemen are here." She sounded portentously excited. Then they had whirled, clattering their way down the back staircase, restraining their gait with one accord at the door dividing Stateliness from the Ordinary. The swinging mannered flights of the great stairway impelled an obedience to propriety. Even Nicandra's little dog, Nettie, checked any exuberance and hesitated behind them to the door of the morning room.

". . . might stop a few earths perhaps. Hounds could run through the place tomorrow. . . ." it was Dada's voice, and it sounded desperate.

"Go *on*." Lally had given Nicandra a little push – no. She hadn't. It had been something in her breathing that conveyed impatience. She followed quietly, a well-mannered guest, as they crossed the crowded length of the morning room. Low winter sunlight betrayed all it touched in shabbiness and dusty surfaces. It was a delightful, careless room, untidy and rather deficient in comfortable chairs. Everything expelled from other places found a haven here,

59

including the only good pictures in the house – a couple of Rose Bartons, bought by Aunt Tossie at a Church Sale, were considered quite pretty and of local interest, but insignificant compared with the photographic portrait of the first Nicandra, standing stripped for a gallop, but without Fagan, much to his disappointment, at her head.

"Oh good, you're here," Dada turned away from the fire where the group of three stood. "Robert's here, dear fellow." A dreadful disturbance overcame him. He could not remember the name of Robert's friend. ". . . anyway, here's Nicandra and What's-her-name. . . ."

"Oh, Sir Dermot, you know I'm *Lally*," she laughed and helped out the moment with sly ease, loosening the way through Nicandra's formal how-do-you-do's.

"I'm Andrew Bland," the tall friend said. Nobody shook hands. Robert smiled gently behind his shyness. Andrew Bland withdrew for a minute with a distant grateful silence, confident, apart, approving and curious. Silence concluded, he was the first to speak. "Do you use Stinko, sir, when you're stopping?" Dada was delighted. "I do. I do. Yes, I do. I cut up a sack and I dip the little bits in Stinko. Marvellous stuff. . . ."

Robert spoke to the girls: "They're having Manahans Band tonight," he told them with nearly religious approval. They paid him no attention. "Oh, Sir Dermot, please let's come stopping with you." Lally was a child, innocently flattering. She gave Dada confidence and importance. For this moment he mattered more than the boys. Did he wish his Nicandra had the same spark? Nicandra put up a hand to the loose hairpins in her bun, and looked rather miserable. Robert felt his heart move for her. "Oh, I shouldn't think of it, if I was you," Dada was pleased: forbidding a dangerous toy to a child, "you'll smell too awful tonight." He must have noticed Andrew's smile dawning, for he shied violently away from his unrestrained remark. "Why don't you go down to the Lake Field," he said to Nicandra, "the yearlings might amuse them. We have quite an interesting fellow," he turned to Andrew, "out of Nicandra by The Jesuit." Andrew's smiling ceased. Now he looked alert and responsible. This subject was what really counted.

In the gun room, where coats hung and hats of all kinds and all ages lay about on tables, Nicandra squeezed her Henry Heath, its brim bound with corded ribbon, over her bun of hair, while Lally, peering into a mildewed looking-glass, felt her way towards a becoming line. Picking up their chamois leather gloves, they joined the boys in the hall.

Nicandra led them by all the ways she had known and disregarded since childhood. Beyond the long line of windows, past the Conservatory and the Laburnum Walk, they came to the winter-bound Pleasure Garden where yellow jasmine crawled over a tree stump, hamamelis, the wych-hazel shrub, thrust out golden hedgehog flowers along its leafless branches, and the stream coming from the kitchen garden – a winter river now – hurried into the culvert that carried it on into the baby lake in the field outside the Pleasure Garden.

Robert said: "I'll stay here. I want to spy on the shrubs." Curious fellow: still, he was a man for the dance. Without comment, they left him to plod about and peer. Nicandra's little Nettie stayed behind too, she scuffled around in the undergrowth alert for game of any sort – a blackbird squatting low, or a rabbit with fear in its silly eyes. The other three walked, single file, over the stone bridge into the field where horses stood and stared.

It was now that Nicandra fell into a sudden easy accord with Andrew. He listened, quiet and attentive, while she conned over the breeding of the yearlings, answering his questions with knowledge and certainty. They talked until the horses, squealing and nipping at each other, turned away to hurry purposefully across the field and stand afar, clouds of their breath plumed against the winter air.

Lally had no share in the informed conclave. She found nothing to say about the yearlings and shrank quite sensibly from their forward advances, staying silent and watchful while Nicandra talked and lifted solemn grey eyes to Andrew's, sure of his entire attention. To rivet all attention on herself was, to Lally, as natural as breathing. The occasion to hold and secure it came almost immediately, when Nicandra's precious dog was heard crying pitifully in the depths of the watery culvert. It was not a cry of contest with any game – it was a faintly choking cry.

Tears streamed down Nicandra's face. She stopped calling "Nettie, Nettie." She lay on the ground, her ear to the culvert, listening. She imagined Nettie, held up by her collar, the water backing up to drown her.

Andrew said: "I'll go for the spades. Come on, Robert, you know the place."

"I don't know where they keep the spades," Robert stood, hopeless and static, his bulk exaggerated by his suit of plus-fours and his tasselled stockings. "I'm too big to go to ground," he wailed gratefully, watching Andrew failing by any contortion to cram his shoulders into the mouth of the culvert.

"Let me, let me, I'm the littlest," Lally was lying on the grass beside him when Andrew dragged his head out of the culvert; like a small dark eel she wriggled her way into the watery hole. "She can't turn in there – she'll drown too." Nicandra foresaw a double horror.

It was Robert who padded solemnly across the little bridge, waded into the pond to the culvert's egress, and wrenched the grating from its mouth, setting free a rush of mud and water from which he lifted out, first, Nicandra's dog (exhausted and bleeding but quite ready to bite), then Lally, every stitch she wore soaked and clinging close as a swimsuit to her solid child-size body. He held her against his tweed-upholstered person while he waded out of the pond, but put her down immediately when he touched dry land.

"Oh, thank you," she said, elated, triumphant, then: "Oh, *Robert*," and her voice fell. He was a disappointing hero to share her brave adventure. But in a moment, the others were beside her, praising, questioning, almost adoring her courage. No one commended Robert's practical act. "Her collar was caught on a root." Lally gasped and coughed, she even spat, her teeth gleamed against the mud. She was a star. The drama gave rise to a sort of wild freedom between them. They laughed and talked together. No one listened, except to Lally. They ran like a group of children back to the house. Nicandra held her dog to her heart. Robert and Andrew each held a cold, wet hand of Lally's, half lifting her off her feet between them. "We put her through the drain," Andrew explained her condition to Dada.

"Oh, did you? Good girl!" he commended Lally as kindly as he would any keen bitch, and asked nothing further. He had to get on with Stinko and stopping. He turned back to enquire: "Which drain? Might get in there. Mustn't forget that one," and hurried on his way.

Now, still clutching the slices of unyielding satin to her, Nicandra wondered how it was possible to acknowledge fitly the immediate and selfless gallantry she had seen. A small opportunity arose when Lizzie came knocking at the door for the ceremonial delivery of two silver-bound shoulder sprays, one, a gardenia, the other an orchid, and a card which said: From Robert. She decided at once that the orchid should be for Lally.

Lally said: "Oh, scrummy – oh, divine." She was wrapped in her bath towel.

"Robert shouldn't," Nicandra was troubled.

"Silly old him," Lally laughed and held her orchid against her bare shoulder.

Not on that evening, but long afterwards, Nicandra was to understand something of Aunt Tossie's efforts for this celebration: this party for her darling, into which she had thrown heart and soul and quite a lot of money. Then, great kindness and great love were only to be expected and accepted. Aunt Tossie was the fountainhead of both, the medium through which Dada might be approached for favours. Money and generosity gave her a kindly power over Deer Forest. With this power and position, there existed a proper distance for her to keep, and on that evening she was to bridge it fatally; worse, there was a strident note of comedy debasing further the shaming accident. . . .

Before the party, there had been much careful planning and changing of plan. All the forceful tact Aunt Tossie possessed was needed to convince Dada that only champagne, the best champagne, would be appropriate to the occasion, and then to compel him into the stony depths of the cellars to root with Twomey along the half-empty bins where forgotten treasures spoiled. Days in advance the bogs had been walked and snipe shot for that famed Snipe Pudding of Mrs Geary's – a pudding more gently extraordinary than any game pie.

On the morning of the Hunt Ball, Aunt Tossie made her descent to the kitchen where orders for the day would be given. She wore her new heather-coloured cardigan; a blue veil (heather and scabious was her idea) preserved her hair, carefully waved for the night. Her ringless arthritic fingers guided a slate pencil. Her writing on the slate was that of a child making pothooks and hangers. Mrs Geary understood it quite well and disagreed with it often. But, today, she gave almost pious attention to every scrape of the slate pencil. This dinner they planned must capture the living memory of every lucky guest. Neither she nor Aunt Tossie, sitting there in dignified order, could foresee that the memory to be implanted would not be of the rare perfection of each course, but of a social mishap, a horror that would engross unbelieving attention and sear its recollection, like a scar, into Nicandra's loving.

Aunt Tossie had a faint dribble of desire at the corners of her mouth when, at length, she laid down the slate pencil and rose from her chair to face Mrs Geary, her companion in what was to be an immortal triumph: its finale that most acceptable of puddings – before diets and regimens were conceived: a really beautiful Trifle.

"Layer it up, up into a glorious round mountain," Aunt Tossie adjured. "Plenty of brandy, and don't plaster the top with cherries, just one, perhaps on the tip-top, and only a touch of angelica."

"Oh, Holy God!" Mrs Geary exclaimed, her genius and her dedication alight.

Many other matters and activities were to fill Aunt Tossie's day, all directed towards the success of the evening. Without her personal suggestion and direction, anything might go wrong, or be forgotten. The fish for instance: Twomey must be reminded to collect that from the station. Flanagan, the distant fishmonger, had sworn it would be on the early train from Waterford. Twomey could forget any vital message to be executed on his morning bicycle trip to the village; any message except the daily gamble to be placed with the bookmaker, and the newspaper with yesterday's racing results. Twomey was getting on, of course, that must not be forgotten. But her own feet, her veins, her weight, and her rheumatism were troubles to be ignored on this day and night when her darling girl was to shine in a proper setting. The setting comprised holly, not very luxuriantly berried, a small greenish collection of ciprepediums, and plenty of ivy.

A vastly increased supply of turf and logs was required for the many fires the occasion demanded. Two boys, one of them Silly-Willie (simple still, but useful sometimes) carried, between them, great baskets of fuel to hall, drawing room, morning room, dining room and six bedroom fires. It was quite a performance.

Evening dress, too, was a matter for Aunt Tossie's close concern and consideration – Dada's pink evening coat, its lining and facings frail and splitting with age, must be handled carefully and aired thoroughly; white tie and waistcoat freshly sparked up, and jewelled cufflinks traced to some forgotten place of retirement.

It was one of Aunt Tossie's more endearing habits to discuss with Nicandra every item in her own wardrobe, and tonight was an occasion for special deliberation. Gigi, no quieter or graver in her advancing years, screamed and flapped, furious at being caged: a necessity, even Aunt Tossie allowed, when velvets, silks, taffetas and bright sequins lay deep on the bed and overflowed the chairs in her bedroom, changes of fashion and flaws of past time limply exposed in the morning light.

"I think I might look quite lovely in *that*," Aunt Tossie held blue velvet against her tweeds and woollies.

"I like you best in black," Nicandra said. "What about your black velvet with the huge skirt, wear that."

"Well I don't say yes and I don't say no, I say, well, yes, perhaps," Aunt Tossie gave the matter further consideration. "No," she said at last, "the lace corsage and the boned neck, a bit ageing, don't you rather think?"

She strained the black velvet across her distinguished breasts, then turned from the looking-glass, "Nip out all this lace and fuzz and, Bob's your uncle, what do you get? A sweetheart neckline."

"Oh, you've got a Kestos brassière – quel absolute chic," Lally picked the bust-bodice out of the pile of underclothes Lizzie had folded and laid, a picture of precision, on Nicandra's bed. She stretched its modest cups on her hands.

"Aunt Tossie," Nicandra explained. "It worries me rather. Still I know she knows."

"May I try it on?" Without waiting for an answer, Lally stripped off the accepted bandaging of the day. "Oh, m'dear, too naughty for words." She screamed with laughter.

Nicandra looked disconcerted and prim before a great light of kindness broke, telling her to spread a little happiness at any cost to herself. "I'll lend it to you, Lally," she said, "just for tonight."

"Oh, Nico, I wouldn't dream," Lally fastened a button more securely on its elastic strap. The mild uplift of her breasts was frightening in its unexplored possibilities: "If you really mean it." Her acceptance was inevitable, as immediate as her plunge underground of the afternoon. She danced away to her bedroom to dance back a minute later: "I wasn't going to tell you, but I will." She had a mystery to share, there was a tinge of the forbidden in her voice. "It's called 'Odor-O-No'. Mummie says it could give me cancer, who cares? I'd sooner die than smell, wouldn't you?"

"Yes, of course," Nicandra sniffed suspiciously at a vacant, scentless strength; "Where did you find it?"

"From an advertisement and guess what it said – 'Are Your Armpits Charmpits?' Mine are a worry, what about you?"

"Oh dear, I do wonder. I pad about with Ponds Extract and Lizzie sews dress preservers into everythng."

"You can forget all that with 'Odor-O-No'. Try a dab."

"Strong stuff," Nicandra dabbed nervously. Her arms, raised in turn, had an air of nonsensical melancholy. "Did you really ask Kevin Kelly for it?"

67

"Ask the local chemist? Too embarrassing. Anyway he only knows about greyhounds and worms in sheep. Armpits would paralyze him. He's very religious."

"He does keep Aspirins. I buy dozens for the Curse."

"I expect what you need is a good curetting."

"A good what?"

"Remind me to tell you. The other thing I'm on to is this pill for obesity. I can't wait. They say it's pure magic."

"We aren't really fat, Lal, are we?"

"Yes, I am, for my height. You know what I heard Cousin Deirdre saying to Mum? She is a ripe plum was what she said. Oh, the cruelty – giving Mummie ideas."

"Too beastly, and when you think of the shape of a ripe plum."

"I hate her," Lalage spoke seriously, "I'd like to stick a knife in her, and when I got it in – you know what I'd do?"

"Pull it out." Nicandra saw no other solution to this ugly and childish idea.

"No, when I got it in, I'd twist it." Lalage's eyes widened, their pupils melting in the pleasure of her thoughts. Once, she had emptied her full po over a sleeping brother. That was in the nursery years. Since then, nothing had happened to modify any bad intentions.

"I want to *be* happy but I can't *be* happy till I make you happy too," Lally sang. She was back in the present and she knew how best to fill every moment of it. Beyond the open door between the two rooms there was silence; each girl concentrating fiercely on making the very best of what looks she had.

In turn, each caught the other, avid in front of the cheval looking-glass, tilting on its mahogany frame; their reflections lighted by the obscure flattery of fresh candles in swivelling brass holders. Nicandra looked away from what she saw: Aunt Tossie's lavish present, chosen from Debenham's Catalogue: white satin, bateau necked and beaded, its length stopped an inch too far above the long-toed silver shoes. Its grace, spread narrowly on her bed, had ravished her. Now she was shaken by doubts. She felt her bones, a cold skeleton, inside an expensive shroud. Aunt Tossie, ever loving, ever kind, had made an expensive mistake. Her resentment and disappointment became part of the awkward thrust she made to fasten Robert's gardenia to her shoulder strap. The gold safety-pin, carrying a fox's mask, refused like a horse at a fence, to go through the beaded satin.

"Till I make you happy tooooo." Lalage came hurrying back. It was the Kate Greenaway look for her; Kestos and green ribbon gave a faint flatulence to the high bodice line – dressing-table muslin skirts were pulled into a flounce at the hem; again the green ribbon tied in a silly bow. It was not fancy dress, more the naughty nursery look. "Can't see in there to fix my orchid." It was the excuse for her deep delaying gaze into the looking-glass. Nicandra stood aside, the bruised gardenia still in her hand. Mirror, mirror, tell me true, went through her mind as she watched Lalage's reluctance to lose her image. It was as though she sucked her body away from the glass before she turned to Nicandra.

Nicandra was standing waiting for a second turn at her reflection, her attitude a droop of pure unhappiness. "I don't like myself," she said. Immediately, Lalage knew just what she could have done with that masterpiece in satin. Poor love, just wrong, always, she thought contentedly. Aloud, she said: "Nico, what a gorgeous gown – so grown-up – not like silly itty-bitty me." The kindness in her voice avoided unspoken criticism and commiseration, "Let me," in a moment her quick fingers had Nicandra's gardenia and its drift of green spray firmly in place.

Cheered a little, Nicandra picked an invisible hairpin from a rosy plate, part of the muddle on top of the white-painted chest of drawers that had once held her baby-clothes. "No, don't, leave it alone," the irrepressible cry of one born knowing sprang from Lalage as she watched Nicandra's efforts to control the blonde strands of hair blowing, light as ducks' down, on the back of her neck.

"It's too untidy," Nicandra said screwing in the hairpin. "Perhaps now we should go down."

It was Nannie's voice before the after-tea sessions in the drawing room. Perhaps she had never quite recovered from the efforts to please she had made then. She looked round, unseeing, at all the discarded clothes and bath towels looped on the bed and floor. Lizzie would put everything away; she would turn down the bedclothes at a neat angle and put in the hot-water bottle as late as possible. None of the muddle in her room mattered. Only the meek little dog in its basket was important.

"She'll be all right," Lalage, its rescuer, said, impatient to get downstairs where life waited.

Cold hung, a draughtless presence, in the heights and widths of the staircase. Accustomed and unaware, they did not even shiver as their warm bare shoulders met its blue embrace. At the stairfoot, Silly-Willie, on his way to some fire with a vast contribution of logs, put down his load and goggled at them. When they came nearer he did a little dancing step and curtsied low. Nicandra smiled and acknowledged the obeisance as if it was from a dog doing its trick. "Is he all there?" Lalage asked when they were out of hearing.

"Almost. The nuns did a wonderful job on him, after his mother died. Mrs Geary looks after him now. He's quite useful, loves cleaning the boots and the brass and all that stuff."

∾∾

In the drawing room there was none of the untidy, unmatched squalor that made the morning room a place

70

where troubles or pleasures could have their breathing spaces. The morning room was for comings and goings, where odd chairs changed their places for different conveniences, and shoes and boots from the fields were not forbidden. During springs and summers, the sunlight came in unshaded through high windows and spread a dry pallor along floorboards. The carpet and chintzes accepted the merging of their colour and gentle rot as, in happy age, the mind obliterates the glories and cruelties of youth.

The drawing room was quite another world. Three windows had their green blinds perpetually drawn against morning sun or any damage from afternoon light. Their sashes were lifted regularly to air the room, and shut again with religious punctuality. There were no stripes of shade down the folds of the yellow brocade curtains. Their pelmets, white and gold, were a rich memorial to a grandmother. That they disturbed the Italian plasterwork somehow added to their important grandeur. In the same way, Sheraton and buhl commodes and cabinets, card and console tables, and tiny escritoires by Hepplewhite contrived a harmony, crowded, but inevitable.

Blue Worcester plates took up nearly the whole of one wall; others overlapped in a china cupboard. The portrait of Nicandra's mother, in Court dress and feathers, had not been moved. Saucy and impolite, her gaze was slanted away from proper procedures. To have taken the portrait down would have marked her flight, distinguishing its importance beyond the dignified acceptance of the Family. One did not speak of those things.

Aunt Tossie was alone in the drawing room. She dropped her lifted velvet skirts (she had been warming her bottom in front of the fire burning fiercely in its basket grate) as the girls appeared. She saw only her darling come down the room – Nicandra might have walked alone, so unaware was Aunt Tossie, for the moment, of the little friend. Lovely, lovely, she crooned to herself. She was quite uncritical of the sad, grand dress; she understood only the pale, still doubtful, beauty, so wrong for its present period, so touching in its failure to be recognized or to please. She had bought this expensive dress to capture notice; she felt it like a blow that the little monster sidling along, sleek and positive, dark hair in brisk waves, silly doll-dress denying fashion, had all the qualities that Nicandra lacked. Dangerous little thing, she thought as she smiled her warm welcome.

Lalage was well aware of the forbidding quality behind the smile. She knew she could never trespass on any liking from that robust and distant lady. She felt a flash of guilt about the borrowed Kestos.

Aunt Tossie's bosoms needed no aids beyond the velvet bodice holding them; holding them separate like two great spoonfuls of cream. The black lace veiling had been snipped away. She had pushed a handkerchief, light as a breath, into the cleavage. A black feather boa, perhaps bought for the Black Ascot, curved lavishly round to cancel any suggestion of nakedness. She did not need diamonds to complete her magnificence. "And how is the poor little dog?" she asked.

Dada came in; Hunt evening coat, waistcoat fitting him with the same exact pinch as waistcoats had when he was twenty. He looked as clean and pretty as a Chelsea china figure. But his sad little face had no shepherd's jollity about it. "And how's the little dog?" he asked.

The great lady and the little gentleman stood together on the hearthrug. Behind them hung a gilt looking-glass, Chinese in its style, cool as a breeze in its execution. A solitary statue, a small silver tribute to the first Nicandra, glimmered alone in the centre of the wide chimney-piece, and below it garlands and Greek ladies twined and danced on their marble plaque. Dada nodded up at the silver horse. A second nod was towards his daughter. "Nicandra also trotted up." Lips glued to his teeth, he indicated his approval to Aunt Tossie.

The boys came in. "How's the little dog?" they said together. Robert, half a beat behind Andrew, felt, as usual, a fool. It was as though each had prepared a remark to cover his entry. Robert was embarrassed by such silliness. Andrew's smile dawned on the joke, enjoying it. Not yet a member of any Hunt, in his black tails, he was as evasively elegant as a departing swallow. His slow swoop across the floor to the fireplace was meticulous in its denial of grace. He settled, as though with a folding of wings, beside Nicandra. This pleased Aunt Tossie; an omen for the evening.

"We're all here, aren't we – let's have a glass of sherry," she said to Dada.

Dada looked startled: "Yes, where's Twomey?" he asked.

"Busy, I told him to leave it over there."

"Ah," Dada said, "good idea." He almost bustled to the far table where glasses and decanters provided him with an interval of escape from the lonely speechlessness that only Aunt Tossie understood. Robert followed him, ponderous and thoughtful, his white tie limp from over-handling. Don't they teach them *anything* these days? Dada wondered.

"I like it dry as a bone," Aunt Tossie was saying.

"I'm a medium kind of girl," Lalage giggled.

"Must I?" Nicandra looked into her glass.

"Yes, darling. Drink up." Aunt Tossie handed her own empty glass to Robert, with a nod towards the drinks tray – her meaning was quite plain to him. He trudged back and forth, careful and dutiful.

"Don't you really want to drink it?" Andrew had talked to Nicandra a little aside from the others.

"No." The mermaid's eyes were lifted, long and despairingly.

"Should we change glasses?" He took hers and put his empty one in her hand. No word spoken before he said: "May I have the first dance?"

Her eyes rounded in gratitude. "And the third and fifth and the seventh, all the odd numbers."

73

"I haven't got my programme yet, have I?" While shaken by delight, she managed to assert herself primly.

Andrew looked round the great, rich room before he swallowed her glass of sherry. Dada was sending a horse on for him tomorrow.

"Dinner is served, Madam," Twomey announced quietly from the doorway.

Without a moment's delay Aunt Tossie got up and sailed down the long room, the ends of her boa floating out behind her, careless majesty in her gait. Three glasses of very good sherry had put her right with the world. She felt ageless and she felt hungry. Alone of them all, she knew how good dinner was going to be. "You here, you here." She directed them to their places. Like a great-breasted pigeon, she preened her feathers along the low corsage of her dress, and spread her velvet skirts into perfect order as she sat down.

Robert, on her right, cleared his throat and thought for a moment before, looking from the silver basket of white flowers in the middle of the table, he said: "Your Christmas roses are wonderful. My mother's are miserable – all a mass of awful spots. What can she do about it?"

There was no effort or affectation in his ease with old people, or in his good manners. Through the first course, clear soup so strong that it almost jellied in an empty soup plate, he talked to Aunt Tossie while she supped up her soup delightedly and gave him gardening secrets for his mother.

Then it was Andrew's turn, and the turn of his father's generation. He conveyed the idea that she had known all of them in the beauty of her youth and theirs, and most of them had been her beaux. In exchange, Aunt Tossie remembered winners they had ridden, fours and sixes they had hit, centuries they had made, and their handicaps in polo.

Champagne came with the fish. Hours previously the fillets of sole in their bass carrier-bag had travelled by train, and on the handlebars of Twomey's bicycle, to the kitchen and to Mrs Geary's genius. Yesterday they swam to their deaths, tonight, tamed to perfection, they lay in a discreet miasma of herb-scented butter.

Aunt Tossie, calculating astutely that fasting gives an edge to appetite, had put Nicandra on Robert's right hand. After the first glass of wine, bending solidly towards her: "The orchid was for you," he said.

Nicandra felt his hurt as absolutely as if she loved him: "Oh, Robert, Lal was so longing – you do understand? Just think what she did for my midget."

And for herself, Robert thought, remembering her disappointed distance when he extracted her from the culvert.

"I think I like my gardenia more." She touched the bruised petals. With satin sliding over her unpropped breasts, she looked like an overgrown, dressed-up child. Robert actually trembled in his longing to protect and to keep all trouble from her.

Across the table, Lalage put her mind to the subjugation of Dada. No more the cutie, she was the serious seeker for information: "Tell me about afforestation. . . Why are beech trees dying? Are ash and oak and alder the native trees? . . . Why was Nicandra beaten a length in the Cunnyngham Cup?"

"Didn't give her running – mares can be funny."

She didn't ask him to enlarge further on that long-ago disappointment. She nursed him back into the winning story. "Three in a row, how marvellous." Her intimacy with those splendid past days was owing to her father's priming. As Sir Dermot's lawyer, he knew the difficulties of extracting even a yes or no from him. Tonight, Dada and that little girl, whose company he had so much dreaded, had their heads nearly touching as they bent towards each other, she asking, he elaborati ıg.

While he waited to hand her the fish, Twomey was not amused. Lalage looked up only when Dada, having completed a diagram of salt and pepper pots, directed her

75

attention to the flat silver dish she was delaying in its stately passage round the table.

"Another bottle, Twomey," Dada murmured as he helped himself to fish. "Keep tambourine a-rolling," he said to nobody before he went back into a silence that remained unbroken while he ate his fish.

Hearing the sound of a cork popping, Aunt Tossie drained her glass in readiness for Twomey's round. She knew that her irresistible hunger for the snipe pudding would lower the happy euphoria of the wine holding her airborne, almost exultant; for the maintenance of that happy state more champagne was needed. When Twomey doubtfully filled only half her glass, she gave him a glance like a whiplash. "Madam, Madam, five to come," he hissed respectfully, his whisper turning into a sigh as he poured the amount required. The slight upwards twist he gave to the bottle took the place of the wry smile he would never allow himself to give.

When she explored the depths of the snipe pudding for a bird she fancied, Aunt Tossie's pleasure rose to its height. "There it is. Dear little thing." Complete and unbroken, the wild corpse kept its tiny crouch on her plate while Mrs Geary's finest and most secret sauce was spooned round it. Aunt Tossie put the long-handled gravy spoon back in the napkin-swathed pudding bowl and waited in happy expectation for the sea-kale. It would be the earliest, thongs milk-white and small as a baby's fingers, were even now draining on toast. Snipe don't sing, they only drum their wings, she remembered, as she cut through the thread-like neck, and holding the bird's head by its absurdly long beak, crunched through the white skull and sucked out the strange delicious brains within it. She wiped her lips on a vast white napkin and emptied her glass of wine. She had no hesitation in her pleasure. Slightly overheated by food and wine, she uncoiled her feather boa and put it to fly and float from the back of her chair.

"Have two," she said to Andrew who was delving dextrously about in the bowels of the great basin, "nothing more delicious, is there?"

"Are you sure about two?"

"Yes. I'm certain."

He found Aunt Tossie most agreeable, and wondered if it was true that she was very rich. A bit intoxicated, he thought, as she leaned away from him, pulling the dress up on her fat shoulders, and began again on some exploit of an uncle (to him an ancestor) already recounted during the fish course.

Between Dada, who had, naturally, nothing to say to her, and Robert, who preferred other subjects to hunting and horses, Nicandra was spending a disconsolate hour. Always longing to give and to please, she responded carefully and with an entire lack of interest to Robert's well-sustained efforts towards her attention. They discussed the rudiments of the Charleston, that still over-sophisticated exercise in dancing, a world apart from the slow foxtrot and not yet a familiar of Irish Hunt Balls.

"I can show you how," he promised, "but we would have to hold on to the back of a chair."

"Could you?" she said. "How lovely." That ended the Charleston. "I forget – are you at Oxford or Cambridge?"

Robert hesitated – would she accept it? "Actually I'm at a Business College," he said.

"Oh, you *are* clever." A businessman. What a dreadful future. How could the Bishop, his father, and a far-away cousin of Dada's, ever allow his son to go into Business.

"What do you want to do?" Robert asked.

I want to fall in love, she thought, looking away from him with helpless distaste. Aloud, she said: "How do you mean 'do', Robert? Everything one does, of course."

"What's everything?"

"The horses, the river, race meetings, shopping, I love. And I adore reading."

"Who's your favourite author?"

"Dornford Yates, by far."

"I haven't read him yet."

"Oh, what a treat for you. I'll lend you my *Berry and Co.*" She thought: If only there was a Jonah calling me M'Lady and running frightful risks chasing after spies all across Europe in a great Bentley.

It was with the trifle that the gross and embarrassing incident occurred, the event that Nicandra was to remember, squeamishly and for always. Time passing never softened the impact of that moment when she looked down the table to where Twomey waited for Aunt Tossie to give her attention to the pudding he offered. Well above the rim of the Waterford glass bowl, the great trifle rose in a stalwart bulge of whipped cream, topped by a single cherry.

It was Twomey's appalled stare downwards, past one great, creamy heap to another, that concentrated Nicandra's shocked observance. Aunt Tossie's left breast bulged out, pale against the background of black velvet. Suddenly, all saw, and all talk stopped. The silence welled through the room.

Only Aunt Tossie was unperturbed by the presence of the dreadful thing that, freed of its supports, hung bare and toppled over. She helped herself to trifle with splendid insouciance.

"Ah, dear fellow," she said to Andrew, "pick up my feathers for me would you – I think the room's getting a bit chilly. Do something about the fire, Twomey, please . . . . Thank you, dear child, how kind," and she re-coiled the boa's black feathers with appropriate deftness.

In the persistent silence only Dada found his voice. He gave an indistinct signal towards the sideboard and a bottle of rather sweeter pudding wine. "Quite nice." He paused before he added: "I think." Then they all talked wildly. Even Nicandra, feeling sick as if she was eating Aunt Tossie, had a question ready for Robert. "Do you know the Froth Blowers

78

Anthem?" When she turned to ask him she saw that he was blushing painfully. Aunt Tossie's misdemeanour became to her forever more indecent.

The road to the Hunt Ball was a long one – Dada drove the car, bestowed on him by Aunt Tossie years ago, when he had been rather upset. It had proved quite an exciting substitute for lost love, and a pacifier in that time of grave trouble. He considered it more dangerous than any horse he had ever ridden, and drove it on a tight rein, seldom exceeding 35 m.p.h. Even so, he had survived some narrow escapes; always the fault of a Rotten Fellow's hopeless driving. Tonight he chose an even longer road than the direct route to the ball, hoping to lessen any chance of approaching headlights.

Nicandra and Lalage sat with carriage rugs over their knees in the back of the big car. Aunt Tossie sat beside Dada, a hot-water bottle at her feet and another in her lap, dreaming the time away and sobering up. Now and then, a hand inside her fur coat, she clutched at her bosoms and pushed them farther down inside her dress.

Lalage grew desperate at the slow speed of their progress. I could beat him on my bicycle; if it was daytime the ass-carts would overtake us, she thought. Wiping breath from the window, she peered out at the landmarks, all so distant from the place where she longed to be. Every moment of pleasure missed was painful to her. She could hear music. She could see dance programmes filling up, and not a name on hers. Her distress was evident to Nicandra, who felt nearly as embarrassed by Dada's miserable driving as she had been by Aunt Tossie's disgraceful exhibition. She wondered if the boys were discussing this as they whizzed along the nearer road in Andrew's fast car.

They came at last to the great, bulky empty house, staring across to parklands through the inspired grouping of its trees. Ghost of the family that had failed it and sold it, still a stubborn Protestantism held it aloof from usefulness to any new owner. Now it was due for demolition. Its death had been postponed, which had enabled the Hunt Ball Committee to hire it for the triumphant last appearance of a house that had outlived its glamour, and all kind importances.

Two men with stable lanterns in their hands waited on the grand sweep, vast as a sea shore, before the house. They guided cars to the curving verges of grass, once mown close, now high and grown with thistles.

Lalage jumped out of the car and waited, hopping from foot to foot like a child longing to pee, while Dada and Aunt Tossie slowly disembarked. Nicandra came last, and full of apprehension. The muffled men with the lanterns lighted their way into the house – up a vast perron, where once guests had sat in the sun before luncheon, and on into the hall, music belching into its emptiness.

Two loyal members of the Hunt, a hawk-faced lady and a meeker male partner, his coat a warm flame in the dark crevice where they sat, took their tickets, and money from Dada, and handed programmes, a Hunt button engraved on their backs and a tiny pencil attached to them by a red string. "You're a bit late, aren't you?" the stern lady said. She was shivering in her dark fur coat. "You know where the cloaks are? Old Gwen's bedroom," she said to Aunt Tossie. They had both known the house when "old Gwen" was its chatelaine. Then, they were as young as Nicandra and Lalage. This reminder of a living bedroom was the shaft of an arrow cleaving an accurate way through time.

In the bedless bedroom, a fitted canopy stretched out squarely over nothing. A forgotten lithograph, the Hounds, the Hunt Servants and members of the local Hunt (numbered for identification) still hung on a wall, stubbornly reminiscent of better, or anyway, different times. Aunt Tossie, a survivor from those days, and unconscious of a further decline, looped her feather boa strategically, and called to the girls to hurry.

A sad old woman rose from her chair, as from a dais, to take their coats and hang them on a row of hooks nailed against a wall. A housemaid had been disinterred from the past for the occasion. She was too well-trained in the proprieties to smile a recognition at Aunt Tossie; and Aunt Tossie did not remember her.

It was Nicandra who said: "Aren't you cold?" as she took off her coat. A gust of winter air shook the shuttered windows into a mild clatter of protest.

"Oh, no, miss. I love to see the style. The style today is only gorgeous." She belonged to the present more than to the past of that bedroom. Her eyes ate up Nicandra's beaded satin, and shifted disapprovingly from Lalage's muslins – a clothes snob to the last.

"You *must* be cold," Nicandra insisted. She had found someone to pity. "Don't you want a cup of tea?"

"I'm only killed from tea." Nicandra recognized a raffish, twinkling suggestion that something stronger might be acceptable.

"Come along, girls. Come along," Aunt Tossie was all for the fun of the fair.

Downstairs, it was warmer. Chimney-pieces and brass-bound grates had been torn out, dismembered, and sold, but fires still roared savagely, or sulked monotonously under cavernous chimneys. The draughts that had drawn them when politely caged, were now either depleted or charged to fury.

Holly and trails of variegated ivies were nailed to the deeply shadowed squares where pictures had hung, their absence now heavily distinct on the wallpapers – Victorian damask papers, shredding in places to much earlier designs.

Through a string of three rooms they came close to the Ballroom; only an ante-room divided them from it. Dada, looking very small and distinguished, was waiting for them. The boys advanced: relieved from the onus of making Dada speak, they were quite eager in their delayed approaches.

"Ours is nearly over," Andrew said reproachfully, stooping towards Nicandra.

"It doesn't really matter," her response was awkward enough. Even more awkward when she said, "Do you think you could get me a small glass of whisky?"

"Scotch or Irish?" Andrew's enquiry came sharply. He had not expected to pay for any drinks tonight. "Irish," she said at once, surprising him again as he left on his mission.

"Don't wait for us, *please*," Nicandra said to the other two. "Oh, really, please don't."

Robert hesitated – knowing the destiny of the whisky, Lalage took a chance: "Of course we will," she said – and how right she was.

"Thank you so much." Nicandra took the glass from Andrew as if it was a chalice, and turned away.

"Where are you going?"

"To the Ladies' Cloaks. I won't be long."

"Drinking Irish whisky by herself in the Ladies' Cloakroom?" Andrew looked dazed and slightly shocked.

Lalage was laughing. "You won't see her for another half an hour." Acting as quickly as when she had gone to ground after Nicandra's Nettie, she took his hand, lightly as a tame bird arriving to perch on a finger; with a touching confidence in his response, she turned her little monkey's face up to him, dropped the hand she had touched and, without a backward look led the way to the Ballroom.

Robert stood alone and waited; he was patiently expectant of Nicandra's disappointment when she should see him. Aunt Tossie was deep in talk with a friend she hadn't bothered about for years. Dada had disappeared on some sort of little prowl of his own. Anything to get away from the noise, Robert could imagine him thinking.

Aloof and separate from her ugly dress, Nicandra's beauty had an air-blown helpless quality divided from her proper self – the self that carried whisky to cloakroom maids and, in the act, lost her man. As she came uncertainly to him, Robert felt for a moment the deep pleasure and well-being of sun on his shoulders. She could never share his contentment, but there were ways in which to please and help her. She was a bad dancer and he would be happy to improve this lack and ignorance. Music and dancing were incorporated in his awkward body and gentle mind. On the dance floor, his shape blew away in the secure grace of his dancing. He wished they might share this brief delight. Tonight he knew he was more likely to find the right and athletic partner in the wicked little friend who knew how to dance and how to steal, and how to do both quickly.

"Robert," Nicandra said, and again, "Robert," changing the inflexion of disappointment to one of pleasure. "Robert you're waiting, I'm *sorry*."

When he put an arm round her she was unyielding and at odds with the rhythm; he persisted, compelling her compliance not to him but to the music. "Ah, you're there," his voice sounded inconveniently deep. When the band stopped they were both on a tide of pleasure; yet, she stepped away from him as though evading her share in the pleasure. "Thank you muchly," he said.

They joined the drift of crowd towards the sitting-out places and the too few chairs. Groups drank champagne and screamed with laughter. The loudest and most determined joker was a son and nephew of the house, staying in some house party for the ball. He seemed bereft of sense as he pulled ribboned holly sprays from the walls and fed them to a sulky fire, cheering as they crackled and spurted heatless flame up the chimney. His eyes were wild, and he blew on a hunting horn. The girls mobbed him.

"Does he mind dreadfully, do you think?" Nicandra stared and listened. "About the house, I mean."

"Not a lot, I don't think, he hunts the country now."

"Yes, of course, that must be a comfort to him."

"Yes, of course. Lots of noise." The horn sounded again shrill and pleading – a "go home" note over the dying house. The huntsman was young and rather drunk. Nicandra stood, transfixed in unwanted pity.

"Would you like a glass of wine? I see your father has an open bottle." Robert had to say it again before she heard him and looked across to the table where Aunt Tossie and Andrew were drinking and Lalage was jumping up and down, opening her mouth to catch with complete dexterity the pieces of biscuit that Dada, suddenly lively, was throwing into it. As they watched, Andrew picked her up as though she was a little dog and carried her, kicking, back to the ballroom. ". . . . or would you rather dance?"

"I don't think so. What would you like to do?"

He didn't want to see her hurt, longing eyes. After this dance, Lalage must give up her predatory conquest. Till then he would keep his love safe on a desert shore. "My mother tells me there's a marvellous Regency conservatory, better than any house in Kew Gardens. Let's look for it." He had guessed correctly. She was ready for a refuge and he would find it and bring her there. How easily she bruised, he thought. What did Nannie put on bruises? *Pomade Divine*? And he was offering her a derelict conservatory.

After a time, and the search became a Treasure Hunt, they found the window, shuttered and barred, that opened into darkness. It was not outdoor darkness, but a place where a star shone through glass. Carrying an oil lamp, lifted from its brass standard, Robert lighted their way. They saw a long pool, a puddle of water shrunken to the rotting lily roots on its muddy floor. Three downward steps stopped above a tidemark of dried moss and waterweed. Happy and beautiful objects were still in their perfectly positioned places. Two plaster horses on folded knees leaned their heads prettily, coquettish, fresh for mischief. A lead Cupid aimed his arrow from the top of a marble pillar. Branches lay across the mouth of a pottery urn, their budding twigs stiff and still in a difficult death. Tubs, their ribs opening, held the corpses of camellias, their desperation for water manifest. Robert and Nicandra stood quietly in front of a bronze, a lover's head perhaps, placed unnoticeably some time ago. Like confessions of happy confidences, two chaises-longues turned to each other, broken canework unwinding down their legs. Robert picked up a wineglass from the low table that stood between them and scratched with a fingernail at the dry stain on the bottom of the glass.

"And another one," she held it towards him, a very long tumbler.

"Whisky for him and she drank wine," was his verdict.

It was all so despairing that Nicandra felt quite jolly when they had closed the window and barred the shutters on their escapade and Robert had restored the lamp to its standard.

Aunt Tossie and Andrew were sitting together, an empty bottle and one half empty, between them – they looked inordinately distinguished in their black clothes. Aunt Tossie's bulk was poised with extreme elegance. Every feather in her boa fluttered and caressed as she lifted her arm and her glass. Andrew sat close to her, immensely sad and trusting, as though she was his refuge.

Aunt Tossie looked up. For the moment all the world was her playground. "Darling, do have a glass of wine. You look cold, darling – are you cold? Where have you been? Robert, find two more glasses, please, if you would."

"Where's Dada?" Nicandra asked, not from curiosity, more for something to say.

"Dada's *dancing*. With Lalage. It's the Blue Danube, so he can. Isn't that lovely? Two Tinies swirling together."

85

At the word "dancing" Andrew had risen slowly to his feet. As though he remembered his manners, he looked an invitation at Nicandra. She intended to say: Sorry, I'm dancing with Robert. She said: "Yes." They moved away together towards the music. The waistline of her white dress, belted solid with beads and diamanté, gave her the look of a page walking with a courtly gentleman disguised in black – doublet and hose lying in a chest at home – an elongated miniature by Hillyard, a gentleman up to no good.

Aunt Tossie could never bring herself to disapprove of any man, however loaded with mischief; she preferred men like that. But, always kind: "Well, Robert, dear fellow," she crooned when he came back from the bar (where he had bought a third bottle of champagne). "Sit here, near me, and let's be cosy . . . oh, well, perhaps just a touch," she turned her eyes away from the bottle and gazed absently at the passing crowd until her glass was quite full. Nicandra was happy. Dada, dear fellow, was happy. How many years since he had whipped up the spirits for any party? Obviously this wicked little thing appealed to him. Another wicked lady once had him in thrall . . . . Her presence and her loss had been equal disasters. There was little for his comfort. He was too old to breed or to ride another Nicandra. All the good rides went to younger amateur gentlemen. Life dithered on nervously, and he approved of nothing in it. He felt rather shy and silly, when he came back to the table with Lalage, skipping along and grabbing for his hand as she went.

"Oh, so wonderful," she sang a bar in perfect tune, "such a swirl! Oh, thank you."

"Yes," he said modestly, "I think I had the riding of it." A dream was explicit in the phrase . . . to get away with hounds, on a good horse, with a good start, and then ride your chosen line of country to the finish of a hunt. The past showed in his eyes. There was a quickened magnificence about him, Nicandra, back from the ballroom, thought, as she had thought once before when he came riding towards her through a spring morning, transformed from little Dada into some kind of royal in his own right. Then, it was a letter he forced her to give up. Tonight someone else was his comfort.

"Well," Aunt Tossie said, "and how was it, my darling?" Impatient to play her loving part in Nicandra's fate, whatever might befall her, she looked up from her glass, raising her head like a bird that finishes drinking.

Nicandra's eyes were full of tears. "Sorry I didn't hear you," she said crossly.

Recognizing her proper place, outside success or failure or even heartbreak, Aunt Tossie turned at once to her brother-in-law: "And did you have fun, naughty old thing?"

"Couldn't stop her, caught hold and fairly hopped it with me," he spoke almost under his breath. Aunt Tossie knew she had embarrassed him, but it drew attention away from Nicandra.

Dancing with Andrew should have been as magical as when, in dreams, she had danced with Berry or Jonah. Tonight, she and Andrew ought to have hummed along, two messages meeting on a wire. It had not been at all like that. Andrew's reserved, night-club hesitation was foreign to the music, and quite foreign to Nicandra. Stiff and inelegant, she followed him, more anxious than ever in her life to please. Rigid attention cramped all response, her feet were corpse-like in their obstinate denial of accord – only his patient skilfulness forestalled disaster. He persevered silently while the music played, and drew a deep breath when it ended.

Now, as he drank Robert's champagne, and saw her, silent beside him, her head set downwards, a columbine on its stem, and as modestly inaccessible, Andrew knew that good manners and good sense told him to redress the misfortune of that last experience. He leant over to whisper: "The next?" She was beautiful, she was rich. Each must recognize the invaluable importance of belonging to the Anglo-Irish "Family". That little wanton who had so suited and amused him had all the qualities necessary for a love affair, but none of those he calculated as obligatory in the girl that he might marry some distant day. Lalage was not on the list.

"Dada's simply dropping," Aunt Tossie told them. "What about beddy-beddy-byes?"

"Oh, not yet, please," Lalage jumped to her feet with the music. She danced a step before Robert, as before a vast idol. He shook his head. Then, captured, he followed her to the dance floor. He supposed he would be the one to drive her home in Andrew's car.

Later, in the hall, darkness grew again in empty spaces as candles guttered down and lamps blinked quietly as closing eyelids. The ball was over. Robert knew, as he waited while Lalage laughed with some stranger, that he was standing near a death-bed. Solemn and clamorous, a choir of young people filed across the hall to the staircase. The men wore the facings of distant hunts; the girls' dresses were short and narrow as striped rushes. "Old Man River," they sang, "he must know something . . . ." they processed, always singing, not knowing that they sang a dirge. They turned and went up the flight of stairs, a frieze of well-behaved actors.

"Aren't they heaven?" Lalage was back with Robert. "It's the houseparty from Mount Martin." Her eyes were full of tears as she stared after them. The reverence she had for glamour touched him. "Lovely to be going home with you, you can't believe how badly that old fool drives." Her bad taste distanced her again.

Sleepy and cold in the back of Dada's slow, unheated monster, Andrew put an arm round Nicandra's shoulders and pulled

88

her close for warmth and company. "You're cold too," he whispered, and laid a hand on her satin-covered knee.

Nicandra knew that this was a forbidden approach. Serious, and reluctant, she pushed his hand away, and waited for the kisses on the cheek allowed within the code.

Mistaking her refusal, Andrew put back a less prudent hand to find it struck away smartly as she retreated from the arm round her shoulders. The car was so big that when she leaned back into her corner there might have been a cold room between them.

Andrew was not going to accept rebuke or defeat from this untutored beauty. He was a beauty too. Like a game-cock in arrogance, he lifted her back across the dividing space and pulling away the collar of her, inevitably musquash, fur coat, he dropped his mouth low on the back of her neck, drawing kisses to and fro and nibbling gently across it.

Nicandra's response, the release of her body, was absolute. There was a wild quality in her innocence that startled him; it was as if he had violated and deflowered her quite by mistake. In her acceptance she broke the code of propriety, went beyond the established manners in a light encounter. She should have laughed and snuggled and taken kissing only as a passing pleasure. As it was he had to find his own way out of an embrace involving him far more seriously than he intended. Although, in manners bound, he held and played with her hand for the rest of the drive home, he felt that he could have done instead with a nice talk about hunting.

A thermos of soup, cups, a plate of sandwiches waited on an ugly silver tray in the hall; a domestic attention marking the end of the party. The fire burned hugely; Silly-Willie had been kept out of bed to feed it. The warmth of the hall was exaggerated by the absolute cold of the night outside. This house still lived; there was no possible reason to question the permanence of its long-preserved prosperity.

Dada came in last, a frozen leprechaun: he never wore an overcoat. He had put his precious car away, rugs over the engine, the doors of the coach-house clamped together and bolted. There was mud on the heel of one evening shoe .... "Bit of bone in the ground. Not enough to stop them." He meant the hounds.

"Soup?" Aunt Tossie invited.

"When I've let the dogs out," he fussed away.

"Well, children, I really think, Bed." Aunt Tossie threw her coat open. Then, remembering that she had left her boa in the car, with a totally unhurried gesture, she put a hand up to hold it together at her throat. Smiling, she waddled her way towards the staircase – a figure from a Russian fairy-tale, Robert might have thought.

Andrew came back from opening the door for her: "Do you think they'll hunt tomorrow?" he asked.

"I expect they'll draw the woodlands," Nicandra said.

"They'll never get a fox to leave."

"No. They'll be there for the day." Nicandra felt crippled in their joint politeness. She wanted to be alone; to escape with her triumphant discovery. She knew now why she had been born, born for his love only. The tremor that had spread through her neck and from her neck, told her so. She supposed that he must share some, or all, of that ecstatic pang. "I think I'll go to bed now," her undemanding innocence set him free. He watched her climb up the first flight of the stairs, saw her stop and turn back towards him.

"Did you bring your own saddle?"

"No."

"Fagan *will* be pleased – strange saddles always give his horses' backs."

Somehow he felt that she had beaten him at his own game of keeping things on a cool level. He went back to the tray where the soup and the whisky waited for his comfort. He poured himself a large drink. Whisky after champagne? Which uncle had told him that was a fatal mistake? He had often proved that uncle wrong.

Before she undressed, Nicandra pulled back the window curtains, cold as glass in her hands, and stood between them to look out at the changed world. Even the moon was not the same. It hung lower in the sky, nearer, more golden, since now she loved and was loved. Once she had read a caption under the picture of a royal bride-to-be. The royal bride was looking gracefully down into dark water: the caption said: where brook and river meet. She understood its meaning because she was a woman now. For always, she promised her love, stretching up her arms to grip the curtains higher; she shuddered and almost sobbed in her happiness. To hell with Berry and Jonah, and Captain Lawless R.N., for now and always she had a love of her own.

Her dress lay on the floor, the linoleum nursery floor – weighted by its beads, it had fallen into serpentine coils. Her petticoat fell next; then the cami-knickers; after that the suspender belt with its four suspenders clicking in their release. Stockings dropped immediately to her lean heels. A bit raffish in her carelessness she stood with both feet trampling the heap of clothes until her head emerged from the muffling of the white, over-ribboned, nightgown. This unusual carelessness was her only overt act of celebration. The reality was in her mind; so much, so soon. In bed at last, believing and disbelieving, she turned her face delightedly into the pillows, smothering her certainty of kisses.

An hour later, Lalage came tip-toeing into her room where she heard a dog whining gently. It was Nettie, with a nose under the door. Quietly as a mouse, Lalage picked her up and, candlestick in hand, went carefully through the darkened house to the hall door where she waited, the candle flame blowing flat and sideways, until Nettie came back, grateful and apologetic for the trouble she had given. "Bed now, poor mite! Isn't that just it?" she asked. Back in her bedroom she settled the little dog beside the still-warm hot-water bottle in her own bed. Then she undressed with due care for her dress, unbelievably crisp after its night of stress. There were only shelves and drawers in the Nannie cupboard, so she was obliged to hang it by the loops of its sash from a hook on the back of the door. She put trees in her shoes, rolled her stockings into a ball and folded everything else with a natural carefulness. Then, in her neat blue pyjamas, she knelt as usual at her bedside. Practical and calculating, never leaving a stone unturned: "Oh, Almighty God," she prayed, "help me to get him."

~ Part Three ~

Aunt Tossie loved Andrew too. Old ladies have their fancies. Andrew, with his lovely looks, his quiet ways, and his proper manner, went straight to Aunt Tossie's heart and head. His response to her warm generosity, his attention when she swept all importances aside to consider the greater importance of the 3.30 at Newmarket, won her completely.

Andrew enjoyed her company and respected her imperious resilience to the classic effects of drinking. That immunity could not last for ever, he thought, watching her rise to absolutely steady feet after her fourth glass of sherry. So far as Andrew was able to think beyond himself, Nicandra's beauty overpowered him. The vast and easy background of Deer Forest gave hope to a future prospect of marriage. For the present, prospects were hopeless. He had left his regiment (to his father's exasperated disgust) to learn about bloodstock and work for a while for a not over-reputable Irish trainer.

Three years after that Hunt Ball, where Nicandra lost her heart for ever, Aunt Tossie broke into her money-box to endow the marriage of Nicandra Constance with Andrew Julian.

Dada was against the match: "Not a tosser," he said, "and not a very tidy horseman either."

Aunt Tossie said, "Nicandra's not a horse."

"Oh yes, I agree, but it's bad blood. Don't touch it – no stamina – Old Andrew sold up and ran out to

Gloucestershire as soon as there was a spot of bother here."

"They were burnt out," Aunt Tossie reminded him.

"That's not the point."

"No darling, money's the point. Do I fork out?"

"Oh I shouldn't if I were you – what are we going to live on here? Everything going out, nothing coming in."

"If you kept away from the bloodstock sales, Dermot, dear fellow. . . ."

"Oh, be reasonable, Tossie, there's this really interesting filly coming up. . . ."

Despite Dada's sensible advice, Aunt Tossie swept all uncertainty aside and broke into her money-box. To buy happiness for her darling, she bought a rather delightful little house of early Victorian date. It had been a Church of Ireland rectory once, where some forgotten incumbent, a keen hunting man, had built a delightful little yard, adjoining the house and with every horsebox looking into the sun; with a hundred acres of good limestone land, the place was just the thing for Andrew and his horse-dealing. After the marriage, the light of Aunt Tossie's generosity continued to spread its rays across the valley between Deer Forest and Kileady. Andrew gracefully accepted (and expected) all that they were given and welcomed the ritual of Sunday luncheons at Deer Forest.

For Nicandra, it was different. All the loving and giving of small luxuries and necessities that she had not thought of herself, and the expected regularity of their attendance at those sumptuous Sunday luncheons, encroached dangerously on the precious isolation of life at Kileady. Some ingratitude within her shrank from Aunt Tossie's possessive sympathy and understanding. Of course, there was nothing for Aunt Tossie to understand, but her concerned enquiries, sometimes with three meanings embedded in their concern, Nicandra found difficult to negotiate. She was too stupid to parry questions like: "Don't you want a double bed, darling?

I'll give you a Giant's Affair." How to say that they felt better, Andrew felt better, in those close twin beds where they lay near, interested strangers, meeting, or perhaps not meeting, in the night .... Nicandra denied to herself that she and Andrew could think differently on any subject.

She was completely and obstinately happy through these their joyous times, these flying years of the 'thirties. The bond of horses was strong between them. Andrew bought young horses and made them well, Nicandra showed them to their best advantage, she had become a beautiful horsewoman. Sometimes money was made, sometimes lost: life was cheap and amusing, they had a host of friends – of them all, Lalage was perhaps the closest. Lal was a rich girl now. Her clever father was dead, leaving her a small fortune by the standards of the day. Surprisingly still unmarried, she lived with her obedient mother and spent the hard-earned money in a grand manner. She had a couple of not very remarkable horses in training; she bought a double horsebox – the first in the County. Andrew found her hunters for her, not neglecting a nice little profit, after Nicandra had schooled them into perfection. Lal rode them, so neatly and prettily, on as many days in a hunting season as her box could carry them to near or far-distant meets. The double box was a wonderful link between the three happy friends – as often as not it took Andrew's horse on as well as Lal's.

"You and I can share," Andrew would say to Nicandra, and to her the idea, particularly if it was a difficult horse, made her feel at one with him. But she always insisted on taking her turn when hounds moved on to the most unlikely draw of the day. Even better were the days when there was no box and she and Andrew rode home together through the short dark evenings, gentle friends, warm goodnights calling to them, stresses of the day, wonderful or not so wonderful, over and past, the time for loving and giving nearer .... Nicandra, who had never cooked, became expert and devoted; for the timing of a soufflé even love could be denied, the perfect soufflé – her present for him. Her real world provided all such occasions for happiness. She was happy when she starved herself of new clothes and expensive hairdressers, her bun gone, her blonde hair cut short, strict and styleless, by a merciless local hairdresser. She was happy when she sat up all night to spare Andrew a vigil by a sick or calving or foaling animal. She would call him when he was needed. "Get some sleep, darling, it's Listowel tomorrow" – one of his favourite little race meetings. And to Listowel they would start off early, Nicandra sleepless and dishevelled. There had been no time to set about her hair, or her blue-white face, only enough time to make a delicious picnic and pack its basket into the boot of the car. She might sleep then, until he shook her gently off his shoulder, because it was her turn to drive and his to sleep.

Robert found her, smiling and alone, sitting at the back of a stand.

"You look cold," he said. He settled his weight down on the step beside her and dwelt anxiously on her state. There was rain – or was it snow? – in her hair.

"You look fabulous," (he must remember her voice, unconsciously beautiful as the lonely bird). Her eyes were on his new sheepskin coat. "Where did you find that coat?"

There was a quiet smell of money about Robert, his business throve.

"Do you know your size?" he asked. "What size are you?"

"I meant, for Andrew."

"Oh," he said carefully, "I think I've got the last of this breed. Shall we have a drink?"

"No, I have to slip along pretty sharpish and get some money on to Lal's horse before they go out. Now, look what I've said."

"You know I don't have a bet."

"You don't talk either."

98

She looks so silly and so beautiful, he thought; not surprising that she gets the money on. "After this next then?" he invited.

"Love to, and Andrew and Lal?"

She left him. He watched her going down the steps of the stand, nervous and intent as though on a holy mission. She was too tall and untidy, but her quality shone out like a light as she passed into the crowd, and the noise and the tension that are part of even the smallest race meeting.

Before he saw Nicandra alone on the stand, he had noticed a different kind of tension; it was in the bar, where Andrew was having a drink with Lalage, while now, he guessed, Nicandra would be getting the money on to Lalage's horse.

"We'll watch my race and tremble together, shall we?" Lalage said. Robert noticed a long, thirsty – or was it hungry? – look exchanged between them. Poisonous little whore, he thought, and too rich. She looked rich too. That new Jaeger overcoat was belted in a vice-like grip and her perch on the shooting stick was that of a tiny, very well-balanced, bird.

All Nicandra remembered about that race meeting was her pure delight at getting the longest possible odds on Lal's runner and Lal buying a bottle of champagne after her race, the three of them were celebrating when she remembered her tryst with Robert. "One must be kind," she said apologetically, when she saw him waiting and called over to him to join them.

By the end of the 'thirties, Aunt Tossie wondered for how many years she had been paying for interesting yearlings, and with very uninteresting results. It had been worth it. There was a time when Dada could have done something really silly, like . . . well, like shooting himself. Time passes. Tragedy gets tidied away – mortal injuries subside. No point in saying money doesn't help. When Aunt Tossie gave, or spent, she was as exuberant as a child, tossing a ball into the air. "All right," she would say, "but don't be silly about it."

It's not long ago, Aunt Tossie thought (or said to Gigi – who was still ekeing out her parrot's longevity) that we used to be rich, dear bird. But it was not often that events of the past ten years paraded their shadowy happenings for her attention; very uncomfortable some of them were too – one unhappy little gamble of Dada's emptied her purse quite considerably. The endowment of her darling girl had meant a surprising depletion in her income. Some exciting advice – relayed by Andrew from a knowing uncle in the City – had jacked it up for a time, before an even bigger hole was left gaping by the failure of that magical investment. If she could not provide a remedy for life's major troubles, she accepted a way round. There was excitement in some of the greater changes that time dispensed over Deer Forest.

For instance, the afternoon when Twomey's touch with the tea tray's unfolding legs, successful for forty years, failed him, and teapot, Spode teacups, scones, sandwiches and blackcurrant jam crashed to the floor. The shame of it may have caused the slight stroke that overtook him, or perhaps the stroke preceded the disaster.

The upshot of it was: his due pension, and his departure to live with a faraway niece. Dada drove him to her little house beside a lake in Co. Donegal. Twomey sat silent for all the two hundred miles of road, holding his cat under his good arm. His dead hand he arranged, in a careful imitation of life, on his knee. Twomey's niece had prepared what she considered "a nice meal" for the travellers, but Twomey would not allow anything so unfitting as sharing a High Tea with Sir Dermot. He urged him to go to the local hotel, only twelve miles in the wrong direction. The thing

Dada remembered most distinctly about the uncomfortable occasion was the very nasty look Twomey's niece had given to Twomey's cat.

After Twomey: the deluge. Lizzie died, quietly and by herself, giving nobody any trouble. One morning, on his way down to breakfast, Dada saw her kneeling on the left-hand flight of the double staircase; thinking she was saying her prayers, she was bent so low, Dada stepped past her politely. After breakfast someone found her, sprawled in difficult death. Lizzie, mentor and bully of all under-housemaids, was a very important part of the established way of life at Deer Forest. But Mrs Geary was integral to its service. So it was quite an upset, though not quite a mortal blow, when shortly after Twomey's departure, she took to having very funny turns, sometimes active, sometimes depressive. Only Silly-Willie was able to calm or cheer her. When she threw five eggs (and the hens were laying badly) at the kitchen maid, he caught them cleverly as they sailed through the air. The funniest turn of them all took her one evening when, bent on success at all costs, she added a frothing soap powder to her immortal cheese soufflé. Minor disturbances, such as threatening the postman with a knife when, for the twentieth time, her expectancy of a letter was disappointed, were passed over, but the soap powder was a little frightening. With extreme tact and gentleness, Aunt Tossie persuaded Mrs Geary into an Old People's Home.

Following on Mrs Geary's departure, a new and surprising interest opened in Aunt Tossie's life. She, who had never made more than toast at a schoolroom fire, became an enthusiastic, if variable, cook. Her delight in her cooking was that of a very young child offering imaginary foods to dolls or sympathetic adults. Her admitted object was the instruction of Brigid, the kitchen maid, who had absorbed none of Mrs Geary's genius. Mrs Geary kept her secrets. Aunt Tossie had no secrets to keep. With no Mrs Geary to guide her, she plunged her ambitious way through the exotics of the *European Cook Book*. Her morning descent to the kitchen was for her a moment of happiness and importance.

She suspected that for her to cook was a debasement of proper status, perhaps embarrassing for the kitchen maid, at her elbow for lowly tasks, or, more particularly, for Silly-Willie who waited at the stairhead to escort her safely down. She corrected this idea by always wearing a hat, as though she had just looked in on her way to the garden.

For Silly-Willie the household difficulties and decay supplied an outlet for boundless energy. He was drunk with a new importance, knowing himself to be irreplaceably useful. He had learnt the proper way of cleaning and boning Sir Dermot's shoes and "doing" his lovely old clothes. He acquired a new dignity when he brought in the five o'clock tea tray. He did so smiling to himself in rapture at his achievement. His finest moment came the first time he opened the hall door to a visitor and, standing a little aside, intoned, "Follow me, sir," before proceeding with due dignity to announce the guest at the door of the morning room. His adaptation of Twomey's words and manner had in it something like the meticulous grace of his dancing to his mother's music. Now he danced to the airs of a dying house, keeping its remote stateliness alive above the enveloping neglect that clouded the memories of Lizzie and her slaves. Sir Dermot's old suits did not have to go through a great deal of abbreviation and pinching-in before they fitted him. The blue suit that no longer went to the Curragh race meetings or the Dublin Horse Show, was his evening wear. By day the grey alpaca coat, left behind by Twomey, covered him like a night-shirt; the turned-back sleeves often fell over his hands to hang for a moment with a pierrot's sadness.

Dada accepted all the changes at Deer Forest, not so much apathetically as with genuine indifference. Comfort had never been important to him. He was indifferent to good living in the matter of food, or wine, or warmth. He never cared if his feet were wet or dry. In the most dreadful weather he would stand and wait in a wet grove of ash and hazel for a shot at a woodcock. Of course, as time went by, he missed more birds than he killed. One late afternoon, swinging on a crossing bird, he slightly peppered Silly-Willie who only laughed and jumped about delightedly.

One matter Dada found extremely puzzling, but he was far too well-behaved to open the question with Aunt Tossie. What puzzled him was her reasons for meeting all expenses, and some absurd generosities, out of her capital, never opening her legendarily replete jewel box to assuage them. She was distinctly a bit funny about her diamonds, always reputed to be fabulous. The tiara had not glittered in Nicandra's wedding veil. She had endowed the marriage (and he could never really like the fellow) most extravagantly out of her invested money, rather than taking a dip among the jewels that she never wore. There was the time, too, when her refusal to recognize any point in the purchase of a most promising yearling had both distressed and exasperated him. Again, she had kept the lid securely shut on her jewel box.

By slow degrees, the world of the bloodstock sales lost the best part of its consuming interest for Dada. Now, at Deer Forest, two brood mares were all that was left from former dreams and ambitions. Both he and Fagan were outgrowing the proper age for coping with forward two-year-olds – hence the breaking and making of the Hunter class of horse they reluctantly put behind them.

Before long, there was a new interest and activity in Dada's life – an interest provided and paid for by Aunt Tossie, who had once divined how the extravagant purchase of the Bentley and the Purdey guns might, in some practical way, alleviate the loss of her wicked sister, his Love and Life; would at any rate restore something to his self-esteem. Now she decided that an active and harmless occupation was what he needed, a pursuit within the powers she knew to be passing from his skill and prowess with horses.

She bought a vast and expensive motor mower, a machine that required skill and nerve for its direction and management. She pointed out that the piebald donkey in leather boots that had for years pulled the mowing machine which cut the acres of grass at Deer Forest, was at the end of a useful life, and, in any case, the whole performance took up two working days of the farm labourer who drove her in long reins – reins thin as thread and cracked with age: there was nothing economical about that. Countering Dada's insistence on the mechanical incompetence of every man in the place, she stated firmly that he, Dada, was the only one fit to touch the new toy – that great virginal machine louring in its magnificence in the coach-house beside the stately Bentley and broughams and phaetons of other days. Lack of space was not one of the problems that affected Deer Forest. There, nothing was abandoned, nothing thrown away. In the late 'thirties, relics of previous lives and times were preserved in dignity and absolute uselessness.

Not all at once, but by degrees, Dada made a conquest of this stallion of modern technology. He learnt to moderate its speeds, and the cutting levels of its great blades. He had a magic touch on the string that jerked its engine into rather terrifying life. The wide passages he cut so clearly across the overgrown lawns and terraces delighted him. He expanded the area of cut grass to encircle nearer trees – this was his own idea and it pleased him hugely. Crippled as he was from many falls, only lately taking their toll, he found in the lawn mower a kind of substitute for the experiences of earlier, dangerous days. There was the nip of uncertainty: would she start? Stop? Get round that tree without disaster? It stimulated memories; perched aloft in his iron seat with mown grass a violent cloud behind him, he sometimes felt almost as though he was riding round Liverpool again. The sensation was particularly poignant when the weather turned wintry. Apart from this absurd recall, the lawn mowing was a worthwhile employment filling dull hours of long days.

It was on one of the most delightful afternoons of late summer, when Dada was getting round his bends most economically, never losing a yard of ground, that he saw Nicandra walking up the drive. She was alone. This was very unusual; she came only too seldom, and never without Andrew. He would be glad to see her. But not now. He knew she would understand. Important work had to take first place.

The house, grey and unsmiling, looked north down the slopes of Dada's well-kept lawns. Empty windows stared – there was nobody at home except Aunt Tossie in a distant wing, stitching away at another exotic parrot in her gros point. The kitchen was empty because Brigid had special leave of absence to attend a party given for her aunt who was making her profession in the Religious Life. Silly-Willie was killing ducks.

Nicandra was walking very fast, almost violently, through the hot afternoon. She had left her dogs in the car at the gate. There was always trouble between hers and Dada's darlings. She passed a grove of birch trees, their limbs mottled and elegant as a herd of giraffes. The stones in a wall seemed to ripen in the hot sunshine. A rook, picking at a dead rabbit's eyes, hesitated before he lumbered up and flew away. She walked with total indifference to what she saw. She was concentrating on the speed and length which her stride might attain as she hurried up the long slope. At the end of the 'thirties she had other things on her mind besides horses and cooking, dogs, bantams, geese and Love Eternal.

Andrew had not been pleased, not at all pleased, when she told him: told him with an almost religious reticence. In his want of pleasure, in his obvious anxiety, he might have opened a bank statement ending deeply in the red.

"Are you sure?" he asked. His anxiety, his thought for her, went to the quick of her loving. She lifted a radiant face for his kiss.

"Of course I'll be all right, don't worry," she said. When his kiss only brushed her cheekbone, she pulled herself away to stare into doubt.

"Aren't you pleased?"

"Oh well, of course I am. In a funny sort of way."

"Funny? What kind of funny? It's not funny exactly."

"Can't you understand? How do you think we can possibly afford this sort of thing?"

"Aunt Tossie would love it all. She'd help."

"Oh, I expect so. It's not just that, it's going to bitch up everything. Do think, darling."

She remembered the years of forethought and carefulness (methods described by Lal, always her sage experienced friend), and she thought of them without regret. They were part of her loving. Now, in spite of all her regular care, this had to happen. Before she told him there had been a kind of subdued glory, a triumphant secret warmth had been hers. Now she must deny it. The glory dwindled into a nuisance, a practical difficulty, since that was how he saw a child.

"How long? Oh, that's not long," he said hopefully.

"Don't you want it? You mean, you don't want it?" When had her secret become "it"?

"Can't you see the muddle it's going to make? Nannies, schools, God knows what .... and you know the Bally Raggets are thinking about me, joint with old Billy Naylor. We could have such fun," he pleaded.

"It's a rotten pack of hounds and a rotten little country." She spoke
her mind for him. Never for herself.

"I'd be hunting hounds." Despair for his pleasure was low in his voice.

"Oh my darling, what must I do?" She came nearer, she would give her life to please him, and this other life was in her gift now.

"Ask Lal," he suggested. "Old Lal is bound to know, and you might see what Aunt Tossie could come up with. Say it's to drain the West Bog."

It was a joke – he laughed. He knew she was on his side now. She saw the impossibility. He kissed her.

Her pleasure was divided with an odd memory, insistent behind her yielding: a little broody hen, persuading stones to be eggs under her spread feathers; after that, a cold nest. The memory left her entirely when she put her hands up to his shoulders, close into that bony warmth until, attentive to his abstracted silence, she dropped them. He was right, of course, this was not a time for love. She acquiesced with a full understanding of his reserve, and with no lessening in her dedication to his pleasure.

Nicandra was breathless as she neared the end of the Avenue. Here, every autumn since her childhood, she had been moved and pleased by the sight of cyclamen growing low and lavish in the leafmould under the copper beech where the driveway forked, left and right. One fork went to the stableyard, the other rounded the lawns and continued on to the gravel sweep and the hall door.

Nicandra waved and smiled at Dada, but did not try to speak above the enormous racket of his engine. "I don't know why I came, I can't possibly tell them," she thought as she watched the tiny man, perched up high as he circled meticulously round about on his chosen futureless employment, shouting: "Wor'-oss, Wor'-oss" to the dogs that followed him, as faithfully as seagulls follow a plough, when he made one of his grand and speedy turns.

She felt as distant from Dada as on that faraway teatime when he had turned down *Dora's Dolls' House* in favour of his photograph album – though now she thought of him with a gentle benevolence, the distance between them was changeless.

With Aunt Tossie, it was an entirely different matter. If she knew the truth today, her sympathy and her sense of drama would be equally engaged, and with her money, her right to know, to know everything . . . . not how Andrew had insisted, of course . . . . but Aunt Tossie's loving and monumental generosity would be a lasting shroud for unhappiness. Much as she dreaded the near embarrassment of asking for money, the West Bog and its drainage was the best and readiest solution to their problem. Not really a Problem, she assured herself. After all, six weeks, there could be only a shadow of "it" – "baby", "embryo" were words she didn't speak, even to herself.

The house was her object now: the house where, she told herself and believed, she had been so happy in a bright, unshadowed childhood. She saw herself as such a jolly little girl. She must have been quite a joker with that bantam on her head, pigeons fluttering noisily on her shoulders; it had all been wonderful outdoor fun. Her love for Maman, with its consuming passion to please, belonged to the times before Maman had, as she now realized, so gallantly followed her love. She no longer linked the flight with her own act of disobedience over the spinach, ably abetted by Aunt Tossie. The happenings on that day belonged vaguely to the moment when she had seen, not a butchering, but the butcher's ugly pleasure in a sacrifice. Pity for the lamb, its feet tied, its pale head held on the ground between Anderson's boots, had never been quite lost in an adult's sensible acceptance of such things being inevitable prior to Sunday's luncheon.

Both before, and for long after Maman had left them alone with each other, the useful and interesting occupations Aunt

Tossie found, or invented, for her, were always in unhappy contrast with both love and its cold aftermath. And, again in contrast to being a useful, helpful, sensible little girl, was her cosy friendship with the changing series of under-housemaids who laughed so readily at her jokes and gave her lumps of sugar from morning tea trays – sometimes it was a peppermint. Mind and don't suck it near Nannie. They were all in a delightful conspiracy of naughtiness.

Then there was Silly-Willie at the Gate Lodge. Before Aunt Tossie had sent him away to that Special School, Nicandra had been such a good little Queen to him. She had enjoyed bringing him goodies from the kitchen – ends of puddings in one of the dogs' dishes, the last remains of cakes, meat, bones – only chicken bones, because they were so bad for the dogs. She ordered him to dance for her before she bestowed the treats. Once, that was after Maman had gone, and when his own mother was distant, she had compelled him to eat a whole snail, slashing his legs with a nettle till he obeyed, and the stinging of the nettle really enlivened his dancing. And there was another "it" in the rela-tionship between Queen and subject – a little incident to leave strictly alone in the dark sludge of memory. After Maman went away it excited her to hurt somebody. There was nobody to love.

Today she was hungry only for the house. She reminded herself that one day it would be hers and Andrew's. Surely the Estate owed her something immediately. They should not feel aggrieved at her asking for money; when she went into the cold hall she felt that it would not give her back much, if anything. The hall had always seemed as unfriend-ly as an abandoned church – it belonged to the days of Lizzie's strict attention and Twomey's quiet, dignified foot-steps. The two tiny suits of armour still stood where they belonged since some remote knight had given them up (sent them to the attic of the day, like old hunting boots). Here they remained: first in the Tower, now in the house that had succeeded it. The slots and slits in their visors were full of dust, their drooping gauntlets gripped on nothing at all. The huge "club fender" of early Edwardian times should have held on to its proper suggestions of Christmas, when a group of laughing guests sat there, full glasses in their hands, while child actors performed in a glittering pantomime, entrances and exits from behind the Christmas tree. Maman was a true victim to any sort of party. Of course there had been many Christmas parties after Maman went away, Aunt Tossie saw to that – but they were not memorable. Thoughts of that previous one only crept their way back with the forbidden thought of a child.

She went through the hall to the ante-room below the great upward-plunging staircase. Again, without Lizzie's care for its brass rods and polished margins, it rather slunk upwards, its dignity lessened by the light to which it climbed. Sunlight poured down from the window in the upper ante-room, to the twin flights of the stairs. Some evenings she and Andrew would separate on the halfway landing and go up by different flights to meet and kiss at the top. Anything, Nicandra knew, was worth doing to keep this dream living. She knew she could not fail him. As a presage, she didn't go up to the top alone. She turned her back on the light and opened the door on to the smaller staircase.

Dust everywhere here too. It lay thick on the margins; a bat, alive or dead, clung on the corner of a picture frame. There was a sweet horrible smell of bats in the lavatory. The two nurseries were damp discarded places, their ceilings blistered and flaking like old orange peel where rain had forced its way backwards from blocked gutters.

Here, through the space of a breath or two, she could live for a moment in the rapturous evening when she and Lal had dressed for the Hunt Ball: the evening that had given her Andrew. From that night their courtship had been her life. Could he get leave for this dance? For Punchestown? For the Horse Show? Since their marriage, three years later, his will and wishes had been hers. In their fulfilment, her won happiness was as complete as that of a warm purring cat. A barren cat, she reminded herself quickly, is just as happy. Happiness is vulnerable to its own destruction. Nicandra was dimly aware of this possibility. So a blind obstinate energy kept her constant in her refusal to allow any eventuality to mar her Love Affair.

Her exalted moment of remembrance expired, she sighed in her relief and in her certainty of purpose. It was only from idle curiosity that she went into Nannie's room. There the presence of the past startled her, not altogether pleasantly. It differed from what she liked to think of as those warm closeted nursery days. This nursery had been better preserved in its decay than her own bedroom. It was still a nursery. A chair, amputated to accommodate Nasty (and she had been nasty) Nannie, still sat near the fireplace; the cold grate was still guarded by its high wire fender. A round table covered in cracked oilcloth stood bare of bowls, jugs, cups and saucers. The brown teapot with a slightly broken spout sat like a cold little sentinel on the hob, jackdaws rustled above it in the chimney.

The awful sensation of a dead nursery comforted her; she did not want nurseries to seem cosy and beautiful. Employing only a cool curiosity, she had defended herself from sentimental pretences. Discarding pretence still further, she opened one of the drawers in the white chest of drawers, slamming it shut at once on the unfashionable baby clothes that Nannie had left in tidy small piles, washed and mended as though she had planned for them an after-life in which Nannie's memory should have a lasting importance. She felt angry at the idea being thrust on her, and more determined in her purpose of obtaining money for the drainage of the West Bog. She only dreaded that she might be asked to give some positive details of the scheme she and Andrew supposedly envisaged.

It was tea-time in the morning room. Aunt Tossie lifted the top half off one of yesterday's scones and spooned blackcurrant jelly on to it. Dada sat low, his knees well below the level of the table. A nursery high chair would have been better suited to his bent and miniature height. He gazed longingly at the sandwiches, Gentleman's Relish, but he did not take one – neither did Aunt Tossie eat her scone. They were waiting for Nicandra to come in. They had something rather awkward and difficult to tell her. The western sun shone, drenching the morning room in an excess of light. Dogs gasped and changed places; long ago cushions and covers had placidly yielded up their colours; Aunt Tossie's parrots fainted into their backgrounds, curtains dangled the edges of their rotten linings in the glare; the evening was brimmed with lassitude.

When Nicandra came into the morning room, the air was stilled for a moment. The sudden sight of her, the extreme quality of her beauty, always moved Aunt Tossie into an ecstasy of appreciation: appreciation and regret for Nicandra's shocking waste of its potential. Why must her blonde hair, bleached now by the long summer's light to a ravishing pallor, be chopped so harshly? Why not use those enormous silly grey eyes that never had a wayward or mischievous look in them? The very unattractive grey flannel trousers, who could guess at the legs they hid? The charming breasts were lost in the folds of a faded Aertex shirt of Andrew's. Revealing sweaters were in fashion now – after all it was 1939, not 1914 – so why not wear one? Aunt Tossie knew that a slavish contentment in marriage should never obliterate further effort. That was the fatal way – sometimes she trembled for her dear one. A trapped rat is safer than a prisoned lover.

"Hullo my darlings," Nicandra stood in a blinding shaft of sun, one hand held her shirt up to her chin, "How *are* you?" The "are" was prolonged. Dada felt foolish in her concern.

"Darling one, you're looking wonderful." Aunt Tossie shuffled the cups and saucers, "Sit here, near me, and try one of my scones – made only yesterday. Silly-Willie popped them back in the oven and buttered them up himself. Isn't he getting clever?"

Nicandra shuddered.

"I've left three for you," Dada suggested the sandwiches.

"Please, a cup of tea," Nicandra proposed weakly. "No milk, oh, thank you." Very apologetically, she moved a dog from the corner of the sofa nearest to Aunt Tossie and reached for her cup and saucer. "Oh, Dada," she was conscious of some uneasiness – was he hurt by her refusal of one of his favourite sandwiches? "Actually I think I'm rather hungry – I've been longing for a sandwich. Can you spare one? Gent's Relish, how perfect." She ate a sandwich. She looked rather queasy, and very anxious. Aunt Tossie considered if this was the right evening to tell her the news.

"How's the Crippen colt?" Nicandra asked.

Dada answered cheerfully: "All right – going to the November Sales – don't think he'll do a lot – very unattractive – small – back of his knees – beautifully bred. Don't know what went wrong. The mares are going too. They might do something for us."

"Dada!" It was a cry of consternation. "You're giving up? You can't think of it – no horses."

"Oh, a time comes," Dada spoke the words as though he was quoting somebody else.

"It's not just the horses," Aunt Tossie longed to get it all over with. "The place has to go too – and the house." She looked round the room in a tolerant way, "Giant liabilities. Can't pay these iniquitous rates. Can't mend the roof, and it's pouring water – we've made soul-searching economies, and the Bank is still perfectly livid with us." She spoke rather grandly.

Nicandra was silent, stunned in disbelief. An agony of love overcame her. This was why the house had turned its back on her approaches, showing her no return, no promise of refuge when she had come, hungry for its comfort, its assurance of the future.

"Who do you think is going to buy Deer Forest?"

"The Agents have some splendid tycoon smelling at it. We don't know his name yet, but they're sure of him." Aunt Tossie sounded confident.

"We're to perch here till he decides to take over." Dada laughed merrily.

"That might be quite some time, we think he's English. All this bother with Hitler and Poland. Yesterday's *Times* had rather a worried headline."

Nicandra shrank into her corner of the sofa. "No, thank you." She refused Dada's offer of a second sandwich. "I feel rather sick," she said.

"Oh my darling, not fro-up sick?" Aunt Tossie asked as she might say: "Do hope it's not something nasty settin' in?"

Nicandra shook her head. "It's just – I can't believe it. Is it all settled?"

"Almost. We'll be all right – you mustn't worry," Dada said.

"I mean to buy a caravan – do they call them 'Mobile Homes', what an awful name! – Gigi will love it."

"This lawyer fellow says I can have a flat in the stableyard."

"Think of all the fun doing it up. Plumbing too," Aunt Tossie put in.

"But why must you? And what about old Fagan? And all the other men?" Nicandra was looking for difficulties.

"They'll be taken on – I've insisted," Dada sounded like a great benefactor.

"And Fagan needn't move," Aunt Tossie reassured her. "Dada will be over the Pigeon Cote and the old dog kennels."

Nicandra drew a deep breath. It had to be said. Only she could say it. She must not fail him. "Have you thought – what about Andrew and me?" She choked back further words. It was an accusation, and in the poorest of taste.

There was silence. Aunt Tossie pushed her chair away from the tea table and reached for her latest square of needlework – a parrot clutching its way up the husky stem of a palm tree. She said gently: "Don't be hard on us, darling. The place is in ribbons. And, oh, the Bank. . . ." She shivered.

"We don't talk about this sort of thing, do we?" Dada meant Wills and Successions. "I don't know if you realize, but your Aunt made over most of her stuff to you when you married this fellow. And I've been bleeding her white ever since. Stop the rot. Stop the rot. Stop the rot." He cried out three times in his pain.

Nicandra was angered by "married this fellow". She knew what "this fellow" meant when Dada said it like that. Her darling was belittled. If they guessed why she was here, beset by care, unable to eat a sandwich, how would they react? "We have our problems too," she said sullenly. "I must go." She got up, "Oh, I must – I've left doggies in the car."

That was an unanswerable reason. They did not try to stop her.

Silly-Willie met her in the hall, he came from the farthest door; his step was as fast and light as his dancing. Every step he took, Nicandra thought, he was dancing on a grave; not Aunt Tossie's death, nor Dada's, but the death of a house. He was in power now, the only useful slave left to them. Not surprising that he danced. He would rule them out of necessity. How well would he care for them? She thought he gave her an intimate, probing look as though he was thinking "does she know?"

Nicandra went down the steps and under the dark carriage portico that put its pillared bulk between evening light, or the light of the moon. She was going home to Andrew. She was shaken with her longing to see him again. How long was it, three hours? It felt much longer. The smell of Dada's cut grass was in the air. The thought of his busy mowing, so useless and so trivial as a defence against the disaster that encircled the house and their silly lives overcame her. With the pitiless unknowing complacency and contempt of the young, Nicandra resented their trivial employments of time, so far distanced from the terrible hazards of loving.

Presently Dada would go to the yard for his evening duties: a light inspection of the yearlings and a long and absorbing confabulation on their prospects with Fagan. Bloodstock was about as useful as Aunt Tossie's embroidered parrots, perched, or flying, or elaborately caged, on every cushion and stool in the house. Soon there would be no more cushions or stools for her to decorate. She could quite see Aunt Tossie unpicking the oldest and least favoured work and starting the canvas over again. Soon it would be the time for her evening drink: "Just the one, Gigi, don't you think?" she would croon when the old bird, freed from her cage, crawled up to crouch against her cheek. "Well, you're wrong, darling. Granny's taking a tiny one along to the kitchen. You want to come with me? You shall." In the hall she would put on her hat and, lulling all suspicions of decay and its mortifications to rest in the conviction of her own economical and resourceful genius, with Gigi on her shoulder, she would stand at the head of the basement staircase screaming (Gigi would scream too) for Silly-Willie and Brigid to come and take her instructions and give their assistance while she created some nauseating delicacy for Dada's dinner. Luckily enough, as she often admitted, unashamed and amused, Dada would eat *anything*.

Once out of sight of the house with its menaces and disappointments Nicandra ran down the drive, jogging and shaking to set herself free from what was not a baby. She ran desperately, soliciting a fall. When at last she fell, she waited, lying expectant on the stones, before, in a small anguish of disappointment she picked herself up. The reassuring love she had expected from the house she found in a different measure from the three little dogs, friendly, even worshipful, and proffering no accusations of her neglectful absence – their care and pleasures important to her, she leaned against the car and waited while they took to the woods and the wild. She did not court disobedience or fuss them by calling. She knew they would come back to her. Beyond the gates and the Gate Lodge, derelict in its faded prettiness, her real world waited, and in it the life that contained all happiness. "You're happy? Are you happy? You *are* happy?" she asked the dogs when they returned, relieved and refreshed, to hop bright-eyed and panting into the car. She drove out through the gates and along the demesne wall; the grip of blackbeaded ivies was close in its stones. Behind the wall, beeches and chestnuts were just faintly jubilant in their near escapes from the weights of summer. The lift of autumn in the air went contrary to the trouble she could not make herself consider.

In the village, she stopped to buy groceries; first on her list came cheese, then butter, then two pounds of very thin rashers of smoked bacon – Andrew only liked it smoked, and cut very thin. She waited, fatally near to the racks of wine, while an obliging boy shaved the slices from a fresh side. Suddenly reckless, she chose a bottle of wine – a vintage they should not afford. Its purchase lifted her heart so much that she bought another. Replete in a small guilty elation, she was on her way back to the car when she met Robert. She stopped. "Hullo, Robert, you do look green."

Ponderously unattractive and sick, that was how he looked. Pity rose in her, "What's the matter?"

"Touch of trouble on a lung – nothing much – everything under control."

"Everything under control", what a phrase! Of course, he was in Business now – a Business man. Did they say "Executive"?

"You aren't looking so very well yourself." He sounded anxious, but warmed to have something in common with her. She looked more untidy and uncertain than usual, he thought, and she was carrying far too many parcels.

"Oh, I'm all right," she sounded impatient. Then, remembering her manners: "What are you doing? Just shopping?"

"Not exactly. I've sent them a big consignment of wine, I'm in that as well as the grocery, and I'd love to know how it's selling." He indicated the glass-enclosed office in the back of the big old shop, "He's the Fortnum of the South. He gets his tea from us too."

"Oh, you *are* clever," she said, "are you making lots of lovely money?"

"Yes," he said gently, "I've been pretty lucky – may I have your parcels?" He took the load from her and walked rather slowly to the car.

When she had opened the car door and quieted the protests of the dogs, he put her parcels in, packing them together as neatly as any shop assistant. When he straightened up from his arrangements, his face was as pink as a very good ham, and his breathing sounded a trifle odd.

"Thank you so much," she said. "Don't overdo things, dear Robert. Promise?" She had to be giving something, he knew, if it was only a word. He turned away from her and went back to his business.

As she drove home by all the familiar back roads that shortened the distance to Kileady, the shopping euphoria dropped down into black anxiety. She would have to tell Andrew how little they could hope from Deer Forest, then or in future times. I'm a worry, I'm a nuisance, she thought, and took a hand off the wheel to scrape a tear from her cheek. She wished so desperately that she was coming home with good news. Money in her purse, their purse, was always good news for Andrew.

The sturdy drawing room (living-room was still an unborn word) of Kileady was devised to accommodate and celebrate the outdoor life: many dog baskets sat on its beige carpet, many pictures by Lionel Edwards and Snaffles hung on its ivory walls. Low tables from the General Trading Company, their surfaces faced with glazed maps, somehow invited the pleasant idea of a drink. In contrast, the curtains were velvet, heavy with gold braiding, a present from Aunt Tossie. They were lined and inter-lined, excluding any breath of draught, giving an enclosed night-club feeling when the parchment-shaded lights were on. Although they had cost a mint, Aunt Tossie felt they were well worth the money, a fitting background for her darling. Her darling rather hated them, but – still more – hated to hurt feelings. On this bright evening, they were looped back by twisted and tasselled cords; light came streaming in through the sashed plate-glass windows. The house had been a rectory once, large enough and plain enough to contain a rector's brood. Now, dogs, cherished like any other brood, took every advantage of Nicandra's tender indulgences.

Andrew and Lalage were sitting, on carefully opposite chairs, looking at each other. He had just told her his bad news. "And after that," Lalage was saying, "I think a little drink, please."

"All right. Get it for yourself." With resolute discourtesy Andrew reached towards the silver cigarette-box on the just-too-distant table. "Please," he said. Lalage was taking a cigarette out of her shagreen case. She put it in her mouth and snapped the case shut. "Lazy sod. Get up and give me a light, *and* a drink too while you're at it."

Andrew laughed. This was a kind of play-group affair affected between them. There was a whisper of whips through it, a distant whisper. For years she had waited, teasing him with abuse and flattery along with the frequent loan of valuable conveniences, such as her horsebox. She knew his tough unconcern over her other love affairs put an edge on his interest, an edge sharpened by her money. The irresponsibility of their odd relationship just suited him. She was, after all, Nicandra's greatest friend. "That's why I'm telling you," he said, "because you're my darling Nico's greatest friend." The extra depth in his voice was an answer in the game.

Lalage knew why he had told her. She guessed what he needed was information, then money. She would play along, another intimacy in their relationship was always of value to her – one of the opportunities her looks alone would never yield to her. Lalage had the style that goes beyond looks. This evening she was wearing a little suit from a woman called Chanel, something that she had drabbled and subdued into an obscurity proper to its country background. Its quality was, she knew, changeless. She wore no jewellery, except a gold and platinum twisted ring that some friend had given her, and the heavy signet ring, perhaps it had been her father's, that weighted one hand. Her hands were deeply sunburned and so was her throat; the collar-bones within the gaping shirt were dark as treacle.

Just back from the South of France, Andrew thought jealously – together with York or Doncaster, such jaunts were forbidden pleasures for him, especially now that this new incubus had been fathered on him, all three were beyond possibility. While they sat there together, drinking and smoking, Lalage considered Andrew's looks with discreet dissecting pleasure. She approved the beautiful careful clothes of the 'thirties that he wore with such distinction: the swinging tweed jacket, the striped shirt with its careful collar and gold safety-pin, the blue bird's-eye tie, all became him immensely. The shoes, handmade to last a life-time, should have been symbols of polite security, but there was no security. In this new emergency, Lalage looked behind the mask of prosperity and saw a valid reason to get closer to him, yet never to lean or serve. Kick him, she thought with brutal accuracy, that's the way to his bed. She knew the spark their play could generate, she was helpless in her own cruel naughtiness. Grief was not her concern.

"So?" she said, "You've had a long holiday from the kiddies."

"Nico's been happy as things are – were," he added mournfully.

"Yes, she loves her animals," Lalage aimed an accurate kick towards the brown Lakeland terrier that was approaching her. In the course of Nicandra's day, drinks time was biscuits time for dogs, "And what does she mean to do about it now?"

"She's worried, but she does see the point."

"The point is – *you* don't want children."

"I've nothing against the poor nips," he said crossly; "only, not now, we can't afford them now."

"Getting rid of them can be quite expensive too."

"How much?" he asked.

"About £100. You might get it backdoor for £25. Then, anything might set in after that job."

"Can't take that on of course." He looked quite despairing. "The whole thing's impossible."

"Financially?" Lalage looked into her drink, swirling and looking as if she saw money in the bottom of her glass. "Where's Nico?"

"She's gone to see Aunt Tossie."

"Bad news there, I've heard."

"She'll part with one of those diamonds she's been clinging to."

"Don't be silly, they must all have gone years ago, keeping Sir Dermot out of the Courts. He's really let himself go since my old Dad died. Too silly."

"Criminal, actually," Andrew sighed deeply over the excesses and idiocies of the previous generation. He got out of his chair slowly when Nicandra came in. She was preceded by a cloud of dogs. Lalage noticed that she did not stop to praise or caress one of them.

"Oh, Lal," she said. "Oh, good," her voice was lifeless. "Has Andrew looked after you?"

"Yes. He even made toast."

"Oh why? Kate left sandwiches ready, darling."

"*And* we found the sandwiches."

They sounded like two naughty children raiding a larder in a nice book for girls. Nicandra had no part in the adventure, no share in the fun. She remembered the horrid phrase: "in her condition" – tears were close. "Must feed the doggies," she stooped over them. "I wonder if Kate put the stew in the oven? I did tell her."

"Yes she must have. It smells delicious."

"Stay to dinner, why don't you?" Andrew said.

"Yes Lal, why not?" Nicandra echoed sadly. If ever she needed Andrew to herself, it was tonight.

"Well, perhaps – no, I don't think so," somehow Lalage conveyed a feeling of being unwanted.

"Oh, come on," Andrew insisted.

"No. Really. I have a runner at Naas tomorrow."

The contrast in their present lives could not be made more explicit. The distant race-meeting was exactly the place where Andrew would most wish to be. But Nicandra knew he would stay with her. The guilt she felt in depriving him of any pleasure was like a stitch in her side, yet the thought of the long day and the long drive were beyond acceptance. She was bound to be sick before the last race, either then or on the road to the meeting, or on the road home.

"You don't want to come, do you?" Lalage asked.

"Oh I *do*. But the bantam eggs are hatching tomorrow."

"You're quite right. Terrible drag to get there. And, anyway, we aren't trying." She looked at Andrew.

"No, I'm staying here." The self-sacrifice in his voice was poignant.

Sacrifice taken for her, Nicandra knew, accepting it as a certainty of his love and care. She had to keep him. He had to share all her bad news. He would never leave her alone with it. When Lalage had gone out to her car, she put down a dog and took Andrew into her long arms. "Well? What did they say?"

"Not a chance darling, and I couldn't ask because – guess what – they've put Deer Forest on the market, and" – the thought of others always first – "I wonder if they always have quite enough to eat."

"Oh, talk sense," she was proving herself beyond reason, and unsuccessful as well.

"You don't know, you can't imagine, it was *Indian* tea today. I could have cried. All right, I am silly, I'll feed the doggies," she drifted out of the room.

She was preposterous in every way, Andrew thought. "Dogs first" – that would take an immoderate time – perhaps long enough for a third drink. He deserved it. He could see no improvement in prospect anywhere. The bottle was in his hand when Nicandra came back from the kitchen. "All right, I know," he said, "it's my second – don't scold."

"You need it, sweetheart," it was the lover's voice, yielding, as if they were in bed. He put the bottle back on the tray. Her indulgence left him without any need.

"Open this," delightedly she held out a different bottle and a corkscrew.

"You don't happen to realize how broke we are?" He was looking at the label.

"Yes, but we've had such an awful day. We need something to keep us going."

He put the bottle on the low table and laid the old horn-handled corkscrew down beside it, a patient sacrifice to the economies that her careless pregnancy necessitated.

The opportunity to retrieve herself by usefulness came to Nicandra almost immediately – Lalage was back with them, downcast, apologetic. "Too miserable," she said, "the car stopped with me, not a spark of life. Could you, one of you," she looked from Nicandra to Andrew, "drive me home?"

"Of course, darling. Unless you'd stay the night?" Nicandra was always ready to give succour in times of trouble. Ready to confide her own difficulties too.

Andrew got between them, almost shouldering Nicandra out of his way. Tiny Lalage seemed to shrink to child-size below his near height. "I'll take her," he said, determination in his voice as though Nicandra had denied him the right to live.

"Please let me, you haven't brought the horses in yet," she was concerned only for his convenience.

In a silence full of his broken intention, she caught the look, passing helplessly between him and Lalage – a look that joined her love and her friend as clearly as if she had found them in bed. The whole truth, nothing but the unbelievable truth, was manifest in that short exchange. Nicandra's big hands hung by her sides, her world shifted place, all certainty lost and gone in a salty fog of despair. She had to believe. She must behave. She turned away from them.

"All right," she said, "You go."

"You're sure?" He sounded grateful – that was more frightening.

"Yes. Do go." She turned back towards the kitchen and the dogs' suppers. As she went she picked up the expensive bottle of wine.

"Don't pull corks, Nico," Lal spoke as if she knew something. It sounded like a midwife's warning. Nicandra couldn't watch them going out of the room together. She couldn't look out to see them in the yard. She could not discredit this terrible truth. Its alloy changed and weakened all she knew, all that was hers. She had never counted how much she gave with such ardent pleasure. Now, in a full moment, everything she had spent was lost and gone. Only this nightmare of unreality would continue.

Nicandra, whose living was loving and giving, felt a vindictive suspicion rising like scum to the surface of her acceptance. Outside, on the mean sweep of gravel, she could see Lal's sleek expensive car overwhelming the place, expressing money in every line, expressing all that Nicandra could not give. Alienated from her proper self, trust and faith extinguished, Nicandra walked out of the house, half blind from tears, and shaking. She was going to prove something.

The door of the car was unlocked. The ignition key was still in place – she could feel Lal's little body in the car; the driving-seat was moved so close to the steering that Nicandra found no room for her long legs. She thought of that small compact body with absolute hatred. There was a picture in her mind of short desirous legs and sunburnt heels. She slammed back the driving seat and looked at the unfamiliar dashboard with all its foreign signals. At her touch on the self-starter, the engine responded obediently.

What must I do? she asked, as Lady Jane Grey had asked when going to her execution. What now? What came first? Two horses were leaning over the gate into the yard. They came first. They were real and living. They must be stabled and fed. Their needs were well known to her. Their proper care was in her blood. Automatically, she led them in and gave them their feed. When she shot the bolts of the loose boxes home, she thought inevitably of the saying about shutting the stable door after the horse has bolted. When she walked back across the yard her precious little house stared at her malignly, its nest-like quality defaced. The blinds pulled, by her domestic decree, halfway down the windows discouraged all hope. They were part of another life, neat signals towards its ending. Back in the house, she went from one ordinary object to the next, chairs, tables, bookcases, touching and leaning against them as if for help. Their immobility had no reassurance. Connection was gone between what had been and her present distress. She thought of the baby only as her last blunder in loving, a mistake leading her nearer to this dreadful woe.

I'm not crying, she told herself proudly, her throat working against her sobs. A dog came to her anxiously; at its concern, tears ran lavishly down her face, past her snivelling nose, into the corners of her mouth. The thought that she had failed him so awkwardly added to the weight of her pain. What to say? Did he realize what she had seen and must acknowledge?

However deep the trouble, dinner, like brushing your teeth, had to happen. I've lost Andrew, she thought, and I'm peeling potatoes. It can't be true. But Pommes Anna always went with Chicken Stew, it was a custom. The meagre little peelings falling from her knife into water eased her, their ordinariness was a link with real life. She felt grateful because it was Kate's day out so that she had this to do. Kate's day out had always been Nicandra's day for experiments made to please, and sometimes to displease, Andrew. Tonight there was a terrible neutrality between cooking and such love and service. She remembered the wine that she had bought and decided, almost viciously, to defy his dismissal of her extravagance and open the bottle. She drove the corkscrew in, twisting it like a knife in an enemy, stretching her shoulders back and pulling, with no result. Her will to pull the cork redeemed for the moment her grief. She stooped, put the bottle between her knees, straining and tugging, her hands searing to blisters on the rough horn handle of the long corkscrew. It was when the cork yielded that pain struck, paused, and struck again. She knew exactly what was going to happen now – she would lose her baby and he would commend her. Too late, she had found out a gift for her dear.

She was propped in bed, a soaking bath towel between her legs, when Andrew came back. She heard him calling for her quietly, then loudly. He needed his dinner.

"In bed?" he sounded amazed when her answer reached him. She heard him coming upstairs in quite an ordinary way as if nothing had changed, nothing had happened.

"What's the matter?" He was staring towards her, his hands on the rail at the foot of the bed. "Aren't you well?" His voice was patently unbelieving. Her answer waited. What was this distance between them? Only that now she knew.

"Rather good news, darling, you're going to have top treatment. Lal's given me – us – the money."

"You don't need it," the "you" was insulting, "I've lost the baby."

"Oh," the relief in his voice was tremendous. "Are you all right?" he asked politely.

She wanted to touch something, to hold on to something before she spoke, but there was nothing stable, only the hem of the sheet, twisting and giving way in her grip. She was mumbling words, the cool words she had rehearsed to herself were lost. In her absolute despair she cried out, the cry came through her whole shaking body into her voice. A child's voice was screaming in the darkness.

"I know. I saw you. I *saw* you."

"Oh, come on! Don't fuss, sweetie." He came round the bed and sat beside her. Her great distress really worried him. But it did not move him to pity her. She was behaving pretty awkwardly, was what he was thinking. He had to accept the truth of her accusation – he remembered the unfortunate moment of betrayal – but he was sure of finding a way round the difficulty. He needed them both. It was a requirement, Andrew's requirement. They were two sides of a coin and the coin was Andrew.

"I thought you understood – that's what's so great. You know it's you." He took her by the shoulders – "You and you, all the time you." He dropped his hands to his sides and stood like a little dog, found out, and admitting: "Yes, I know I have a silly sort of fancy for Lal. Tell you the truth, I wouldn't mind a month in the sun with her. After that . . . ." he shook his head to denigrate any idea of a lasting affair . . . "she's not in the running."

"And she gave you all this money?"

"Yes – for you – after all, she's an awfully old friend."

Nicandra's arms were flung out, wide against the pillows. In bed, where there was no witless, careless dressing to lessen her beauty, she was purely ravishing to look at. He did wish that custom and her total generosity had not made everything so easy as to be negligible. There was no game to play.

"Oh, God, I do love you. Have anything you want. Have a divorce."

His laugh was genuine. "You are a silly old toad." He looked at his watch, such a reasonable gesture. "Look, stay where you are – don't get up for dinner. I'll bring you yours."

Nicandra felt her way deeper under the bedclothes – she put aside what she had seen, that look, deeper than a kiss. A merciful wave was closing over it, healing her despair. Cry no more, ladies, where had she heard that? Anyway, why more than one lady? One was enough. She put her cold arms to bed and lay warmed and breathing slowly in her relief. Trust was back. She felt no unhappiness about her lost baby, only gratitude because Andrew was free from its inconvenience. And now, this testimony of love, her dinner in bed, she accepted with a shudder of pleasure. Andrew, always properly shielded from any domestic servitude, was muddling about in the kitchen now, a foreign place to him. He would be setting her tray, loking for knives and forks, salt and pepper, plates to heat. There were no Pommes Anna to puzzle him, but would he find the croûtons for the top of the chicken stew? Would he see the open bottle of wine? . . . Oh, poor love . . . her anxiety overcame her. She was sitting on the side of her bed, trembling with worry for him, undecided whether or not it would be safe to discard her bath towel and go to his help, when she heard a footstep on the stairs and bundled back into bed, anxious to conceal the unattractive evidence of her nasty little experience.

It was Kate – Kate looking young and jaunty, and quite unseemly, out of her cook's uniform of blue dress and white apron, or checked, to preserve the white.

"I only came in on the red, raw minute," she said, "so you'll excuse me, madam." She meant the pink jumper, tight skirt and high-heeled shoes. She settled the loaded tray on Nicandra's knees and shook out a white napkin.

Nicandra stared at the food and its arrangement – croûtons on the chicken, toast, butter, even a salad, no Pommes Anna, of course, but a glass of wine and a glass of water, and all the china matching. She touched things gently, unbelieving: "Did Mr Bland do all this?"

"Oh, God help him, poor gentleman," Kate laughed, pleased at male incompetence, "he was only looking for the oven when I got in. And he's on the telephone since. I'm keeping his dinner warm."

"Thank you," Nicandra said. Her joy wilted. It was only in her imagination that he had puzzled his way through kitchen labyrinths to bring a tray to her bedside. Did it have to be on this evening that Kate, that notorious hedge-row flirt, should have come in early to steal his mission of mercy and love?

"You're not sick, are you, madam?" Kate's voice was full of warm concern as though some conspiracy held them near each other. "Will I bring you a hot bottle?"

It was her panacea for every ill. Before she called the police she would bring a hot-water bottle, probably in its knitted jacket, to the victim of a murder.

"No, I'm all right, Kate, thank you."

"I'll go so and see to his dinner. And I'll bring up your bottle when I come for the tray."

Left alone, suspicion cruelly linked with anxiety overcame any reason other than love, to account for Andrew's absence on the telephone. Of course, it was obvious that any chance for contact would be stolen when she was out of hearing. The shrivelling mistrust was back with her. She saw that the need to be watchful and attentive, and at the same time generous and understanding, was to be part of her life for every hour of every day. For so long as she and Andrew were together, a pulse, a nerve, something integral to her loving would break free from her control to distort the nearest moment they might share. Even tonight she must be wise and womanly. She must not ask who was on the telephone. At the idea of such restraint tears blinded her. The tears were like another person's, crying for herself. They were salt on a forkful of chicken.

He came back, looking pleased and well-fed. His heavy wireless set was in his hand.

"I thought we might hear the nine o'clock news – I've brought you a hot-water bottle." Her heart jumped in recognition of his thought. "Kate thought you looked cold." He contradicted her assumption.

"I don't think I want it," her voice distanced any obligation.

"All right. I'm always cold." He lay back in his own bed, perfectly at ease, his feet just clear of the eiderdown. His hands were on the hot-water bottle, the hot-water bottle was on his stomach. "I rang Lal," he said.

130

"Why?"

"To say I wouldn't cash her cheque. Why did you think I rang her?"

"Because you couldn't help it," she wanted to say. Instead, she said, "Would you put my tray down somewhere, please, if you would."

"Yes, in a minute. Lal says we're to keep the money. She said you'd need a little break after all this bother." There was a knock on the door. "Oh, here's Kate coming for your tray. Good. I needn't move."

Kate bent over Nicandra to pick up the tray: "And you didn't eat the half of it," she said reproachfully. She felt a proprietary interest in these two beauties lying there in bed. For her, whose man had failed her tonight, they made a picture of all happiness attainable. She was glad to see such a love story come true before her eyes. They're only stars, she thought. She's beautiful, of course, himself too, isn't he – you'd have to pity him. She waited at the door to say: Goodnight. God Bless, and listen for their answers.

"Did Lal say that?" Nicandra asked when Kate had shut the door.

"No, I think I said it. Why don't we? We could get a glimpse of the sun, I love the moon," he misquoted, coaxing.

"Darling, you do want me?" She was the captured bird again, wings folded in acceptance.

"Of course. Shall we get the nine o'clock news?"

He looked away from her to twist the knobs on the wireless. She understood the concentration necessary to attain any audible message from the BBC in the South of Ireland. All the same the interruption was untimely. Why bother with the news now? He must have heard the racing results at six o'clock. He was sitting up, holding the clumsy wireless set on his knee with one hand, searching through the muttering frequencies with the other. There was no hand for her to touch. "Oh good," he was saying, "marvellous tonight." He turned the volume higher as a restrained, gentlemanly voice announced: "England has declared War on Germany. . . ."

"How too really awful," Nicandra said with awed lack of interest. "It can't make much difference to us here though can it?"

"Except that we won't get to the South of France now."

"No – how sad."

"And I'll be recalled."

"The regiment can't want you back after all these years."

"I expect so – even an old fogey like me," he laughed.

Was he laughing at the absurd idea of being an old fogey? Or was there something else just evident in his cheerful voice? . . . . Recalled to the colours . . . . Rejoin the Regiment. The unspoken words had a fanciful storybook-by-Henty quality, far away and distant as bugles blowing. So why did that thread of excitement in his voice frighten her? Once again tonight, uncertainty dithered at her heart. What a goose she was, she the loved and wanted one, to be afflicted even for a moment by any threat or doubt. She caught his hand away from the radio. Even tonight, there could be some comforting pretence, an assurance of love.

~Part Four~

*I*t was during the first year of the war, when Nicandra and Andrew were in England, Andrew with his regiment, Nicandra devotedly Following the Drum, that Aunt Tossie bought a secondhand caravan. Although the promised purchaser for Deer Forest had not materialized, "be prepared" was her motto, she said. The preparation of her new home gave her unlimited freedom to spend what she called "her last pennies" in adding touches of luxury to this latest economy. As she often pointed out to Dada, the electric current her caravan required for light, heat, and the fuelling of her hot-water bottle, was minimal compared to the amount eaten greedily by her own vast bedroom, not to speak of the morning room and the dining room, ever since the electrification of Deer Forest, which she had installed as soon as the Electricity Supply Board made it available. Dada had always been repelled by the new convenience and its expense. He hated the stuff and never asked for more heat than that supplied by a couple of good logs in the morning room fireplace. He considered Tossie's caravan an expensive and unnecessary joke, but recognized that the only thing to do was to let the old girl have her head in the matter. She would come back to her bridle when winter set in.

Aunt Tossie planted her caravan in the most sheltered place she could command that was convenient for service from the house. The place she chose was the wide path underneath the morning room windows.

Here the sun, when it shone, shone with vigour, most of which Aunt Tossie's caravan obscured from the windows behind her new residence. One of the windows was, rather inappropriately, French, giving her easy access to the house, should she require it. She often remembered that charming song, "Where my caravan has rested", and hummed its air lightly to herself, and sometimes to Gigi.

Gigi loved the caravan. In her rather frail and unattractive old age, the sticky warmth, shot through by slivers of smelly air, suited her exactly. It was not a parrot's odour that hung on the air, for Gigi's cage was scraped clean and freshly sanded every morning when Willie – William now – came out of the French window with Aunt Tossie's first cup of tea. It was the compressed, deadly whiff of old apple cores, or worse again, the nail-polish odour of abandoned stumps of banana, forgotten in odd corners by Gigi when she left her cage to make love with Aunt Tossie.

Aunt Tossie noticed nothing unpleasant. She loved her caravan, so beautifully warm, and with everything to hand: the blue biscuit box with Pussy on its lid, the whisky bottle in the po cupboard (the space dividing the curtained Elsan from the rest of the caravan was so short that she had really no use for a po) and her spectacles, ever near, not as in other days forgotten in the morning room when she was already in her bed for the night. Now they lay, conveniently near her pillow, on top of the book from the Travelling Library. William changed her books, under the advice of the librarian, who was also the hurling critic for the *Cork Examiner*. He was sympathetic to Mrs Fox-Collier's type of fiction. She liked a nice story, he knew, and he reserved the Georgette Heyers for her, no matter how many other ladies listed them as first favourites. Of all these subscribers, Aunt Tossie was the only one who sent him a good Christmas present, together with a little letter of thanks for his interest and help.

For Dada, the days of breeding losers were sadly past – just as well since English racing was at a dead-end owing to the war. But Dada was resilient in his ability to spend money. Unfortunately, he had an unfailing eye for seeing potential improvement in any obscure three-quarter-bred two-year-old that caught his eye and could be bought for reasonably small money, to be sold, when fed and gentled in long reins by Fagan, as a prospective winner in a light-weight Hunter class. Together, Dada and Fagan would spend long exciting days scouring the countryside for possible purchases. The shadow of a horse on a distant hillside was enough to get them out of the car and on their legs across country for a closer view. Crabbing their discovery to each other was half the fun of the chase. Fagan was on good terms with any small farmer, no matter how far from Deer Forest he lived, who might own something worthy of a trip to spy out its potential. All this business kept Dada in happy contact with the world of horses and prevented him from worrying himself about trivialities such as blocked chutes – blocks often halting the water supply to the lavatories or kitchen sink – together with wind-stripped roofs in the farmyard and gates off their hinges everywhere. There were more important matters than these to discuss with Fagan in those intimate conversations in the saddle room where once the possibility, even probability, that the favourite for the Derby, now a forward two-year-old, had been bred at Deer Forest, was their everlasting and unrealized dream. There were still happy and interesting hours of discussion in the saddle room, and on wet afternoons in the woodshed, while Fagan split logs for the fires in the house. On other days, as much to amuse the dogs and keep them on their toes as to keep the butcher's bill in check, Dada, accompanied by Silly-Willie with the game bag on his back, would set forth to shoot rabbits and wood pigeons, with an occasional pheasant adding a touch of class to the bag at the end of the day.

Besides all this for Dada to see to, there was the car, seldom on the road now – petrol already getting difficult – except for those little horse-coping flurries with Fagan and, occasionally, to take Aunt Tossie to church, where she loved to sing. Dada really enjoyed washing and polishing all the old fittings on the still-splendid Bentley. He trusted her care to no one but himself. Still more important and time-consuming was his mowing machine, which required to be kept at the peak of her performance. "Doesn't give her running otherwise," he would think, busy with his pliers and oil-can. December, January and February, once the top of the year's pleasures, were now blank spaces. There was no hunting for him, no grass to cut. If grass did spring up lavishly in the mild Irish winter, the going would be too deep for mowing. "I wouldn't ask her the question, she'd only bury herself," he thought gloomily, but he never relaxed in his care for his dangerous Treasure.

Silly-Willie was his attendant sprite, Ariel to his Prospero in all activities, outdoor or indoor. Dada much regretted that he had not, in earlier times, made full use of the lad's extraordinary weight; wonderful to have had him up riding work on some of the horses let in lightly by the Handicapper. He sighed over that waste of a possible talent, but he still found Silly-Willie (now William, of course) useful enough when spread out, small as a frog on dry land, beneath the Bentley, obediently carrying out orders about greasing and cleaning. The garage bills saved were considerable. In another age, the boy would have been a useful chimney-sweep, just made to fit up any chimney in the house.

Silly-Willie was a master hand at de-fleaing the dogs. He prepared their dinners more carefully than he did his own, deeply concerned if any dog did not eat up as voraciously as he thought it should. The dogs loved him as he loved them. They flew to his beautiful whistle, even when on the hot line of a rabbit. Nettle, the Killer, a fierce opinionated person who would have been hero of a rat-pit had Silly-Willie been sweeping chimneys, was, of the three, his favourite. Perhaps it was because he displayed all the macho habits and appearance that Silly-Willie must always fail to express in his own sad little person. The fact that only he could get a worm pill past Nettle's terrifying teeth and murderous protests, gave him immense satisfaction.

Silly-Willie's indoor duties and responsibilities were never skimped or put aside to make room and time for outdoor sports with Sir Dermot. He would stay up till twelve o'clock at night to tree wet shoes and bone dry ones; brush clothes and fold trousers back in their creases; set trays for morning teas and, lastly, give the dogs a run so that there was no excuse for little mistakes in the kitchen where they now slept, all except Nettle, who joined Sir Dermot in his icy bedroom. With such a night behind him, he was never late with the early cup of tea. Again, at eleven o'clock, he would come tripping along to Aunt Tossie with coffee and a small brass can of very hot water masked in a clean, warm towel so that she might wash her hands – she did not wash much else in the caravan.

"Ah, William!" Aunt Tossie would welcome his coming as quite a surprise. "And have you fed the birds?" was often the opening for a fascinating talk. The bird-table was one of their joint interests.

"The weather is what's beating us, Madarm. They're just not hungry." Though regretful, he was resigned to the flighty ingratitude of birds.

"Oh dear, not even my robin?"

"And I tried him on the mouth-organ, imagine."

"And you couldn't coax him?"

Willie shook his head, admitting defeat.

139

"I expect we shall have another cold snap," Aunt Tossie said easily, "that will bring them back – I shall ring when I'm ready for luncheon."

"And look at your bell where it's gone – under the couchette." Silly-Willie made a point of calling things by their advertised names. Aunt Tossie was not sleeping in a bed, or on a bunk, but on a couchette. He lay on his face to reach for the bell on its flex. "Take care of it now, Madarm, for I wouldn't hear you calling if you lose it, and I won't trust you out on your own on the steps of the Mobile Home – they're treacherous steps."

"No. I won't venture without you," Aunt Tossie would promise, and wisely so. She had once fallen, heavily and painfully, down the three steps, and was lucky not to have broken a hip, always the first defeat in advancing years.

Silly-Willie would shake his head warningly and speed away to a myriad other duties to be discharged before he announced: "Luncheon is served, sir." He would then proceed to the dining room, where he waited with meticulous ceremony although his head was not so far above the height of the dining room table. He insisted on Brigid's carrying his own dinner into the old servants' hall where he ate in lonely state. He considered this division from the kitchen suitable to his status. Although religion and prudery forbade him to enquire into the alarming advance of Brigid's pregnancy, and he avoided allowing his eyes to dwell on her changing shape, he still continued to voice his disapproval of her condition in many subtle and covertly hurtful remarks, such as: "So-and-so had a White Wedding – did you see the picture in the *Examiner*? A White Wedding is a lovely thing, wouldn't you agree?"

Occasionally Dada would bring the car round to the hall door. Then Aunt Tossie, enormously wrapped up and escorted by Silly-Willie, would come out of her caravan and join him for a visit of inspection at Kileady. It would be a surprise visit, made to ensure that Kate was properly fulfilling her function as caretaker. Since Aunt Tossie no longer had much sense of dirt or neglect in any form, still less any wish to make trouble, these pryings were depressing rather than useful. The cold unused air of the house, the fogged unopened windows, the stripped beds with their damp uncased pillows, saddened her. Downstairs, the Snaffles pictures and the Lionel Edwards' landscapes with a distant pack, in their total recall of such a different and proper way of life, distressed her. The *Tatler*, the *Field* and *Country Life*, lay in neat glossy layers on a table, outdated by many months. Unopened copies of *Horse and Hound* lay sad in their neglect. Aunt Tossie, as she sighed and gathered up the papers to read in her caravan, forgave the extravagant carelessness that had forgotten to cancel their weekly arrival.

In the stableyard Dada was poking his disapproving nose into all evidence of neglect. The oats in the feedhouse, for instance: only fit for the bantams who were fluttering round teasing for food as soon as he opened the door. Nicandra's geese seemed to be taking life quietly enough, Kate fed them, he supposed. In the barn, he tore out wisps of hay, putting his hand to his face to smell the quality which he considered very moderate. Smelling the hay, kicking at the straw, investigating every empty bin in the feedhouse satisfied his disapproval of the absent owners with their sad lack of proper method. He was particularly distressed by the absence of a lock on the saddle room door, damned carelessness . . . someone should write to the fellow about it. Inside the saddlery was stiffening to a crisp beneath its bluish mould. If Dada had known how to click his tongue in disapproval he would have done so, over the two Whippy saddles, his expensive wedding present. Typical of Andrew to leave things so disorganized. He supposed the man they had left in charge did come to put the horses in at night, and give them a feed of some sort. There was so little grass in the paddocks they were practically eating their own footsteps.

In the field, when they came shoving and purring up to him, he knew they were looking for apples, or some other nonsense of Nicandra's. The thought saddened him for the horses. Nicandra should have stayed here and kept an eye on her place for the duration of this war. He supposed "things" would hot up some time, then Andrew's regiment might be sent abroad; there, something unfortunate might happen to Andrew. He didn't like to think of Nicandra as a widow; on the other hand, she certainly would not stay a widow for long, and in the interval they could hope to see a bit more of her, and without that rather silly fellow. Dada was not so much hard-hearted as he was concerned over this dilatory war – he had only just come in at the end of his own war, that trouble with the Boers, and then he was involved more in the transport of horses than in active service. As he was never one for reading the newspapers, or listening to that ghastly wireless, except for the Racing Results, this war seemed to be jogging along very uninterestingly. Tea, he had heard from William, was soon to be rationed, lemons impossible, and wine unobtainable. He had no pressing anxiety about the generation now involved in this hesitating combat; he knew so few of them, except for Andrew and, vaguely, Robert. Robert, he understood from someone, was keeping out of things, and that he disapproved of enormously.

Together again, cold and tea-less, Aunt Tossie and Dada locked the doors of Kileady, and clambered back into the old car. It felt warm and inhabited after the deserted house – yesterday's nest, Aunt Tossie thought, and, "no eggs in the nests of yesteryear" came into her mind. Dada, who never wore an overcoat, looked cold as the bones of any frozen bird. As he waited patiently for the Bentley's great engine to warm up, Dada was comforted and rather pleased by the sensation of Aunt Tossie's hot, well-wrapped bulk beside him. He was pretty sure he caught a whiff of something on her breath, and wondered if she had been stealing to the sideboard – bless her, he thought, and so typical of that fellow not to have put his drink away before he left. When she took a very long hunting flask, encased in leather, out of her handbag, saying: "Have a sip, darling," he shook his head. "Do you good," she insisted, so he was obliged to obey her. She was always right; when he screwed back the silver lid and shut the flask up in its case, the leather straps that had once held it on her side-saddle still intact, he felt depression and disapproval melt from him magically. "You do look after me," he said, "don't you." The little drink seemed to seal their easy companionship.

Sometimes in the tidy Gloucestershire manor house where Andrew's mother lived, at other times in small, bleak hotels, he and Nicandra met as though in a foreign country, and ate and drank expensively – why not? He implied an unspoken necessity to live in the present. They were two beautiful people, wherever they were seen together, their joint glamour affected them both rather joyously. Nicandra, who was so modest and unsure, caught the infection, the slight fever admiration evolves in its subjects, it gave her a certain power, a temporary ascendancy now that she had no domestic cares, no happy drudgery to tire her for his sake. Their joint entrance to a crowded room in a country house, a bar, a chic restaurant, had a valid and exciting strength, far removed from the daily demands and dependencies of Kileady. There was no "perhaps – perhaps not" about lovemaking. Every meeting was an encounter, and each parting was under its own shadowed threat.

One day, in February, the threat came out of the shadows. Tea, early morning tea, had been brought to them in the brisk blue and ivory bedroom of his mother's house. Nicandra sat up and thanked the old housemaid who padded across the deep rabbit-coloured carpet, looking like a senior rabbit herself, to open the blue padded curtains on to just risen sun shining on red dogwood.

New every morning, the look of Andrew's dark head, half lost in the pillows, surprised and enchanted Nicandra. Perhaps today they would escape again from his mother's cool, well-behaved and tactful efforts for his company. Perhaps she would be understanding and leave them time alone together. She couldn't guess that such times could sometimes be difficult and uneasy. Without their horses and dogs, and the racing results, there was not a lot to talk about. There were hours when Andrew sustained good humour with whisky, and Nicandra yearned silently for evening.

Now she must nudge him awake to drink his tea. Dearly as his mother loved him, the hour of breakfast was a fixture in her day. He sat up, brown and bare, hair shuffled about like a little boy's. The tea-cup shook in his hand.

"Do you think," he said, "it's about time for you to go home. What do you think?"

Witless, she cried out: "Why?"

"Well, we aren't meant to talk, are we?"

She knew what that implied. "Let me wait till you go."

"I wonder about the dogs rather. Are you quite sure about Kate?"

"Yes."

"Oh well, if you're happy about them. And Maeve is due to foal any day now."

"I'm no use with foaling mares."

"Look, darling, to please me. . . . I want to think of you at Kileady. . . ."

She was a child, coaxed back to school after the holidays. She yielded, as a child must yield, graceless and unhappy, but obedient for love's sake.

"I want to think of you there. I want to find you there."

Relief put something like a caress in his voice. It had been easier than he had expected. Grateful, he moved his hand across to catch at a lank blonde strand of hair and twist it short, so that her head turned to him. No further tenderness was due so early, and with breakfast so punctual. Reading his lack of intention correctly, she got out of bed: "I must go to the lav," she invented the need.

He watched her trail away, barefoot, her long white nightdress dripping over hands and feet. "Turn on my bath, would you?" he called after her. She didn't answer, just made a sign with her shrouded hand. Andrew wondered if she could be crying. Letters took so long, he wondered too, how soon and how privately he might telephone to Lal.

The crowds on Paddington Station, the waiting in the queue for tickets, the absolute necessity of finding a seat, all these imperative actions had their share in quelling the pain of parting. Waiting at the barrier, she saw him coming back to her, a cardboard box of terrible food in his hand. He found a way through the crowd as tidily as though coming from behind to win a race, and went past the barrier without a platform ticket – a nod from him was enough. In his distinguished company, it didn't seem right to travel second class, but it was her usual sacrifice of comfort. He put her bag up on the luggage rack, and stood, uncertain how soon to say goodbye. "Don't wait," she said, "please." They didn't kiss, and she didn't look after him, dodging his way against the contrary surge of travellers – some Irish superstition in her blood said: Never say goodbye twice, and don't watch him out of sight.

"Is this seat taken?" a purposeful woman asked her twice.

"Oh, no. No, I don't think so." Nicandra picked up her handbag and the *Evening Standard*. Andrew had bought it forgetting that there was no racing today. Had he left it on purpose for her? That was it, she was sure, and felt comforted to think how easily he could buy another.

The long journey through the night began. The purposeful woman had two daughters, a husband, and a large amount of luggage, overtaking every inch of space in the carriage. Quite soon, a travellers' companionship came to life between them. The woman, with her entire family to feed and scold, was aware of a cold desolation pervading the opposite corner of the carriage: the beautiful woman, shrinking into the upturned collar of her Jaeger overcoat. No doubt there had been a parting. She offered a sandwich. In accepting it, a curious sensation came over Nicandra, a feeling of relief and freedom, because she did not have to protect Andrew from what would have been his certain recoil from familiarity with these kind people. She felt guilty in this freedom, and even more alone when she lent Andrew's *Evening Standard* to the man, before reading it herself.

As the train clanked and droned along, past Reading and far into unknown Wales, she was subject to their pleasure in telling her of their West Cork lives, their difficulties, their successes. They owned a small hotel, and they had just put running water into four bedrooms, and the low-pulling flush type in all toilets. Now, since the war, they were in trouble for lack of visitors. However, since everything has its compensations, this gave the kind woman more time for reading. The long echoing platform of Cardiff Station was no longer than the list of her favourite authoresses, as well as the plots of several historical novels. Nicandra had not read the books mentioned, but she nodded in a kind of glacial sympathy over the intricacies of their plots, in which invented lives linked up with political periods. Whether disastrous for the heroine, or felicitous for the villain, such times provided a reliable background for the fluent pen of the novelists. ". . . and I like a good story," the woman concluded, before embarking on the education and differing childish ailments of her daughters, and the best use for leftovers in the conduct of a small hotel.

Behind her attention to this flow of entirely foreign information, Nicandra found a hiatus of oblivion for her present acquaintance with grief. The trivial realities recounted so unmercifully, and at times inaudibly, against the growling chatter of the ongoing train, were like a forgotten bedtime tale, bad dreams kept in waiting behind the story.

"Perhaps we'll meet up again on the boat," the woman said, standing surrounded by her loving family on the platform of Fishguard Station.

"Oh, I do hope so," Nicandra said. Left alone, the empty train a dead thing beside her, and the boat, obscured in darkness, looming indifferent to its transport of her unhappiness, she had nothing to do but follow the crowd of passengers to the gangway. While she stood in the queue, Aunt Tossie's expensive little alligator travelling case heavy in her hand, the anodyne of boredom slipped from her. What to do while she waited to hear of his death? What must I do? Lady Jane Grey was with her again in the delay. If she fell and hurt herself now, only a stranger would pick her up. She went carefully up the gangway and down to the Purser's Office, with the consolingly immediate question of a cabin. . . .

"Anything booked, madam? Sorry, only a berth in the Ladies' Cabin."

Only a birth in the Ladies' Cabin. That spelt out her future she thought, as she turned away from the caisse. Perhaps a cup of tea would be a possibility. Then she saw Robert, smiling delightedly and bustling towards her. "Nico," was all he said but everything he wanted to say was in the way he named her. He was close now, a great, kind buffoon, a friend who didn't matter much in whatever way he spoke her name.

"Andrew?" he asked, lighting on her one importance.

147

"You know," she said, "careless talk, all that nonsense. I'm going home now."

"Oh, my dear," he said, "let's have a drink."

She waited sadly, without any thought of pleasure in the prospect of his company while he worried the barman with determinedly complicated instructions. When he came to her table, bringing two vast champagne cocktails, she thought only how much she would have preferred the brandy without the champagne. Robert was a familiar, too connected with her life to be the valid shield against truth that her strangers in the train had been. "You're still busy?" she asked. Meaning: you're not serving in the forces yet?

"Yes. I go back and forwards. Well, cheers," he said. He must have caught that from his executive friends.

"Thank you, darling Robert," she moved her glass faintly and gave him a distant smile before she drank.

"You're going home?" he asked, "Or to Deer Forest?"

"No, not Deer Forest. I have to run our place till . . . ."

Till Andrew comes back, if Andrew comes back, he knew what she could not say; and he knew something he would not say.

"You're looking better than last time I saw you," she gave him a kind survey, "perhaps you'll be in this thing soon."

"Perhaps," he sounded unutterably calm in being safely out of it all. "How are Sir Dermot and Mrs Fox-Collier?" he asked.

"They're trying to sell Deer Forest. Did you know?"

"Only a rumour. Someone said their buyer had run out."

"I wouldn't know. I hope so."

"Are you going to stay there and starve?" he asked.

"Oh, Robert, what a silly thing to say."

"Yes. I know." He finished his drink. "Bed now, I think." He picked up her heavy case. "Where is your cabin?"

"I was too late. I'm in the Ladies."

"Nico, that's nonsense. Have my stateroom. The Purser will find me something." He spoke with total assurance.

Going back and forwards on his business, she thought, and put her teeth together on the idea of Andrew, soon to be in cold, discomfort and certain danger. In contrast she saw Robert, comfortable in his stateroom with two beds, not berths; it might be graceless to refuse, but she could not sleep in that double cabin. Robert might have thought how absolute, in the second bed, would be Andrew's absence.

"Thank you so much," she said, "but the Purser was such a dear man, fixing me up – I can't run out."

Watching her as she walked, rather uncertainly, away from him, he saw her stop to ask a stewardess the way before she wandered on, companionless. While her absolute silliness alarmed him, it provoked, at the same time, an ardent longing to keep her safe from all ills to which such idiocy is heir. He would pursue and protect her because, bright as a light glaring into the future, was his remembrance of Lal, whom he had seen that evening, running – a whippet out of the slips – into the dark echoes of Paddington Station. Now, since he had found Nicandra travelling alone, he was sure whom it was Lal ran to meet. A man of business, he looked surely into a long-time future. Picking up small strands of the present, he remembered that his car would be waiting for him at Rosslare Harbour, and wondered patiently if she would let him drive her home. If not, there would always be good things to bring, an excuse to see her at Kileady. He knew this war would last longer and its attritions be more severe than anyone envisaged in 1940.

Sunday afternoon, the sixth Sunday since she parted from Andrew, and spring was here, and she was alone. Small daffodils, mean and clear in contrast with overbred luscious successors, spread low as water round trees and in forgotten corners. On banks and ditches, primroses repeated their faithful pattern, always the same and always a heart-breaking surprise. They grew lavishly between the bank and the split rail of the paddock where Maeve wandered and fed, indifferent to the ecstatic gambols of her colt foal, safely delivered since Nicandra's return. Nicandra stood and leaned on the gate from the yard, waiting for the pleasure that should be hers in the happy sight. She waited, and turned away. She would watch over everything, but without him the fun was gone. Near to the house, her bantams clustered round her, flying out of rhododendrons and ivy stumps, bright and friendly, as in her childhood. Her passion for them was spent. They were healthy, thrifty little birds. She knew some of the flock by name, but didn't bother to call to them. As she had brought no food, they dispersed in a careless, disparaging kind of way, back to their own concerns.

The sun shone almost violently for spring, lavishing warmth into her shoulder-blades. All the agreeable suggestions of spring were heavy on the air. All well, all to be avoided. She knew what she ought to do, what she should want to do, on this Sunday afternoon: drive to Deer Forest to see Dada and Aunt Tossie. She had not been there for a week. They didn't need her – they were so happy together with their small, sterile occupations, their contentment somehow aggravated her single loneliness. Their sympathy for her was evident in every word, spoken or unspoken, but when she left them she knew they would settle back in enviable contentment among their accustomed little doings. Spring was here, so Dada would be up on his mowing machine as soon as he could see the least growth on his lawns. Perhaps he would take a stroll with his stick and his dogs, on this quiet Sunday afternoon, spying on the few wild pheasants near their nesting time.

On Sunday morning, Aunt Tossie would have got herself out of her caravan, and gone heavily and purposefully through the cold house to the kitchen, there to organize Sunday lunch for two with as much attention as though she planned for ten. They were happy in the timing and strictness of their day's events: the arrival of the postman; Silly-Willie's morning trip to the village and his return with the *Irish Times* and the messages. Aunt Tossie's little nips from the bottle in the po cupboard were one of the pleasures; so were Dada's closeting with the telephone, placing not always such very small bets; all this acceptance and contentment while decay rotted the house round them, the house that they were quite prepared to sell, their happy shelving of responsibility having reached that limit.

Andrew held strict and uncompromising views on their behaviour, and on their silly, spendthrift old age; views that Nicandra shared even more closely because he was not there to support them. As she turned in through the dislocated iron gates, she knew exactly the importances she was going to hear about: a mare, the only mare on the place, would have slipped her foal; no hen was laying; Silly-Willie had sucked a toffee while serving lunch. He said it was a throat pastille, but Dada had smelt raspberry drops, and said so. William had been near tears but he had to learn. She could hear it all beforehand.

The Avenue, as always in springtime, held on to its beauty, unimpaired by neglect. Light, slanting through its double line of lime trees, lay flat on the ground – better than bird-song, more cheering. Halfway along the contrived windings of the drive, she heard the furious sound of Dada's mowing machine, and on Sunday afternoon. There must be an abnormally early growth of the grass. Once, when she was a child, a sidecar had rattled past her and she had known something ominous was in its passage; now, again, a suspicion of trouble was vibrant in the bright afternoon.

Rounding the last bend of the driveway where, behind its verges, snowdrops planted by some great-aunt stared at the ground, she saw him. He was bent forward as though sitting up the neck of a horse. Dogs tore round him. Grass billowed in angry clouds behind his furious progress. Nicandra jumped out of the car and stood, a hand over her mouth. He was out of control, she could see, and there was nothing she could do.

"Hullo, darlin'," he yelled when he saw her, "she's taken quite a hold."

In the insane, terrible noise of a mowing machine gone mad, she saw him try to make the turn round the tree at the bottom of the slope, a winning post, as it were, on his substitute for a racecourse. She saw this last dreadful horse take charge and batter its way against the seamed and solid trunk of the Spanish-chestnut tree. She saw Dada flung to the ground and ran to where he lay, small as a doll, with his anxious dogs around him. "Bloody old fool," he said, "just tipped off her." And he shut his eyes. Was he concussed and unconscious, or was he dead? She didn't know. Dogs sniffed at him and turned away, all but one who sat down, obstinately whining for him to speak. She looked up to the house, calling for help, and could only be sure of an unbroken silence. There was a look on its many-windowed length suggesting that it had been struck across the face and knew its life was over.

It was Aunt Tossie who came tottering out of her caravan, fat, bent, an animal from its cosy lair, from its full-fed after-lunch nap.

"I heard the engine stop, oh, darling, it's you," she called on one breath, and came hurrying down the hill in her slippers and no coat, her bosoms flailing right and left. Nicandra's memory skipped back to a long-past dinner party. There was an aggravation of that remembrance when Aunt Tossie leaned over Dada, her bosoms touching him when her hands felt for his pulse under his tweed cuff: more closely, when she fumbled for a heartbeat against the narrow blue stripes of the flannel shirt.

"He's dead, darling," she said and kicked a dog away from him, practical in her intention, before bursting into terrible sobbing.

The lack of restraint embarrassed Nicandra. She felt a little sick. "You can't know," she spoke crossly, "we must get the Doctor. Where's Willie?"

"Fishing. And Fagan's out with the Sunday Harriers. Let's get Dada into your station wagon."

"I can't let my dogs out – they'll fight with Dada's. They'll all be killed."

"Oh, let them fight it out," Aunt Tossie dried her eyes and spoke as though of a free-for-all, a spree, or a picnic. "You're the youngest, you take his head, I'll take his feet."

They carried him between them, his eight stone heavy as so much lead. An arm trailed a hand, and the hand caught once in uncut grass and had to be put back across his chest. In the back of the wagon, he lay among the thick smell of little dogs. They seemed frightened of him, and backed away, hair rising; too well-mannered to bark. On the short drive back to the house, Aunt Tossie scolded ceaselessly. . . . "I told him not to get up on that thing, oh why did I give it to him? . . . and the going was much too deep today . . . he's so obstinate, and quite sly too. But he's such fun . . . slow down, slow down, there's a huge pothole coming. Don't bump him about darling, please. . . ."

They were at the flight of steps that innumerable people for uncounted years, family or guests, had gone up or down in happy and unhappy days. Now the problem of carrying the Master back into his house seemed insurmountable. "Go in and ring Dr Tynan," Aunt Tossie said, "I'll stay with him in case he wakes up. He'd be worried to death, I would, wouldn't you?" She sat with him for an hour before the doctor, who was out with the Sunday Harriers, arrived. Nicandra set out again, "the doggies need a walk", to find eager helpers at a neighbouring farm. Death, or the prospect of death, provided them with entertainment for a long Sunday afternoon. They carried him into his house and tramped loudly and carefully up the flights of stairs till they brought him to his tidy, icy bedroom where a Sèvres china basin and jug still stood on the marble wash-hand stand, where it had stayed since Maman's time. A window was half open to the long spring evening, ready to admit the evening chorus of the mating birds. Someone said a little prayer while they waited for the nurse to come and lay him out.

In death, Nicandra thought, as she made tea for the women and poured out drinks for the men, he was hardly more of a stranger to her than he had been in life. She sat with Aunt Tossie in the morning room, among all the embroidered parrots looking down their crooked beaks, waiting, while upstairs, nurse and her friends, Silly-Willie, their messenger, set about their secret, private business with Dada. "I'll stay with you," she promised, "as long as you like."

"Oh, darlin', no." Aunt Tossie sounded surprised and quite decisive. "William is all I need – he'll be back soon."

The funeral, mildly heralded in the press, brought a surprising and unexpected crowd. Contemporaries from the racing world, and young representatives of blood-stock sales regretted his death politely from at least two pews in the little Protestant church that Dada's family had built and endowed and neglected. A companion in arms from the Boer War arrived when the service was half over. He was correctly and exquisitely dressed, and marched, as if on some soldierly duty, up the aisle to lay his wreath against the enormous coffin. It had been ordered specially large by Aunt Tossie, who thought it was more dignified than the tiny one that would have fitted Dada's body more accurately. It was all most touching and, in a way, Aunt Tossie enjoyed every moment of it.

"Please," she said at the church door, "come in – just a tiny drink . . . so dear of you to come all this way. . . . He'd have loved it, wouldn't he? Don't you think so?"

Nicandra, standing beside her, grave and beautiful, felt further isolated and even more unmoved than she had felt on the Sunday of Dada's death. If the funeral could have brought Andrew back to her, even for one night, she would have been nearly grateful for it.

In the hall at Deer Forest, its walls sweating under the unaccustomed heat of a great fire, there was not quite enough drink for the crowd of chattering mourners. It was a disappointing finale, but at least there was a plethora of sandwiches. Brigid, nearly in her birth throes, had been summoned back to cut and butter and trim them. "I could live on these for days – aren't they delicious? Egg and parsley, my favourites," Aunt Tossie said when the friends had left, all in their turn punctiliously shown out by Silly-Willie, waiting, minute and dignified, at the door.

"But what shall you do, Aunt Tossie, what shall you do now?"

"I'll just nip into my caravan, and William will bring me two hot-water bottles and all these sandwiches."

"But Brigid will have her baby any day now – what about that?"

"I don't mind a baby. She can bring it here. I shan't hear it."

"You won't like it screaming in the kitchen."

"Shan't have so much cooking to do now," Aunt Tossie spoke in her most practical voice.

"What if you get a buyer for the house?"

"Shan't sell, it's mine for life. Right of Residence."

"It's on the market."

"I can't see any buyer arriving – not with this war. And it's going on for years. All our Generals muddling their battles – you'll see. It's never going to end."

"Please," Nicandra whispered, "I can't bear it."

"Have a little nip," Aunt Tossie said, "if they've left us anything; you'll feel better."

"No. I must drive Brigid home."

"Do her good to walk. Get the thing over with."

"You don't mean that."

"No. Of course I don't, pore gal."

"Goodbye then, I'll come back on Thursday. You're sure you don't want me to stay?" The last was a cry to be needed.

"I'm quite sure, my darlin'," Aunt Tossie got up, as much for an optimistic stroll towards the drinks tray as for a goodbye kiss.

In the kitchen, Brigid and Silly-Willie were drinking tea. They put down their cups and got off their chairs when Nicandra came in. Light filtered down on d sty beams from the prison-high windows. The Aga, which had long ago replaced the Eagle range, was very cool. Brigid was wearing a winter coat, buttoned tightly across her baby. Nicandra looked away. She thought she had seen the baby move.

"The Aga's very cold." She put her hand down, flat, on one of its lids.

"We've been sparing the anthracite," Silly-Willie said, "now Sir Dermot (R.I.P.) won't be needing his bath before dinner."

"But what about Mrs Fox-Collier's bath?"

"Only once in a while," Silly-Willie spoke authoritatively, "and we have the Baby Belling for her hot bottles," he added, and fussed away before Nicandra could ask about anything else.

"And for herself at all times Madam prefers a nice slice of cold ham," Brigid explained, as if to a stranger. Nicandra felt a stranger too, helplessly strange as she stood in the great, disorderly kitchen while Brigid rinsed out the tea cups.

When the door of the car was opened, the dogs rose, as one, to welcome her or to be released. She felt apologetic because she dared not let them out with Dada's pack around. Later, as she waited for them, as usual, in the gateway, Nicandra felt it only polite and natural to ask Brigid, silent beside her, some question about her baby. "Do you want a boy or a girl?" was all she could think of.

"I don't mind." The placidity of the answer, expressed in her demeanour towards this unchurched event, woke in Nicandra all the sickening regrets she had denied herself – not so much when her baby was due – as now, when it would have been a person. When she saw Brigid dispose and settle her position to give herself and the baby ease, a small dreadful loneliness crept round her heart, like a warning of indigestion. Now, her ardent wish was to be rid of this pregnant girl, whose nearness brought to life the idea of a lost person. I lost her, she said to herself, I didn't kill her. I didn't have to. Together she knew they would have done just this. And on Lal's money. It never happened. Twenty-eight days is nothing, nothing at all. She stretched out an arm and pulled a little dog on to her knee.

When Brigid had climbed, solemn and careful, out of the car, she drove home through the unsparing beauty of the spring evening. There was no necessity, other than the dogs to feed, and her geese to house, for hurrying home. There, all nestling comfort was barren. Pleasant acts, such as turning on lights, putting a match to a well-laid fire, having a drink, eating dinner, were barren now. The hunger in her heart was not transferable. When she crossed the rattling cattle grid and drove up the short avenue, tidy split rail on either side, she felt no sanctity of ownership, no anxiety as to what might have happened in her absence. Usually, she was torn with anxieties, visualizing a mishap to a foal, the fox raiding her flocks of geese and bantams: now all things dear and precious to her had acquired an unimportance because love had failed. She was unwanted.

The small circular stableyard was delightfully sheltered, holding the day's warmth in its bowl. On the central round of grass, crocuses were in flower. Now she was back, all was tidy again. Nicandra got out of the car slowly, it was like a long sigh, and stood beside it, desolate. In the yard, dedicated to living country things, and in contrast to the dull, innocent little house beside it, Nicandra's clothes, worn for Dada's funeral, seemed absurdly out of place, and entirely beautiful. In the waisted black coat, its gored skirts twisting in a perfect flow as she moved, in the eye-veil blowing flirtatiously from a tilted hat, the long leather gloves, fit for a wedding, carried in her left hand, she walked in beauty that was nearly theatrical against her stolid background. From the field gate, into the yard, her five geese came clattering towards her, to stop, horrified at this stranger in black. Her voice coerced them; she persuaded them slowly towards their house, safe from foxes.

Just awake and staring from a window, stupid with sleep, Andrew fell in love with this distant and beautiful goosegirl. He watched the gander turn away from her and saw her stoop to land him a lightning slap with her long gloves. He heard the gloves clap against the bird's solid feathers; neck thrust forward towards the ground, it turned back the way she had directed – at this small, distant act of violence, he laughed, amused and delighted. For a moment, she pleased him entirely. Why can't she stay like this? Why not keep this magical distance? Why take such satisfaction in mended socks? Always bending over the kitchen stove, when they might be having a drink together in the proper hour before dinner. She would reappear from the kitchen, a

158

deep flush on her cheekbones, to hurry him into the dining room before soup cooled, or a soufflé fell. It was all part of her readiness to give. She has everything, he thought, why doesn't she keep it? Enclose it so that I must find it for myself. Now, watching her spend her usefulness, undirected to himself, he felt powerless in its attraction. He knew he was bound to behave badly.

They met as she came up the four stone steps to the kitchen door, the high-heeled shoes on her big feet as long and pointed as a pantomime pied piper's. Kileady could have been a night-club not their own empty house, his embrace was so discreet: he held things back, he was waiting.

"My darling, my darling," Christ might have risen for Mary, her adoration was so complete. It was she who let him go, rather than the other way about.

"You're here," she said. "I don't believe it. You've missed Dada's thing."

"The boat was awfully late – I couldn't make the funeral. I'm so sorry."

"Why didn't you tell me? Dinner will be awful. And Nooskie has her puppies in my bed. How long have you got?"

"Only tonight. Can't Kate cook dinner?"

"Her mother's sick."

"I don't believe it."

"I don't either. But I do rather understand."

"Let's have a drink anyway."

She sat opposite him. Her London clothes kept her at the exotic distance he longed to preserve. That glowing tenderness was too familiar.

"Don't take your coat off," he said it before he could think. Any uncertainty was precious. She had just thrown her veiled hat on to the floor, and he knew her coat would be next. "It's so lovely, do I know it?" She sat back in her chair, her long arm reaching out for her glass, her blonde hair falling as straight as water across her face.

"I have to cook something," she said, "where did you have lunch?" He shook his head.

"Oh, let me go. You must be wildly hungry."

"No, I'm all right. Tell me about Dada."

"Well, I knew there was something wrong. I heard that ghastly machine going pr-pr-PRROOP. . . ." she became the mowing machine.

"Wonderful for him, really," he said when she reached the end of her tale, not a detail neglected, even the sandwiches, the dearth of whisky, Silly-Willie ushering the guests in and out. He loved her when she was like that – forgetful of him. He would hate to hurt her. She was a wonderful girl and he wouldn't hurt her for the world. If only she would stay like this. They had another drink, and another. They were laughing and kissing briefly as they talked about the letting of the land, the mare and the foal, their idle hunters. . . "And you'll be back soon," she said, "it can't be long."

He looked at her hopelessly. She would never understand. When he didn't answer, she guessed death was in his mind. She got on her feet to hover over him, a wonderful black bird, stooping for its prey, greedy for intimacy. "Let's eat Robert's foie gras. He brought a cask of it."

"Shall we make toast and eat it here?"

"Yes, wouldn't that be lovely . . . like after hunting."

He knew she was suggesting ". . . when we made love."

He didn't smile in recognition, "I'll light the fire," he said.

"No, I'll light it. I know its wicked ways," she snatched the matchbox out of his hand and knelt, black skirts spread round her, as flat on the floor as water-lily leaves anchored in a pond, until the fire caught on its dry sticks and turf.

"Shall I have a bath?" he asked. "Are you going to?"

"I thought, not till bed-time."

"Then you'll fall asleep on me." Of course he shouldn't have said that. But pleasing was always his pleasure.

"I *promise* not," her voice came deep and certain from the inside of her buttoned coat. "I've been keeping Robert's Floris for you. It's in the bathroom cupboard."

"The Universal Provider, isn't he?" he said, without a touch of gratitude.

"And the Income Tax man, he's so dear and wonderful."

"The Universal Aunt?"

"Don't laugh at him."

"I'm serious really," he pulled her up from the floor and held her at arms' length, a hand on each shoulder. "Be nice to him," he said. "I mean it. Seriously. Promise."

"Of course. Have your bath, darling. You open the Floris and I'll open the foie gras. Oh, the bliss of it all."

He let her go and walked away from her, to the Floris and the fragrant bath.

Dinner was perfect. She had stewed tarragon leaves in Campbell's Consommé and added sherry. She toasted bread, sitting on the floor with a long-handled toasting fork, supplying a hot slice whenever needed from the plate into which wood-ash fell. Dogs mumbled and sighed and changed places round them, too well taught to beg. The curtains were open to the creeping clarity of the spring evening. An air of complete harmony and content was sustained in the childish smell of hot toast and the educated pleasures of foie gras and wine – on such an evening, love must be a certainty.

Andrew knew how it would be. He could deny no pleasure tonight. He accepted without protest the last of Robert's foie gras. He hated the thought of her finishing it by herself tomorrow night. With the ritual of letting out the dogs, the uncomfortable notion that he might be going to miss them assailed him unfairly. He hated feeling disloyal, especially to a dog. Disloyalty wasn't like him, he knew. Not like him at all.

On the next morning, Nicandra woke early – Andrew was sleeping. His cheek, flushed like a child's, was thrust deep into his pillow. Not for anything would she have woken him. She lifted herself carefully on one elbow, only to gaze. A rapturous gratitude went through her. His beauty was her life – asleep, defenceless, he was a Holy Child for her. She would make him a cup of tea. She crept out of bed and went downstairs, her bare feet whispering on the carpet. She quieted the dogs almost savagely when she let them out, a threat in her lowest voice – nothing should wake him until she judged it was right. Before he went away, everything in her power would be made easy for him. He was going back to school after an exeat. She was the one to stay at home and take good care of all his possessions. She was warden of all that mattered most to them both, and the thought of this responsibility was healing and comforting.

The sun welled through the kitchen window, glittering through a new batch of marmalade. She felt so well, she could eat three breakfasts. If she was a poet she could write three poems. He had a train and a boat to catch. Before she woke him, she would make sandwiches for his journey, so that not a minute together should be lost. She made three packages of rich, delicious sandwiches, parcelling them up as neatly as if they were for the pocket of a hunting coat. She had folded the last meticulous corner when she heard Kate's bicycle rattle as it was leaned against an outer wall.

"Good morning, madam. What a beautiful funeral. Such a crowd. Everybody's talking about it."

Kate was congratulating her on an event that was in the past. Dada's funeral had been sponged out of her mind. "Yes," she said, "Mr Bland came back for it."

"Oh, he would, of course, so he would. Will he be long with us?"

She stared at Kate. She couldn't bear to say how short a time it would be. "Only this morning – the early train."

"Ah, God help you! Hop back into bed Madam, and I'll bring ye up a cup of tea."

"No, thank you. I'll bring it. He's still asleep."

"He'll miss his connection," Kate prophesied cheerfully.

When Nicandra pushed open the bedroom door, she was disappointed to see that Andrew's bed was empty. She had slipped out of bed without moving her bedclothes, his had been thrown back violently, as if in anger. He was in the bathroom, whistling, a nervous, broken whistle. She had heard him whistle like that on a morning when he was going to ride a really bad horse.

"Thank you darling. Put it there, would you? You are kind." He went on shaving. There was something concentrated and businesslike about his shaving, at total variance from the sleeping child image that had touched her so deeply. Sitting on the edge of the bath, she sipped at her tea, looking into her cup then lifting her eyes to consider his brief presence. He turned round to say: "Get dressed sweetie, you'll catch your death." He looked pained. No wonder, if he was feeling nearly as awful as she did. She must be the brave one. That would help. She was off the edge of the bath and into her clothes with sharp determination. She clattered down the stairs, calling to the dogs, it sounded jolly. She went banging about in a way very unlike herself. She was playing a part. Kate had made hot buns for breakfast, cuddling them in a napkin. Perfect eggs and bacon, coffee in a Cona. She heard him in the kitchen talking rather boisterously with Kate: unlike him. They were playing the same game, of course, Kate's laughter sounded gratified. She loved his attention.

Then he was visible again. "Good morning," he said dourly, as if to a stranger in the house. This had always

163

been a joke between them after any rampage of love. She breathed fully in the implication. She watched him eat, dwelling on every necessity. She could hardly wait for his coffee cup to be empty. She pushed butter nearer to him, and marmalade. Like last night, this morning was representative of what life had always been like between them, what it would always be like. When he was away from her, the mirage would be with her.

He got up, vaguely looking for a cigarette. She was first to the box, and ready first with the matches. They were at the window together, smoking and looking quietly out across their pretty yard. A horse's head stooped across the high door of a loose-box – two of her pigeons plopped about on the cobbles. Beyond the field gate, the mare and foal moved in sunlight. She took his hand.

He turned to her, unwillingly: "Nico. There's something I have to ask you. Will you give me something?"

"Of course." She would give him India, if she had known that over-done quotation.

"Nico?"

"Yes."

"Will you give me a divorce?"

He must be joking. Of course, he was joking. "No," she said merrily. "I don't think I will."

"Darling girl, I'm rather serious."

Blind, not so blind, terror of the truth took charge of her: "What do you mean? Lal? Is it Lal?"

"Yes, Lal. Do you mind terribly?"

"You can't get a divorce, not in Ireland," it was a last protest before she gave in. She knew she would give in.

"Don't you believe it. Lal's brother is brilliant at that job."

Her escape route was cut. Of course, they would have considered the difficulties. Kate came in, looking at her watch. "Don't leave your sandwiches after you," she said, putting the packages down on the table. She hurried portentously away. She was tact itself.

164

It was the sandwiches, lying so formally on a bright salver, she had cut them and filled them up with so much love and forethought, now they waited, tokens of a journey that was to take him away from her for ever. An hour ago, love had been as sure as a bird's wings spread against the morning – love was giving all you had. "Of course. You can have anything. You know I'd give you anything – you know I would."

"And *you* know how you'll always matter" – her mouth groped its way into a new sort of smile – "– to both of us," he added carefully. "Lal is so fond of you."

At that, kindness failed. A breathless, silent scream was choking her. If hearts broke, hers snapped then. He took hold of her wrists and bent towards her, smiling. It had all been easier than he expected. She leaned away, her height and strength exaggerated, her head turned down, her big feet roots of a tree lashed by the wind. She pulled free. "You're going to miss your train. Do go. *Please* go."

"If you won't be friends," he said, surprised and wounded in his nicer feelings, "perhaps I had better go." He picked up the sandwiches. "Thank you for these."

She ran from him, out of the house, into the yard, waiting for him to go. Then back to the house again, to stave off her loss. Her anguish was extreme, stripping all sense away. She would cling to him. They would make it up. Division between them was a monstrous impossibility. There would be no parting.

In the tiny hall, she didn't call. She waited, a hand over her mouth, listening. She heard him moving in the dining room.

Kate came out with a tray of breakfast jumble. "Oh, madam," she was too polite to put an arm round Nicandra, "Mr Bland's left. He said it would be best. He'll leave the car at the station ."

"Yes, yes, of course." Before breakfast, in another life, she had left the car at the door ready to drive him, as far as the boat if need be.

"And he'll be back, he said, in no time at all, he said, and you're not to fret, he said, this war will be over any minute now." Kate stopped, inspiration flagging. He had said: "Goodbye Kate," and gone out to the car, looking not nearly as upset as she felt would have been proper. And no message left, so she had spoken for him.

~Part Five~

One morning, some months after Dada's death, Aunt Tossie sat up in her bunk bed, quietly comfortable. Her velvet dressing-gown kept her beautifully warm, and just one bar of the small electric fire was enough to maintain her caravan at a proper temperature. She missed Dada's company sadly, of course; but his loss had retired into a secondary place when Gigi fell sick one morning and died the next. She still sat, superbly well stuffed, in her cage. In her silent presence, Aunt Tossie missed the evening gossip and nibbling love tokens more acutely than if Gigi had been quite a ghost. "Giving you fondies" William had called it when he brought her tray and found them together. It was William who had taken the dead bird away and persuaded the Post Mistress to carry Gigi to Cork to be stuffed. When Aunt Tossie saw her again, wired to her swing in the most lifelike way, she screamed with pleasure, or horror, it was hard for her to know which; perhaps gratitude for William's misplaced thoughtfulness was her strongest feeling. Pretty soon, Gigi's corpse became much the same to her as Dada's photograph, placed reverently on the po cupboard.

A curious quiet coma possessed her days, uninterrupted by the creation of Dada's dinners, or by the bother of his latest extravaganza. She felt free now to indulge herself in any little privilege she fancied. Shan't live for ever, she thought cheerfully, so why not relax and enjoy the second drink before dinner? There was no longer a cuddle with Gigi to fill in the time until William arrived with her tray. It seemed an unnecessary nonsense, moving into the morning room for meals, and the dignified vault of the dining room was unthinkable; in any case, the descent from the caravan was slightly perilous when she was what William called "a little tired". Aunt Tossie didn't call her happy state "a little tired", she knew she was a little drunk, and enjoyed the short euphoria.

Very soon her cooking had become a lost interest and excitement now that she had no man to please. Why should I exhaust myself, she thought, I *don't* entertain, and I *never* go out. William's four-minute boiled eggs, or a neat little heap of sardines, were quite enough for her. Her only trouble was constipation, but four Cascara tablets soon settled that; and if she was conscious of a slight gasp and shudder when struggling on the Elsan, whisky was the cure for that too.

Naturally, Andrew's horrid behaviour did upset her. She was disappointed in him, and her loving sympathy for Nicandra's unhappiness was boundless, or would have been boundless if Nicandra had come to her with tears and confidences. But she had, too, the rare ability to accept her place as an outsider: she never thought her generosities gave her any rights to affection. Young people had their own lives to live, pore things . . . the muddles. . . . When young herself, she could never have envisaged the peace and comfort of old age in a caravan. Even her gros point had become too much of a business, contented selfishness possessed her – when she folded her soft, crumpled hands against the hot-water bottle on her stomach, she dozed away from all troubles and anxieties, her own or anybody else's.

On one of these quiet, prospectless days, when William had left her with her morning cup of coffee, she sighed her way back among her pillows, before leaning out from her nest to reach into the po cupboard. Some time soon, next Thursday probably, she was going to open and answer all those dreadfully kind letters about Dada, as well as some of the rather disturbing ones in neatly typed envelopes. Aunt

Tossie thought of them as arnvelopes, and would have gone to the stake in defence of her pronunciation. Now she drank up her medicated coffee while she considered the next step in her morning . . . perhaps a biscuit. She was delighted to hear a knock on her door.

"Oh, do come in," she called. "Push, it sticks." In her stately velvet dressing-gown, she was ready to receive at any hour of the day.

It was the grotesquely embarrassed face of Robert that looked round the door. "Oh, it's you!" Aunt Tossie cried out in welcome, wondering who he was.

Robert was accustomed to delayed recognition – he fathomed her doubt without hesitation: "I'm Robert."

"Of course, I'm so senile about names."

"I wanted to tell you – I was so sorry I missed Sir Dermot's funeral – I wanted to say, if there was anything I can do. . . ."

What could he possibly think he could do, dear fellow? "You *are* kind," she said.

Robert had squeezed himself into the caravan. He sat upright on the only symbol for a chair. In the back of her mind, Aunt Tossie knew there was some subject where they had a common interest. In a flash it came to her: "How were your mother's Christmas roses this year?"

"Not very good. Lots of black spots," Robert refrained from reminding her that his mother had been dead for five years.

"I'm not sure if you know," he said, "I thought I'd like to tell you myself. It seems a funny thing to say, I know: I've bought Deer Forest."

"Have you? Have you really? You don't mean I don't own my caravan?"

"Of course not. What an idea."

"But where am I to put it?"

"Don't move it. I like it here."

"Oh, you *are* kind . . . there was a rumour of a buyer, of course we never dreamed of you. Do you mean to live here?"

"Not yet – there's the dry rot to consider."

"Dry rot? I never noticed any."

"And I want to make one bedroom habitable."

"Which?"

"The sunniest."

She stared at him. This talk from a stranger of dry rot and habitable bedrooms was curiously hurtful. Well as she recognized the horrid truth of what he said, she felt herself to be some sort of aboriginal, and Robert a species of kind white settler. She found herself wishing that he had been a nice, thoughtful Church of Ireland parson, like his father, and had not made all this money she had heard about. A tycoon, that was the word. Rather a nasty word too. It was a word that didn't properly fit Robert, sitting there breathing audibly but quietly (he had always been asthmatic) in her caravan. "Anyhow," she said, "I expect it's all in one of those awful arnvelopes that come for my poor brother-in-law, he hated letters," she stretched out a hand to touch the pile on the po cupboard. She didn't seem to have anything more to say. She sat there, grinding her teeth together in an abstracted way. Behind her Gigi, so adroitly stuffed and poised, moved a little on her swing as Aunt Tossie heaved, on her heap of pillows. For Robert, the gaudy bird lived. Each old parrot has her cage, he thought, and his heart was full of pity.

"In confidence, you understand," Robert's voice hardened, it was the voice of a man of business, cool and slightly dictatorial, "I've left the place to Nicandra, that and any money I may have. I rely on you not to tell her," his voice changed uncertainly. "I'm afraid she might be rather disgusted."

"I shouldn't worry," Aunt Tossie reassured him. "Go on keeping out of this war and you're bound to outlive her."

Robert blushed and said nothing. Neither did Aunt Tossie. After a minute's silence, Robert pointed to a green corner of the ceiling. "I noticed the felt on your roof is cracking a bit. Perhaps my builder could do a little job for you there."

"Perhaps." Aunt Tossie withheld the favour of her acceptance with a charming smile.

Robert smiled too. "I wonder if I might take a look at the house?"

"Of course." She reached for her bell and kept a thumb on its button. "William will show you."

So Silly-Willie had become William; the faintest ghost, the last representative of grandeur. But he was wrong. Aunt Tossie had been thinking only of Silly-Willie's feelings when she changed his name.

"William," she said firmly when he came to the door, "would you show Mr . . . er . . . this gentleman, round. He is very interested in old houses."

Always alert to please, Silly-Willie preceded Robert along the weedy gravel path, under all the windows and round the corner of the house to the high, wide steps and the hall door. The thing should be done properly – no creeping in by the convenient morning room window. He turned the big brass handle and, his shoulder only a short way above it, pushed the door open. He was the dwarf keeper of a storybook castle.

"I airs a different room every day of the week," he indicated the lifted sash of one of the half-shuttered windows. Cold northern light came meanly in to match the stilled chill of an empty church. Silly-Willie stopped and stooped so suddenly in front of him that Robert tripped forwards and almost fell into his own house.

"Oh, excuse me and pardon, sir," Silly-Willie stood upright, hiding something small between his hands. "It's her robin," he said, "whatever should happen him." He picked at some sticky feathers. "We won't mention it to the Lady," he indicated a possible want of tact. As a child might carry a small plaything, he held the dead robin carefully in his hand while he paced across the black-and-white tiled floor to throw open the dining room door.

The dining room was composed, and dignified. Nothing showed change or decay. The first Nicandra's greatest silver cup stood in the centre of a long table and, at the head, a place was laid: one silver egg cup, an egg spoon two small plates, a toast rack, a wine glass, and a large white napkin. Robert counted over the items: "Does Mrs Fox-Collier still dine here?" There was a careful formality in the setting that suggested dinner rather than breakfast and a boiled egg. No cup. The wine glass.

"I serve Madarm in the caravarn." He saw Robert's surprise at the table setting. "Sir Dermot's dinner," he explained. "The funeral had me so upset in my nerves I didn't clear my table since."

Robert's memory went back to the long-past date of the funeral. There was something funny in this devoted service. "I expect you're kept pretty busy," he said kindly. "I'll take myself round the house." He wanted to be left alone with his plans and his measurements, and he wanted to locate the source of that evasive grave-like air, not quite a smell, but the hint of a hidden smell that came and went while he waited.

"Oh, sir," Silly-Willie protested, "here, nothing's a trouble." The "here" was magnificently accented. He saw that Robert did not know how to behave. Enquiring about the table laying and now poking at the wainscoting. "Can I help you, sir?" he asked severely.

"I'm looking for mushrooms. Have you noticed any?"

Mad as well, Silly-Willie thought. "No sir, it's too early in the year."

Robert was looking down at a solid white fungus, forcing its way between wall and woodwork. There was something indecent in the determined protrusion. He sighed: "The whole floor will have to come up."

Silly-Willie found the criticism distasteful, the gentleman talked as if he owned the place.

"This is the real decay," Robert sounded resigned. "Have you noticed it anywhere else?"

Silly-Willie shook his head silently. He was appalled at the ignorance of the question. He held the door wide open. "Would you care to follow me, sir?"

In Sir Dermot's bedroom there was no sign or smell of rot. The sun poured in, warming the mahogany furniture it had stripped to its bones of polish, lying across the big bed in a long caress. Robert wished he might think that the bed could tell a merry tale; knowing what he, and everybody else, knew of Sir Dermot's marriage, he doubted this entirely. Under the sunlight, he saw feathers, infinitesimal ducks' down, burst here and there through the rotted silk of the Paisley-patterned eiderdown. He put his hand under it to feel the weightlessness of another time. When he did so he was aware that Silly-Willie drew in his breath almost to a whistle as at a desecration. He wasn't going to like any of the coming changes, Robert thought. Always kind and understanding, he cleared his throat and stooped to put himself nearer the world of this vexed little mortal while he explained the situation.

Silly-Willie scooted aside before Robert could speak. "We have the North Wing to see yet, sir," he suggested time was short.

"I can go over that another time," Robert said. "What about that door? Another room?"

Silly-Willie went across to a closed second door and turned his back to it, all possible discouragement in his stance. "Sir Dermot's Dressing Room. Do you wish to see it, sir?"

Robert felt he had been guilty of some ignorant indecency. But his sound, innocent sense forbade any retreat

from his intention. "Yes please." He spoke a little brus-
quely.

Antagonism was in the air. Silly-Willie took a key out
of his pocket and unlocked the door – why locked? –
before he turned the handle. Robert stood on the threshold
staring short-sightedly, taken aback by what he was seeing:
Sir Dermot's clothes, a lifetime of well-cared-for clothes,
overflowed from wardrobes, wedged drawers open. Folded
as if ready for the leather bag and the race meeting, he saw
Sir Dermot's colours – silks and a knitted high-necked
jersey. Robert cared and knew less than nothing about
racing, but a ghostly breath and cheer for forgotten courage
lived – a spasm in his understanding.

"Would you wish to see anything else, sir? Sir Dermot's
cufflinks? The studs for the evening shirts? . . . I have
them in the safe in the gun room. You can't trust people
up here, we look out for the moths." He raised his hands
and clapped them together in a quick airy suggestion of
practical possession.

Robert acknowledged the Dressing Room to be cousin
to a tomb of Egypt: "Sir Dermot was a wonderful dresser,"
he said.

"No. But He knew who He was." There was a correction
and a rebuke in the statement. Robert felt rather small and
at the same time rather defiant, as if he had been put in his
place, a place from where proper style, as understood by the
aristocracy, was unrecognizable. He respected Silly-Willie's
great snob attitude and understood fully how unpleasant it
would be for him to accept the change he must learn to
accommodate. Perhaps, the sooner the better.

"I'm expecting a builder and a plumber to come here on
Friday," he said gently, "and a lady from Dublin to measure
for curtains and things. Could you get this room clear by
then, do you think?"

Silly-Willie's hands were knotted into fists that swung,
desolate and dangerous, on his long arms. Robert took a

step away, but did not turn his back. "I hope Mrs Bland will be moving in," he said. "She will want to look after Mrs Fox-Collier."

Not only Silly-Willie's face, but his whole tidy body seemed to splinter up into angry dismay. It was a moment before a cloak of long-instilled politeness dropped to cover his indiscretion.

Robert thought he had never seen jealousy so briefly naked, so smoothly concealed. What he had seen was uncomfortably like a threat. He had overheard a secret conversation – some difficulty, some impediment he could not discern was in the air, true and faint as the fog of dry rot in the dining room.

If Aunt Tossie had felt like an aboriginal in the unfolding of Robert's plans for the restoration of Deer Forest, Silly-Willie felt like a monarch about to be dethroned – useful for uncounted years, since Sir Dermot's death he had become something near both Master and Keeper of the house. Besides that, he knew himself to be indispensable to Mrs Fox-Collier. He was deeply concerned for her well-being, and he had no rival in importance since Brigid's pregnancy had come to its term.

"She only lives on nothing," he thought as he boiled the egg for lunch or dinner, and arranged its presentation with careful elaboration. "If it was dogs' dung itself," he murmured, "it should come up on a silver dish." Like a nimble beetle, he was here, there and everywhere in the big house, opening and shutting windows, locking and unlocking doors, carrying dirty linen on the handlebars of his bicycle to the village where Madge, uncomplaining and unable to resist the money, did the weekly washing. He loved every aspect of his responsibilities. When he cycled past the decaying Gate Lodge where Nicandra had teased him so shamelessly, he felt satisfaction warm within himself. He had overtaken so much that was weighted against him. When he bicycled back again, his bicycle wobbling under the load of domestic commissions, he could hardly wait to bring his account to Mrs Fox-Collier, and keep her informed of the sharp economies he had made and the delicacies he had searched out for her. He greatly enjoyed breaking into the monotony of her days (since Sir Dermot R.I.P. had gone) with reports of village scandals and other items of interest. He was quick but respectful in prompting her faulty memory; careful in taking her orders, before making his own decisions as to their execution. He was absolutely useful and he was in power. He needed no helper. Footsore and weary, he went to bed in the distant, dirty servants' wing. There he wasted no time in cleaning, or in emptying the green water, gathered under dripping, leaky spots. His own tin po stayed full for days, before he carried a bucket down to sluice out in the stableyard.

Times were very changed from the days when it was a chance in life and great promotion to be turf-boy and boy-of-all-work to Mrs Geary in the kitchen. Often kind, she could shake him and berate him cruelly before spoiling him with cake – that was when things went wrong between herself and Mr Twomey. He knew he had been a laughing-stock to a changing line of kitchenmaids, he could still hear them whispering their dirty jokes between themselves and the stable lads. Mr Twomey was always mistrustful and ceaselessly watchful, as if he had to keep an eye on the spoons, if he was obliged to call Silly-Willie in to clean up a dog's mess in the pantry or elsewhere. He, in his turn, was always watching Mr Twomey, because he admired his superbly graceful ways. He felt quite pleased and excited when Lizzie was found dead on the staircase, so creating another gap in the hierarchy. From the very first morning after Mr Twomey left, when he brought Sir Dermot his can of hot shaving water, he was like one possessed by an incipient grandeur. From there, correct behaviour grew towards a protective possession of his Gentleman: a gentleman very nearly as small as himself, whose feet, actually, were the same size as his own. He had cried, the tears falling on the back of his hand in pity, when he helped the nurse to dress him for his coffin, in his best pyjama suit, of course. Silly-Willie had insisted on the blue silk dressing-gown too, because *he* knew What was What, and the poor ignorant woman had no right idea about laying out the Gentry.

Since Sir Dermot's death, he was more than ever indispensable. All the ways of the house were his secrets to keep; Mrs Fox-Collier's little indiscretions were among them, whether these concerned the refreshing little drinks he never counted, or the sheets he brought Madge to wash and boil. He could keep quiet and make allowances. All went into the value of his absolute usefulness.

At six o'clock, on the day when Robert had hinted at the news of his ownership, and all the changes which that portended, Silly-Willie was, as usual, in his pantry, composing the dogs' dinners. In Mr Twomey's time, the dogs' dinners were prepared in his pantry since it would be derogatory for Mr Twomey to stand mixing up hearts and lights, table-scraps and well-soaked biscuit under the eyes of Mrs Geary and her assistant. Silly-Willie stuck to the tradition, carrying the makings of the dinners up the kitchen stairs to what was now his – not Mr Twomey's – pantry. As he cut and mashed the food together, trouble and spite seethed within him. When he squeezed the mess through his fingers to obtain the right consistency, he felt an obscure wish, quickly denied, to have his fingers and his hands on the throats of those coming to watch and displace him.

For the year after Andrew left her, Nicandra lived alone at Kileady. She avoided the company and sympathy of friends: most of all, she avoided Aunt Tossie, whose adoring pity she found unacceptable now, as in that bed-time moment long ago, when she had thrust her face deep in her pillow to avoid a good-night kiss.

In her marriage she had been too happy, too secure, for close intimacies, other than that one fatal friendship – and Lal was so popular, there would be mutual friends to take her side. Nicandra was not due for the clear sympathy given to widows, a mellow loving sympathy. The feeling for her would be run through with a latent curiosity as to the inner reasons for Andrew's desertion. There would be a hidden satisfaction for other women in knowing that beauty is not exempt.

Nicandra was stupid; she could only touch and feel. Daily life had a quality completely null now, leaving her purposeless. To restore reality she had to tell herself of her pain – bring it into daily actions. Andrew's gone and I'm brushing my teeth – I'm brushing my teeth and Andrew's gone. The horrid rhythm was present in every necessary act and occupation – to be hungry, though Andrew was gone, seemed an insult to grief. Another landmark in sorrow: she never went into the downstairs lav. It was papered with photographs of Andrew riding winners or losers, Andrew taking a sensational fall, Andrew, the most exquisite in a group of exquisites at some Hunt Ball. An inspired false modesty had hung this gallery with the graceful record of his prowess.

Good manners told her that she must not embarrass anybody. Alone, tears were forbidden, they could become irrepressible in public if not under proper private control.

The sense of their indecency went back to the "brave girls don't cry, do they?" of childhood. "One must be sensible" was a chorus line reminding her when it was time for the dogs' dinners; time to feed the greedy geese, that she had loved and laughed at for so long. Now the horses and dogs and bantams were in that void where sight and taste and smell had no importance, and there were no laughs. There would never be any more laughs.

When Robert found her, she was sitting, stilled into horrible immobility, with an unopened letter in her hand. No one had answered his ring or his knocking. He came in, bearing gifts. He would leave the tidy parcels – scent, pâté, brandy, wine, all with French labels, on the oak chest in the hall. A sound, between a cough and a sob, guided him across the hall and into the drawing room, or sitting room, or whatever she called the room. Here, Nicandra, distressed and shivering, was crouched and sunken into one of Aunt Tossie's presents, an inordinately expensive leather chair. The chair belonged properly to other, jolly days; teas after hunting; drinks before dinner. This was a travesty of its purpose when it arrived "straight from Harrods" as Aunt Tossie announced with satisfaction. Now Nicandra, tall though she was, seemed shrunken in its generous spaces. Here Robert saw more than grief; with his sober purpose he knew why it was different, beyond his consolation.

"I brought you a few contrabands – I left them in the hall – is that all right? The dogs won't . . . ?"

"Oh Robert," she sounded like someone surfacing out of water, a drowner who has touched a raft: who might cling to the raft? He saw the manila envelope she was holding. "You look worried – letter from the Bank?" Half mischievously, he took the sallow envelope out of her hand and opened it. "All right, Nico. You're well in the black."

"Was it only the Bank?" she burst into tears.

Kind, and enormously stolid, he sat down beside her. He took out his very clean pocket handkerchief and in a solemn way, a priest wiping the chalice, mopped at her tears and snivel.

"I am a fool . . . I never do this," she took the handkerchief away from him, folded it up, looked into it, then up to him.

"Andrew's left me," she said. "Don't let's talk about it – not yet – we've started on this divorce, did you know?"

"You're certain? People get so hysterical. It's this war."

"Because he may be killed? It's not that. He just does know what he wants – Lal."

Robert made up his mind. He was a master of unselfishness – they were, fatally, two Romantics. "Don't give him a divorce. That poisonous little bitch will only hurt him and leave him. She's been after him for years."

"Perhaps he's loved her for years. All those horses, and the Box, whenever. . ." She was crying again, ". . . more fool me."

Robert took her hand, not affectionately, more as though he was a nurse about to take her pulse.

"Hold tough," he said. "My advice is. . . ." Selflessness could go no further. And it didn't have to – Nicandra, his darling Nico, obstinate and goose-like in her loving, spoke out for all Romance: "I love him."

He understood. That would be her answer to any sacrifice, and nothing would turn her aside from her purpose. She might have been the heroine of a Scottish ballad, or an early Christian martyr determined on taking a jump into the Tiber, as adamant in her loving.

"Nico," he said, "what are you doing with yourself here, alone at Kileady? Every day? Ordinary days, I mean."

"I was all right when I first came back – looking

after things, you know. But what's the point now."

"You know what does need looking after, don't you? Deer Forest – Aunt Tossie. I saw her yesterday. It's only a matter of time till she sets fire to herself in that caravan."

"They tried to sell Deer Forest – didn't you know?"

"Well, yes. I do know. I've bought it."

"Then why don't you look after it? It's simply rotting away."

She sounded as though Deer Forest was some sort of deserted baby that had nothing to do with her.

"I have rather a lot on my hands just now," he apologized.

"Making plenty of Green Backs?" she asked. Not to be hurtful, she added: "I do hope so."

"More or less, yes," he sounded guarded, "my grocers' interests, you know. I can afford the rescue. I don't see how I can supervise the work."

"Aunt Tossie's there."

"She wouldn't be exactly useful with the builder. Would you do that for me? Overseer of the Works? Irish builders are a destructive lot."

"Robert, how can I? What about here? If Deer Forest is sold, I'll have nowhere else to go."

"You'll have money – and anywhere else you'll feel better."

She looked round her at all the once-loved things. She had to admit the sterile return they yielded to her loving. Without Andrew they were nothing; worse than nothing, hurtful in the remembrances they carried.

"Just go," Robert insisted, "sell up and clear out as soon as you can find a buyer." Get her away from here. Give her something to do. The idea possessed him so strongly that some ray from his conviction reached beyond her obstinacy.

"Perhaps you're right," she looked over her shoulder. "I could go mad here." She laughed to lighten the idea, and added: "Of course, the doggies would love it."

He would be the author of kindness to doggies – he didn't look for anything further – not yet – not ever, he supposed. He was her match in giving. "What about Aunt Tossie? I didn't much like the look of her."

"Aunt Tossie? She's quite happy with Silly-Willie."

"Silly-Willie is going to find her dead one of these mornings."

"What a frightening idea – he's like a Nannie."

"Silly-Willie's not absolutely the full shilling, is he? She doesn't look very well to me."

He saw a new perplexity, a shifting distaste, in her beautiful stupid eyes. If he could give her enough to pity and care for, she might live again. Now he was nearly sure that she would go back to Deer Forest, the idea of the room he would have ready for her flowered delightfully in his mind. It was going to be a big, beautiful surprise for her in that shambling desert of a house to which, for the sake of her own good and perhaps her happiness, he was condemning her. Man of Business that he was, he knew how to procure anything he wanted for her, and how to have it properly installed. He wanted everything to be complete and paid for before his next little venture. The restoration would take some time, but so would the sale of Kileady.

"Can you give me some lunch?"

"Only a scrambled egg."

Obviously she wasn't feeding herself properly. "I've brought you a little pâté," he suggested. Her enclosed forbidding look bothered him. He could not know that it was there because she saw Andrew devouring another pâté Robert had brought.

"I've got dozens of bantams' eggs," she said. "I scramble them in a bowl over boiling water – lots of parsley – do you like parsley? I forget."

Luncheon was a miserable meal – she cooked the

eggs perfectly and ate them without the smallest interest. He almost wished to keep the foie gras for one of the dear girls who didn't appeal to him in the least. On his way out, perhaps he would pick up the pot. He knew he wouldn't. The time might come when an exceptional pâté would be a convenience to remind her of him.

Almost immediately after lunch, he said: "I must go. Thank you. Delicious eggs, Nico." He was struggling into a covert coat; as usual, just not loose enough for his bulk. She thought how silly he would look at Newmarket, or Cheltenham, or Liverpool, and a rush of tenderness came over her. Kind, kind, Robert – all those presents. But how tiring to owe him so much. He was forever giving presents – now, for once, he was asking something from her: to keep a watch on his property. Putting work in her way out of sympathy? No – surely out of his business sense. She was the obvious person to be stewardess of Deer Forest. He had worried her about Aunt Tossie too. She knew she had neglected her shamelessly. But in those years Aunt Tossie had Dada, and she had her own lover and companion, all time lost that was not spent with him.

Robert picked up a terrible briefcase. He was leaving. "Do you really think you can take all this on?"

Relentless kindness welled in her, "Of course I can. Come back soon." She touched her cheekbone to his, then the other side, both in cool friendship. She even said: "What a friend you are, Robert – bless you." But it was with a sense of liberation that she heard his big car going down the avenue. As the sound of the engine petered away to nothing, a glimmer of purpose came into her life again.

~Part Six~

$\mathcal{T}$he prolonged divorce proceedings between England and Ireland had reached no conclusion when Kileady was sold, and the time to auction the contents of the house and its outdoor assets came nearer. The wooden buckets grouped like a family in the yard looked monumentally pathetic. There were terrible decisions to implement in a businesslike way – such as the meticulous collection and expedition of Andrew's clothes and saddlery to his mother's house. Everything else in Kileady would be sold, from the beds – especially the beds, with all Aunt Tossie's linen sheets and featherweight blankets going with them, as well as the great rough bath towels, big enough to comfort even Andrew's length – to the kitchen pots and pans she had worked with so lovingly. She wanted no reminders. She quite looked forward to a penance of difficulties in cooking with the prehistoric implements in the kitchen at Deer Forest. There would be no Kate with her there to share the load.

"No, madam, don't ask me, I couldn't. That big barracks of a place and that little eejit of a fellow around me, he'd give you the creeps." Lavish though she was with loving service in these last months at Kileady, she stayed obdurate in her refusal to work at Deer Forest. Nicandra accepted her default without much surprise. She was getting used to the idea of disloyalty. For the present, Kate's service was selfless and dedicated. Before the auction, she sorted and arranged and re-arranged, putting reserves on objects that

Nicandra, with aimless lack of interest, abandoned to the hammer. She insisted on the inclusion in the sale of small items, one such a bunch of Andrew's old silk ties, which she fastened together with tears. If no one else made a bid for them, she would; doubtful though she felt as to whether her fellow would wear them. To move miles away from the fellow, with petrol so scarce for his motorbike, and then to join that dwarf in the dark kitchens of Deer Forest was beyond her, dearly as she cared for Nicandra.

On the last evening at Kileady, refreshing tears poured down Kate's cheeks as she tied the gander's legs together before shutting him in the boot of the car. "Ah, you ruffian, you slipped me yesterday," she sobbed. Yesterday the main flock together with the bantams, had been shipped to Deer Forest. "Ah, madam, madam," she cried and hugged Nicandra close, "God help you." Nicandra yielded to the embrace without feeling any ability in her to return Kate's affection: "I'll get over it, Kate, don't cry about me, please."

"Ah, but you won't get over it," Kate promised her, "you'll get hard, that's all. That's the wholely all." She watched Nicandra get into the car, heard her call, rather crossly, for the two little dogs. They had hopped in before her, ready and waiting. Kate heard her profuse apologies and endearments to them before she turned back into the empty house. She knew it was unlucky to see the last of a leaving.

It was March, the month for dramatic changes of weather. On this late afternoon, as Nicandra drove along the familiar way between Kileady and Deer Forest, a wild sun with a glitter in it threw bearded shadows across the road from wind-shaken branches. Snow could be near – or a lovely day tomorrow. She stretched a hand to pull a rug closer over the dogs. Then she wondered if her goose had enough air in the boot – suppose she had smothered him? She drew in near a wet ditch, golden with celandines, to reassure herself. When she opened the boot, the gander stretched his neck to the full and gave her a long, extended hiss. "I know, I know," she said, and loosened his poor bound legs a little, before she shut him in again. "Soon now, drinkies," she said.

The unrelenting cold of the late March afternoon reminded her she would need hot-water bottles in her bed. The idea stirred in her mind. The thought of all the meagre discomforts she would face was a gratifying prospect; it was a kind of "to your oratory" comfort – she would sleep in her nursery room. She wished for all the aridity possible, even the cold walk to the bathroom, and probably tepid water. Her conduct of household affairs would be gentle, her authority over Silly-Willie exercised with patience and with sympathy for what he was sure to see as deposition; neither of them must give a thought to those strange encounters when, in her despair for Maman's loss, he had been a whipping-boy for the exercise of a childish teasing. Those dark little cruelties were pushed to a nowhere beyond memory now.

Where the drive forked apart at the bottom of Dada's uncut lawns, she saw, to her dismay and anxiety, her geese heading determinedly for the near woods. What fool had opened the stable door that she had shut on them so carefully yesterday? A strange man was running to head off the flock. Between them, with the habitual assistance of Nooskie and Slipper, they turned the geese away from their purposed direction and outflanked their obstinate efforts to break back towards the wild.

"I'd say they were looking for water. What I say is: a breeding goose needs water. They passed through myself and the bicycle like a pack of eagles. I said to myself they won't last long in those woods, I should get them back in the yard, I said, whatever about the work in the house, the fox won't wait, I said."

"You are kind, you do understand geese," Nicandra spoke gratefully. Of course, he should be indoors, overseeing the demolition, not playing goose-boy with her. As he skilfully defeated the backwards turn of a goose, she felt she had a friend, even if he was the head executioner of demolition. "Perhaps," she said, "tomorrow you would help me to get them down to the farmyard. They would have the pond there."

"I'd say you have the right ticket – water and privacy is what the like of them want. Never interfere with a breeding goose," he advised.

Nearer the house, a great heap of timbers was lying like rotted old bones on Dada's overgrown lawns, a spread of pebbly plaster and deep wheelmarks of loaded barrows defaced and defiled the grass around the pile. Why did the rubbish have to lie there? It seemed a gross rudeness.

"You'd hate to be looking at the lovely stuff that's gone," the man said, "it's only it's the handiest spot to dump it. Listen and you'll hear the fellows at it now."

The profound blows of a heavy hammer and, after a pause, the prolonged shriek of woodwork yielding to some other instrument came through the open window of the dining room, followed by a consignment of the same rubbish that lay on the dump. "We'll have the most of the floorboards up tonight, please God," he said. Nicandra accepted that the dining room was a case beyond mercy.

In the vast empty stableyard the geese, even when reunited with their gander, huddled miserably. When she and her new friend had ushered them quietly back into their loose-box, she saw that the old tin bath, and the hose she had contrived and directed to carry water to it from a tap in the yard, were both dry. The tap had been turned off. She turned it on and replenished the feeding trough before she let her bantams out of another loose-box, where they screeched and clattered. In a moment, the mob flew round her and round the yard, prisoners loosed in a wild disarray. If they could fly back to Kileady, they would. There was a chill spot in her mind at the idea. They should feel only too happy to be here. A glimmer, more a sliver of memory: some previous change for the betterment of bantams that had gone wrong.

It was when she was turning the car out of the yard, where she had untied her gander, to drive round to the porte-cochère and unpack her vast amount of luggage, that she heard a sound, different from, and terribly audible above, the noises of demolition in the dining room: the dogs were fighting. Distracted by her wandering geese, she had left her darlings unprotected and now in danger of ugly death. They were no match for Nettle and Knobble. High notes of anguish came to her past the guzzling growl of a killer. Teeth would be sunk in the neck of one or both of her dear ones. Calling hysterically for help, she ran to the grass sweep where Nettle and Knobble were fastened on their prey. Nothing is more full of primeval terror than a fight between even the smallest dogs, when the will to kill is rampant.

She tore Nettle off Slipper and held the little creature close to her heart while Nettle screamed and punched against her legs. So handicapped, she was no match for Knobble, now almost silent in her dreadful hold on Nooskie. It was only a minute before the kind man and two followers left their work. Jumping down from the dining room window, they came running to her assistance. With some forethought they brought with them a silver pepper-pot – actually it was a sugar-castor, and it did nothing to allay the heat of the battle. Inexpert and afraid, not one of the demolishment hearties moved adequately to quell the aggressor or rescue the victim. They kicked each little dog impartially, keeping themselves out of any real trouble. They advised one another: "Mind yourself now – a dog's bite can be a dangerous thing."

It was Silly-Willie who brought deliverance – he came out of the yard tottering under the weight of two buckets of water, carried one in either hand. With aim and swing worthy of the tallest man, he flung water on top of the dogs and, while they choked, he dragged Knobble away from Nicandra's squealing darling. When, a semblance of peace restored, he rated the dogs, his voice – a child-like and true imitation of Dada's – surprised Nicandra. Oddly enough, she thought it rather an impertinence. Thankful as she was to have her darlings restored alive and not really wounded, she was disappointed and a little resentful at their undistinguished conduct in the battle. She had read about rat-pits. Dog-fights are somewhere on that hideous level of competition.

The men went back to their work in the dining room. She was alone with Silly-Willie. Now she knew the dogs were bound to be a dangerous sort of cannon-fodder between them. Sides must be taken at once, and kept to strictly. When he said: "Sir Dermot (R.I.P.) would have enjoyed that. He loved a good fight," she realized how right she was. "Shut your dogs up at once, please," was her answer.

Silly-Willie felt the flick of a ghostly lash in her quick order. "Certainly, Madarm, and of course – Nettle! Knobble! In the pantry with yous – those two are worse than Christians the way they miss Sir Dermot." He picked up the empty buckets and whistled for his dogs. Why shouldn't he whistle? There was nothing disrespectful about that. But it was rather as though he had shrugged his shoulders. "You do understand," she softened her order a little, "the dogs can't be out together, ever."

"And you'll understand and excuse us, Mrs Bland, if we make the odd breakout," he shelved responsibility on to the dogs, "we're so used to our liberty." He patted them lovingly, and called them after him on a note of sadness and warning. His whistle was as sweet as that of an unseen bird. It reminded her of his dancing in which, as a child, he had so outclassed her. She denied remembrance of a different day when she had whipped him into his proper obedience, that of slave boy whose mother lived in the lodge only by grace and favour. She never told what she had seen. It was a secret then – nothing worth remembrance now.

On her way back to the yard for her car, she met her new friend and his two assistants – a flight of cyclists at the end of their day's work. "See you tomorrow," she called. Her friend shook his head respectfully. "We're not working tomorrow," he was back-pedalling to keep near her, "tomorrow's a Holy Day and we have the place closed up." He cycled away after his mates. When she looked towards the house she saw that the three long windows of the dining room were shuttered closely.

Silly-Willie was waiting to unload her luggage from the car, solicitously obedient to her directions. In the hall, standing among all her suitcases, she felt as though in a deserted railway station, no trains coming in or going out any more. Dust lay, a thick, dirty frost, on the carpet and on everything. The uprooted furniture from the dining room was packed untidily amongst what seemed the living furniture of the hall. Pictures were stacked together. Chairs sat reversed, on the laps of their mates. The leaves of the dinner table, lifted off their pedestals, stood up-ended against the wall. Woodworm powder oozed from one shaky leg of the sideboard. All proportion and dignity was lost. Shock, and with it a kind of shamed curiosity prompted her to look into the dining room. The door was locked and she could not turn the key.

"Excuse me, Madarm," Silly-Willie came hurrying to her assistance, "that door will only open when it will like." He turned the key with a familiar knack. "We" – he spoke for Aunt Tossie too, perhaps – "we have to keep it closed.

We can't have these fellows running in and out to please theirselves."

Peering into the shuttered gloom, Nicandra could just see that the bare empty room, shrunken somehow in size without its furniture, looked only too ready for the final breaking up – a patient prepared and anaesthetized for surgery. Cold as it was, the air held a fullness like bad breath, something elemental and lightly poisonous. Nicandra shut the door.

Aunt Tossie made a great effort to look her best for Nicandra's arrival. There was something like anxiety in her welcome, in the kissing and the promises of fun. They met in the morning room, not in the caravan. The purple velvet dressing-gown had been discarded; Aunt Tossie was gracefully dressed in a loose coat and skirt. The skirt needed two safety-pins (the kind made for babies' nappies that Silly-Willie obtained from the chemist) to maintain its position. The vague disorder of her hair was gently veiled in blue. She struggled out of her chair behind the tea table, where watercress sandwiches and chocolate biscuits waited. For the last half hour Aunt Tossie had longed for a nibble, but restrained herself. Today everything must proceed in its proper way, no shiftless lack of ceremony be apparent. Perhaps it was in defence of her position as Regent that she had left her caravan, an animal coming suspiciously out of its happy hole. If such was her intention, she was unconscious of it, and saw nothing beyond a wish to welcome in her preparations for Nicandra's arrival. A fire blazed and glowed in the grate where water had dripped down the chimney throughout the winter months. The silver teapot gleamed after long neglect in the pantry cupboard. Now that she was back in the morning room, afternoon tea set before her, memories of other days spread their feelers in her mind. She was in no way a dependent old member of the family. Generous and unthinking as she had always been, she could not quite forget whose money, as long as it lasted, had maintained Deer Forest. Remembrance was as unconstant as dust in the wind, inconsiderable and light with mistakes. Everything as it occurred had seemed a necessity, nothing an extravagance or a foolishness. She looked no further than the present moment and its needs. The present moment had always been her refuge. She sat back in it now, more than happy because she was about to divulge a wonderful surprise. Tea first.

"Ah, William," she said in acknowledgement as he put a jug of hot water beside the teapot and shifted things a little on the tray. Tea was something special between them.

"Should I put a bit on the fire, Madarm?" he enquired. This meant that Nicandra, sitting on the hearthrug with her back to the fender, would have to move. "It's all right," she said, "I'll do it presently." Silly-Willie still looked at Aunt Tossie for orders. "Leave it for the moment, William." She knew she had yielded a point. "Take Mrs Bland's things up to her room." Their eyes met. They shared a secret.

"And will I let out Sir Dermot's dogs now, Madarm?" he asked Nicandra. "The poor mites are bawling their heads off in my pantry." The message about deprived orphans came over strongly. Nicandra's heart was touched. "Poor loves, let them out. I'll keep my lot in here. Who wants a chocky bicky?" "Nettle's mad about them," Silly-Willie sighed from the doorway. The subject of dogs was a Tom-Tiddler's ground when all their loves were at variance: jealousy and display as complete as Nannies' jealousies in different nurseries.

"Is it going to be horribly difficult?" Nicandra said when Silly-Willie had shut the door. Aunt Tossie gloated a little over this first intimacy. "They're longing to take Nettle on at the Kennels," she invented. "She's a bit old for a working terrier. It's that wonderful bloodline. You should have heard the Master at Dada's funeral."

"Only think of poor badgers," Nicandra was not going to be reassured or comforted.

"The dogs will settle down, darling, and it's so lovely you're here. Have some tea, have a sandwich – William waded up to his waist for this watercress. . . ."

Aunt Tossie ate most of the watercress sandwiches, pleased that they were well buttered. The dogs ate most of the chocolate biscuits. Nicandra drank a lot of tea. At last she put the dogs aside and, drawing the lengths of her legs towards herself, she grew slowly to her own height: "I think perhaps I ought to unpack." She felt as gripless on life as though she had arrived at a strange hotel.

"You're not in your own room," Aunt Tossie tried to sound ordinary. The surprise to come was so colossal it had to be smoothed over.

"Not in the nursery? Why not?"

Aunt Tossie squeezed her bulk determinedly from behind the tea table. "I'll show you," she said, and the hostessly tang of politeness was in the air. "I know you're going to be absolutely thrilled."

Not thrilled, but frightened and coldly apprehensive, was how Nicandra felt as she matched her striding step with Aunt Tossie's trotting shuffle through the quiet, dusty house. The dogs, tiny giants of strength, pulled hard on their leads. From behind every door she expected a Nettle or a Knobble to pounce out to murder. She knew now how tired she was, and to be tired was nearly a luxury. A loveless bed lost its forlorn quality and became itself – a necessity for exhaustion. Whatever Aunt Tossie had arranged she would accept for tonight and tomorrow night and even longer. But in a week she would be back in the hungry, undefiled nursery bedroom, where tiny Nannie had been so strict and

198

uninteresting a despot. The nursery was a dead world signifying nothing.

As they climbed the separate flights the clear, almost medicated, light of the March evening came resolutely through the Venetian window at the stairhead. Gasping from her unwonted climb and from the joyful stress of expectation, Aunt Tossie delayed to draw a few deep breaths. They waited together in the gallery at the stairs' head where young ladies once practised their party pieces. The red silk behind its gilt lattice on the upright piano was intact – the harp still stood in its beauty, dust-furred strings untried. The curtains were never drawn here because they shed a petal of rotten brocade at any touch. Aunt Tossie delayed another moment, while she drew a few redeeming breaths, before turning, her appetite refreshed, towards the surprise in store. "There: what about that?" She opened wide the door to Dada's bedroom, and waited for the amazed acclaim due to the luxuries and beauties created there for Nicandra's ease and enjoyment.

A chord of absolute dismay struck through Nicandra, it vibrated even to her hands, rigid on the dogs' leads, as they pulled her through the doorway into the magnificence prepared for her. The bed, wide as a street, imposed a vast opulence on the quiet square of the room. Its head-board was blue satin, deeply padded and buttoned into regular bulging cheeks. The eiderdown was blue as sea-mist and, when she lifted it, light as air in her hand. Because blue was the motif of what had to be called the décor, a picture hanging above the bed was blue too – a Marie Laurencin: blue dress, a grey young face and a pale, silver head. There was nowhere the least ghost of Maman and Dada to remind her of a little girl kneeling for her morning prayers, eyes on the bread and butter. Even so, the bed appalled her. Speechless, she could only stand and stare round her at the rest of the room. The fireplace had been blocked out with a marble slab, an electric log fire blazed in front of it. The dogs, off their leads, settled into the depths of a white goatskin hearth-rug, ignoring two lush dog-baskets, hooded and warmly lined. The wallpaper was a sprawl of blue roses. A tallboy was inevitably walnut of the right date, so was the card table on which a blue leather blotter held blue blotting-paper. Writing paper and envelopes were stacked neatly in the several compartments of a tooled blue-leather box. The white brocade curtains and their pelmets were looped and looped again, cord and fringe discreet in their magnificence. White carnations were reflected three times in the triple-winged looking-glass on the dressing-table.

"Well?" Aunt Tossie asked. Nicandra nodded, wordless.

"And the bathroom – you haven't seen anything yet," Aunt Tossie sounded as though the bedroom was only bread-and-butter before cake. "As you see," she opened the door, "everything straight from Harrods – the Customs must have been enormous."

Nicandra could well believe it. Blue-tiled walls matched a blue bath, sunk to half its height. Its taps were gold. The white carpet from the bedroom carried on, "throughout" would be the word, Nicandra knew. The bathmat was deeper than fleece. A long glass shelf was packed, neatly as if by books, with boxes of scent and bath essences – a scent for every mood. Great bath towels hung on a hot rail; tiny towels in huckaback, monogrammed "N" in blue cross-stitch, surrounded the hand-basin, wide and deep enough to bath a baby. A shower and a bidet were cloistered away behind blue curtains.

Nicandra felt overpowered, sick! The best thing in the world would be to feel hunger for anything. She turned on Aunt Tossie. "Darling," she asked, "why did you let him? How *could* you?" Aunt Tossie beamed, "Can't you guess? Dear Robert. All for you, darling."

"It's his house," stubborn in her wilful isolation, Nicandra spoke coldly, "not mine." Robert had cheated on her through this agglomeration of luxuries. Abetted, and probably advised, by Aunt Tossie, he had cancelled out his pretence of her usefulness, a pretence invented to turn the edge of her grief and loss. He was forever over-kind in his spending and giving. When she made scrambled eggs, he brought pâté de foie gras, the real thing always. "I can't sleep in that awful room" she cried out in her revulsion.

"Oh my darlin', you have to give it a try."

"All those roses and I know it will be satin sheets."

Her eyes met Aunt Tossie's. Aunt Tossie's fell away, chided. But her full understanding was there when she held out her great stalwart arms. "Yes, I know. I know," she was whispering. "He is so dear, and he is so awful."

Why did Nicandra helplessly resent this understanding and translation of Robert's long purpose? Why did she connect it with Aunt Tossie's disposal of cold spinach on a cold plate? Because then, a gift of life had been stripped away – the unmade sacrifice haunted her still. Another time, stagnating but unforgotten: a heavy white breast, now discreetly covered by tweed and wool and a Jaeger vest, toppling from its restraints to hang, dreadfully distinct against black velvet, before averted eyes and shocked silence .... The heavy clutch of beads on an ugly satin dress still weighted that same evening, when all she should have remembered of it was: Andrew kissed me. Tears too near, she turned away from Aunt Tossie. She felt like a rat she had once seen being tendered a straw to help it out of a deep tub of water. The straw broke.

Her outstretched arms ignored, Aunt Tossie left Nicandra and sank her weight into a white leather chair in the, to her, still glorious bedroom. But it had not pleased her darling. She thought of herself as tiresome, miscalculating, tactless. "Silly old me" was how she saw her false step towards confidence. All poise shaken, she waited, a tired old woman, for Nicandra to restore her. She knew her place: kind Aunt Tossie. Darling Aunt Tossie sometimes. Such fun – so kind – perhaps so dear. She had never let herself understand the frightening loss of love Nicandra had suffered when Maman ran out. "Running out" was Dada's word for that shaming elopement. She was proud to have assuaged some of Dada's grief. Nicandra had always been evasive, accepting her love with crippling reservations. Where was she now? Sitting on the edge of that lovely bath, revolted and angry at Robert's unrestrained giving. Looking around her, Aunt Tossie could find no fault with the bedroom. In her day, she would have revelled in it. The past and the present mingled in her mind. Other days recreated their importance . . . . champagne in the box at Cheltenham . . . . then, dashing on the money, she had really lived. It was not her money that brought a blissful marriage – her money was nothing compared with his. And he adored her. After his death she remembered vagrant lovers. Dada had never been her lover: her child, perhaps. She sustained and caressed him with kind words and expensive indulgences – a high-powered mowing machine the last and fatal indulgence – comfort was always within her power to give . . . this time comfort had been achieved only by proxy, and its failure was manifest. At the back of her exaggerated welcome lay the horrid truth that she absolutely dreaded Nicandra's coming to cherish and watch over her. She had her established ways. William had his ways too – Nicandra would upset them both. The caravan might be tidied up. Aunt Tossie shuddered. Punctual hours for eating would be put back. Drinks would have their proper times too. There she would defend herself. Her meagre little drinks at odd hours were purely medicinal. Dada had always recognized their necessity for her silly bit of heart trouble. William understood perfectly how to shepherd her from caravan to kitchen if she was feeling a bit shaky. Now, as she sat waiting for Nicandra, the clock of drink time struck in her head. She turned her wrist to see the tiny watch, so typical of its date. It was nearly lost in the creases of old flesh and, without her spectacles, its figures were invisible. She found herself making nervous old lady faces, moving her lips involuntarily, blinking her eyes; all quite unlike herself. With an effort, she lifted her head to achieve her usual proud demeanour. The little restorative drink that made nothing of her age and changed her world was distant. The bottle waited in the po cupboard, so convenient to her bed. Impatience for its solace invaded her entirely. Then, as minutes went by, that tiny familiar stitch of pain crept, alive again, under her arm and grew, a preposterous indigestion, overtaking courage and control as drowning might engulf reason.

She cried out, but not loudly enough for Nicandra, running the cold tap and dabbing at her eyes (big girls don't cry, the ghostly Nannie whisper), to hear – Nicandra thought she was alone with her dogs. She thought Aunt Tossie had gone downstairs. To find her, doubled up in pain, imploring help, sweat sopping into her blue veil, gave a glorious resurrection to her own powers of loving and giving. They had a victim now – a victim who could not escape them. She caught up the cold hands, she stuffed cushions behind the fat shoulders. "What is it, darling? What can I *do* for you?"

Her loving pleading eyes had no importance for Aunt Tossie. "Get William," she whispered. "Ring for him. Run for him. He knows. . . ." Her breathing raced, louder than her words.

Devastated, panic-stricken, Nicandra left her and ran down the stairs, calling for Silly-Willie. She heard him pounding up from the kitchen. How could a creature light as a midge make so much noise? He must have sensed trouble, he was hurrying to its source.

"Ring the doctor, Miss Nicandra," he said as he passed her. He kept on running, turning quick as a bat through

203

the evening: a bat's flight up the staircase, devil's wings on a harmless mouse.

Nicandra felt excluded, threatened in some dim way. Why *Miss Nicandra*? It sounded as if they were back in the Gate-Lodge playtimes. Did he still remember? It was as if, this evening, authorities were reversed. The telephone was his business – Aunt Tossie was her concern.

The doctor said: "I'll be over straight away."

"But what must I *do*?" she was shouting into the telephone.

"William has her tablets," came the answer.

"Brandy? Should we give her brandy?" But he had rung off. She might find some in the dining room. She hurried from the telephone into the hall, corrupting quietly under its own dust. Forgetting that all its furniture was stacked in the hall, from old habit she ran across to the dining room door. It was locked. She set about tearing the leaning portraits of dead ancestors away from the sideboard cupboards where they had been leant against its doors. She found a brandy bottle, but without even a dreg left in it. What to do now? Of course, Aunt Tossie must need air, that was vital. What else? Rub her head, rub the back of her neck with cologne. The bathroom was full of scent bottles. She must hurry.

Where Silly-Willie had darted up the flights, Nicandra hovered upwards, a great white moth in the failing light. Before she reached the top of the staircase, she knew exactly what must be done. She would put Aunt Tossie to bed in Dada's room. From now on that should be her bedroom. All that baby-blue luxury would please her – warmth and comfort would surround her, and loving care. Nicandra's loving care.

It was a shock not altogether pleasing to find Aunt Tossie sitting upright in her chair and sipping from a glass Silly-Willie held to her lips with one hand while, with the other, he swayed a fan, regularly and tidily, near her face. He had opened a window; the March air needled its way through the excessive heat.

"Oo, I am a bother," Aunt Tossie apologized.

"No bother. How could you be a bother?" Nicandra watched Silly-Willie's hands holding the glass and swaying the fan, they were steady and very clean. Nicandra felt she was seeing a ritual of rather questionable devotion. She supposed the clean, dextrous hands derived from his mother's good old housemaid's blood. Everything seemed in order, competently dealt with. No panic evident. So this must have happened before. Why had she not been told about these attacks? It was quite time that she took charge. "All right, Willie," she reached out to take the glass and fan from him, "would you get Mrs Fox-Collier's night things? She must be in bed before the doctor comes." She could see Aunt Tossie stiffen in her chair. She could see a look exchanged, reassuring on Willie's side, reassurance verging on conspiracy. Aunt Tossie's response was harder to gauge. Nicandra proffered the tooth glass.

"William keeps a tiny drink handy – just in case," Aunt Tossie looked ridiculously caught out.

"And I carry Madarm's tablets on my person too," Silly-Willie put in.

"Just fetch her nightdress and dressing-gown," Nicandra's tone was dismissive. Silly-Willie hesitated before he left the room.

"I'm not sleeping here," Aunt Tossie said firmly.

"Just for tonight."

"Not tonight. Not any night. Oh, please not. . . ."

The more Aunt Tossie showed herself obstinate and baby-like, the stronger Nicandra felt her protective love to grow; it swelled out through her – feathers on a winter bird.

"Don't let's fuss, darling, wait till the doctor comes and see what he says."

The young doctor, when he arrived, had been thoughtful and reassuring: talking quietly to Aunt Tossie, not demeaning her symptoms as she wished him to do, nor exaggerating their importance. He agreed with Nicandra on the benefit of a night's sleep in luxury, and showed diplomatic sympathy over Aunt Tossie's insistence on the superior comforts of her caravan.

"For this night only," she agreed, at last, "and I shan't sleep a wink. I know I shan't."

"Take one of these in a nice hot cup of Ovaltine and I promise you, you will." He might have suggested a nice cup of cold poison, Aunt Tossie's shudder at the idea of Ovaltine was so intense. He shed a small rain of tablets into Nicandra's hand: "A light supper, and I'll call in the morning – don't move." He restrained Nicandra. "I'll find my own way down."

But Silly-Willie was waiting to escort him. Nicandra heard their voices joining. Had he waited at the head of the staircase, or outside the door, perhaps? Nicandra wondered.

Aunt Tossie undressed slowly, stripping off clothes only as far as her waist before Nicandra dropped the nightdress over her head. It took minutes before the whole of the sad, slack body was naked and lost under a vast nightdress, with ecru lace insertions, that covered it like a frail tent. The velvet dressing-gown was wrapped round and belted.

Sitting up at last between the new satin sheets – slippery and unfamiliar in their extremity of luxury – her buried feet, with their toe-nails thick and cold, felt round for a hot-water bottle and found it. Nicandra had thought of everything. There was no need for Silly-Willie to come back, knocking on the door.

"I brought up a second hot bottle," he said before he crossed the room to slip it between Aunt Tossie's back and the pillows heaped behind it.

"Comfy now?" Nicandra asked. She enjoyed her own soothing voice.

Aunt Tossie nodded with desperate politeness before she said: "I can't bear it – these awful slimy sheets. I'll fall out of bed – I know I shall."

"You heard what the doctor said, 'keep very quiet'."

"He didn't say 'very'."

"That doctor killed a man with an injection yesterday," Silly-Willie put in. "They say, all the same, he's good," he added: a bright and false assurance to the invalid.

"That doesn't tell me how I'm to find my way to the loo."

"We'll leave the light on," Nicandra promised.

"Can't sleep with the light on."

"The whole pity about it is we didn't take this little turn in the caravan. Everything is so handy there."

Silly-Willie was pulling Aunt Tossie's stockings inside out and folding back the toes, ready for the morning. Looking at the heap of uninviting underclothes, Nicandra felt his hand-maidening was indecent. She wondered if this had been going on since Dada's death and Brigid's departure. She blamed herself at once for a year, and longer, of selfish neglectfulness. "Better leave all this to me," she came between him and the defiling task – defiling to Aunt Tossie. "Is there some soup you could heat up? Some thin toast?"

"There's pork chops only waiting in the kitchen. Am I right, Madarm?" he deferred to Aunt Tossie.

"Ah, my pork chops," she sighed and closed her eyes.

"But the doctor did say something light tonight. . . ."

Aunt Tossie's longing for a pork chop filled the bedroom air with the scent of its cooking.

Nicandra took a middle way: "Put the chops in the larder

till tomorrow," she suggested. "I only want a boiled egg –
I'm not a bit hungry."

"I want two – two boiled eggs – four minutes," Aunt
Tossie said firmly.

"And the doggie dinners, Madarm?" Silly-Willie sounded
reproachful as though Nicandra should have ordered
for them.

"They've had theirs, thank you. Their baskets are in
the car. Would you bring them up to the old nurseries?"

"I was going to make up a bed for you in the double
spare. The nurseries are gone wild this long time." He
smiled a little anxiously, suggesting that it was not his
place to make decisions.

"Thank you. But I'd rather have my own old bedroom."

"And have you a bottle with you I could put in your
bed, Mrs Bland? We will want our own two here." There
was enjoyment, even a sense of power in the way he dealt
with this domestic problem.

"I never have a hot-water bottle. If you would just
leave the suitcases and the baskets in my bedroom,
Willie, that will be all I need." The distance in her voice
grew longer, vaguer. He didn't mean to be tiresome, her
kind heart said; but something within her disagreed with
Aunt Tossie's favour and familiarity towards him.

"Rather wonderful, isn't he?" Aunt Tossie's eyes followed
Silly-Willie out of the door. "Nothing is too much trouble.
And darling, if you could remember to call him William.
The thought of being Silly-Willie rather hurts him."

He had stayed Silly-Willie in Nicandra's mind ever
since . . . well forget . . . . "Of course," she said, "if it
matters."

"I do hope your bed won't be absolutely steaming," Aunt
Tossie went on, "you see, we did think you'd rather love it
in here." "We" again.

"I'll be all right, the doggies will keep me warm."

"Yes. *How* I miss my Gigi, " Aunt Tossie sounded as if

Gigi had once kept her warm in bed – maybe they had lain cheek-to-cheek. Nicandra shivered a little at the idea.

Aunt Tossie shivered too, looking at Nicandra: no husband, no lover. And at her age. "And your bath," she almost screamed in her concern, "not a drop of hot water over there."

"I always have mine in the morning." At the back of her mind stayed Andrew's unemphatic indication: a bath before bed was rather middle-class; after hunting, before dinner, or in the morning, was more proper.

It was late in the evening when, after almost forcing one of the doctor's sleeping pills between Aunt Tossie's clenched teeth, and watching her relax, happy and helpless in its influence, Nicandra decided that it was time to whisper to the dogs and seek her own resting place. Tonight, she knew, it would be awful: the doggies might hate it. The more awful it was, the more for her to work on – occupation was to be her discipline and her religion now. When she found that the bedside light did not work, the irritation only became part of her new code of discipline. She put the dogs under the frosty blankets and glacial sheets of her bed and, as Aunt Tossie had predicted, steam rose. She found the rank discomfort very nearly agreeable. If everything had been warm and clean, she would have felt an alien in the nursery past, and a revenant in the night when she and Lal had dressed for their first hunt ball: the night when her love, her only love, had overtaken her.

Tonight, all maidenly pretences towards prettiness were gone from the room. The nursery had become a junk room – a receptacle for every small unwanted object that changes in the house had ejected from its perpetual place: small pieces of furniture, put aside for repair and never mended; an enamel clock, hands motionless on its golden face; a bow and arrow; a Worcester china teapot – inside it a broken handle rattled; a pile of photograph books.

Victim of the universal compulsion to open a photograph book, Nicandra saw once more the steps of Government House; saw a dead lion; saw dark faces and white clothes. She held the book up, nearer to the hanging light-bulb, and lived again an evening of confused despair: the evening of the day when Maman, faultless and heartless, had gone away, leaving Nicandra with her great store of love unspent. Long ago, that child had crossed over into unreality. But the Nicandra who succeeded her was living on in a repeated loss where remembrance must be deprived of attention, objects supplied for forgetfulness when, beyond all sense, she knew that she would take him back to her heart tomorrow – now. She must keep to the proper new rules, stay strictly attentive to those small springs feeding the sources of habit, habit which would hold back despair. She must be neat and tidy, answer letters; pay bills punctually; feed the dogs regularly; make a real cheese soufflé; grow choice vegetables; shut her mind when a goose was slaughtered for the table; make a list of the silver; endure and moderate the mad exaggeration of Dada's bedroom. She would do all these minor tasks with care and interest. She would be a good steward and put the house back as it ought to be. Not for herself either. She was isolated, ringed round with cold in an endless solitude. She would contain her loss. Sorrow could be contained. What else were widows made for?

For a start, there were suitcases to be unpacked, impossible to deal with that until she cleared all the broken rubbish from her room. In the meantime, they could wait in the night nursery, Nannie's room. Lal had slept there too. She opened the dividing door and touched the light switch beside it. Two lights went on, one by the bedside. That was a neat little piece of comfort. She would exchange it for her faulty lamp. She went into the room and then shrugged backwards at what she was seeing: arranged in an orderly manner as though on display in celebration of some eighteenth-century gentleman's life-style, Dada's clothes, for all occasions, were laid out with the utmost particularity, their smallest details lovingly cherished. When did men stop wearing spats? Chalky pale spats – black laced shoes? buttoned boots, boned to form a second skin. Hunt buttons gleamed, frostily bright. Leather gaiters and spur straps, laid flat in a row on a folded copy of *The Times*, were soft as chicken skin – the strappings on hunting breeches were delicately coloured, buff, rust, yellow. Breeches were scrubbed to the bone – coats hung on chairbacks – trousers were folded flat to their creases, two pairs were in a press as though to be ready for wear – waistcoats for day and evening, cardigans, camel and lovat coloured, not a button missing, were folded as though in a shop and laid on Nannie's bed, together with underclothes, all of the finest wool, pants and long johns and vests, their separate piles tilted a little towards the long-deserted hollow of Nannie's mattress. A leather hat-box, lined in red, held the grey Ascot top hat – the solar topee of Indian days perched on a knob of the brass bedstead.

Who could wear and carry off the neat perfection of Dada's dressing? Who could understand its importance to him and to others of his kind and date: appalled by this sudden testimony to a living Dada, Nicandra looked back for remembrance or for love. Nothing she saw evoked what had never existed. She had not grieved for him and tonight nothing she saw brought her any closer to her silent little father. The distance between them had never changed. From the dreadful evening when he had refused *Dora's Dolls' House* as a substitute for the sympathy she did not know how to declare, until the last minute when, undefeated, he rode to his death on a lawn mower, Aunt Tossie's gloriously mistaken present, she had never known him: poor little Dada. She picked up a blue bird's-eye scarf, wondering if it could be of any use to her. It had not been washed and smelled of cigarettes and, more faintly, of its wearing against flesh. She tried to foster sympathy because she so much needed reasons for loving. Perhaps this prompted her to handle and refold a pair of the pyjamas, stacked on Nannie's bed – at the bottom of the tidy striped flannel collection, were three pairs of blue silk, heavily frogged; there, sympathy left her . . . she was back on her knees on Maman's side of the bed, saying her prayers, knowing she was being hurried away from Maman who laughed and smelt so warm and sweet in bed . . . prayers said, she danced her way to the door, pausing for the admiration they forgot to give, before she left them alone together. That was the day that Dada had lost Maman – that Maman was lost to both of them and Nicandra was left with Aunt Tossie who was so kind and smelt so differently, the soak of scent extinguished in her heavy breath. She had never been free of Aunt Tossie's encroaching love: never, until Andrew became the whole of her life, the object for life itself: a lost object.

Now, when life offered something for her comfort, a responsibility beyond her caring for dogs and horses, bantams and geese, Aunt Tossie had become elusive of her possessive care; watchful, and with guile somewhere in her watchfulness. She was old, of course, an old baby who should have snuggled contentedly into Nicandra's long-delayed love. Perhaps, just as it had been beyond a child to accept Aunt Tossie's unbounded love, so, their status with each other reversed, she had needs Nicandra could not supply. It was Silly-Willie, sure in the power of his service, who came between them. Nicandra was invading a territory where he had been supreme since Dada's death; and indispensable before it. She was aware of a polite enmity, evident in his superior knowledge of Aunt Tossie's needs and fancies. He was involved in her obstinacy about the caravan: over-familiar in his diligent service – tonight she had seen him, his arm enveloped in long stockings, turning them the right side out and pulling them toes to heels. He would have been busy with the dirty underclothes if she had not interfered. It was all wrong: his displacement as personal maid-in-waiting would be a first necessity in the fulfilment of her happy responsibilities towards Aunt Tossie.

Back in her bedroom, the light-bulb warm in her hand, she felt the silence of the big, empty house, not entirely friendly. The audibility of unseen objects tipping and tapping, near and distantly, was distinct in her hearing; there was a shrinking and an expanding in the newly heated air of a room sucking warmth into its foggy damp. A wire coathanger swung its small, bell-like sound against the door between the nurseries. Nicandra felt more comfortable at the contented breathing of dogs under the bedclothes. She fell asleep with both of them motionless and warm at her back.

Defeating her sleeping pill, Aunt Tossie woke in darkness. The bed, with its weightless blankets and an eiderdown rising like a whiff of smoke when she moved, did not suit her at all. She liked to be well tucked-in under six heavy blankets; and she liked linen sheets, turned sides to middles, darned and turned again as time went by. Now, when she pulled the eiderdown up to her fat cold shoulders, it slid away; escaping on a runway of satin sheets. As she woke further she thought longingly of the china po with its comfortable handle and bunches of flowers, sitting empty in its compartment in her distant caravan. She had foreseen trouble in getting from bed to bathroom, and she had been right. The heavily curtained and blinded room was dark as a ditch; no amount of fumbling could discover the night switch by her bed.

Out of bed, and drowning in the obscene darkness of the room, Aunt Tossie panicked. Beset by her immediate problem of getting to the loo in time, she became totally lost in her search for the bathroom door. She dragged desperately at a window curtain; it only answered to some device she did not know about. Darkness persisting, she struck her bare toe on some imperceptible object, and the pain went through her like a knife. She hopped and jumped about, a heavy, wingless bird in her white nightdress, until, by luck, she found the bathroom door. When she opened it, light flooded out; Nicandra had remembered her promise. Even that benefice did not compensate for the cruel diffi-culties Aunt Tossie had suffered. As she sat, relief flowing through her, a resolve was absolute in her mind. No loving coercion would succeed in keeping her caged and closeted for her own good. Her own good, or her own bad, were her own concern, her own sacred cows and causes. Even though Nicandra, this child she so loved, was to be her warden, she could never yield up her independence. She was not, for the moment, anxious about the little nips, often required at non-drinking hours; she was far more concerned for the po in its accustomed place, the electric kettle within reach of her hand, the small tray left ready-set with teapot and tea-cup and milk jug. Biscuits were in the blue box with Pussy on the lid (William never forgot to replenish it with her favourites). The silver tea caddy just fitted on to the tray, together with its caddy spoon, a minute silver shovel that had been at Deer Forest since tea drinking became a fashion. Even to please Nicandra, there was too much familiar comfort to give up.

The vast sunken bath, the enormous bath towels, hot on their rail; the battery of sealed scent bottles wait-ing their release on to steamy air; the bed next door where she felt that long ago she could have enjoyed a good romp – all this luxury was far from seducing her now. Just one night was what she had said, and as she searched in vain for the hidden gadget that would flush the lavatory, just one night was what she meant.

Aunt Tossie left the bathroom door open to light her way back to bed. Exhausted by her wandering, she fell asleep at once and did not wake until she heard the happy rattling of a tray outside her door. William knocked, and came in before she answered.

"I looked in a couple of times and there wasn't a note out of you in the night, Madarm," he said.

"William! Where did you sleep?"

"Out there in the music salon I had a blanket on the settee."

Although it must have been forty years since she had seen *The Cherry Orchard* and hated it, Aunt Tossie's thoughts flew to a younger Firs.

"That was quite unnecessary, and very naughty of you," she said.

"Ah, what harm! And you're looking great this morning." He was opening the curtains to the low glare of a rainy day. "Put on your cardigan, Madarm, I brought up our warm blue, and I'll give you your tray." He looked absurd. The studied elegance of the room seemed to lessen his height. He might have crept out of a shell. Aunt Tossie accepted him as wholly hers.

"No egg?" she had lifted the lid off her hot plate.

"Bacon toast, today," he said. "Too many eggs would sicken you. Eat it up now before . . ." He paused meaningly. She knew what the pause conveyed ". . .before it's gone cold," he finished, looking over his shoulder as if he was being followed or overheard. "I brought it up early, you had such a light dinner, I said you'd be starving."

Crunching up her bacon, Aunt Tossie nodded: "I don't think I closed my eyes all night." She sounded almost ill-used.

"I'd say you were only in the want of your own little couchette, Madarm. I wonder will I warm up the caravan? I will, will I? I will." He both asked and told himself.

Aunt Tossie nodded. "Well, yes, perhaps." She had not

exactly given an order, or withheld one. She was being naughty, as she had been in other times when naughtiness was a natural part of living. Then diplomacy had seen her safe round many an awkward corner. And diplomacy must be her safeguard now.

Nicandra woke to a fusillade of barking from her dogs. Willie, with a tray in his hands and the smell of really hot toast in the air around him, was standing halfway between door and bed. She wondered for how long he had been there looking at her sleeping.

"Oh, pardon. You didn't hear my knock," he said, modestly apologetic.

"Thank you Willie. I never eat breakfast," she lied, and waved away his approach with the tray – was this unkind? Toast to make, and a heavy tray to carry up all the stairs, poor mite.

"Well, perhaps, only for today," she accepted unwillingly.

He still delayed. "And the dogs, Madarm? Should I let my little people out now, or later?"

"Oh, give them half an hour. And shut them up while I give mine their turn."

"Certainly, and of course. Have you everything you need now Madarm?"

"Yes, thank you. What time is it?" She looked at her watch.

"Half past *nine*! I must get to Mrs Fox-Collier." She pushed the tray aside.

"Madarm is very comfortable. We had a good night," he was the bright nurse in charge. Before he shut the door he paused, smiling to say: "Back in our caravan since eight o'clock this morning."

216

He had gone, running down the stairs, before Nicandra could make a comment or a protest. It was the opening of a duel, and the lady they fought over would play them one against the other. Today would be difficult. She saw another problem as she looked out of her window: Nettle and Knobble were sniffing, raising legs, and kicking back at grass in a belligerent and suspicious way. If they met again, what might happen to her own two darlings? The anxiety grew; it was a situation that must be resolved. She would be fair, but she would have to be strict.

The thought of Dada's dogs, troublesome as it was, drew her to take another look at Dada's clothes; somehow, they too must be dealt with. She sighed: another disturbing thought. She looked in to assess the size of the problem, and stood, confounded at what she did not see. The chairs and the bed were empty. The cupboard was bare. Near her in the night, and silently, Silly-Willie must have been in and carried everything away. He was a cat, carrying kittens in its mouth from a dangerous nest to a safer hidden place.

Reason and good sense advised her that he was only forestalling what must be her wish, if she chose to occupy the nurseries. Still, even with due allowance made, these comings and goings in the night disturbed her – this extremity of service was unnatural. It was Good Fairy stuff: sixpence under your pillow for a tooth. That memory flickered to life in this nursery room; with it, other memories broke surface to submerge again purposefully unconsidered. They could have nothing to do with this splinter of mistrust which had already dug its way, as though under a finger-nail, into her difficult mission. These comings and goings, so quiet and so near, were, for all their dedicated industry, a creeping threat to her authority. Willie had chosen his own odd time to forestall any order she might think of giving him – or had he? She could understand, though vaguely, what it meant to be in the thrall of that terrible wish to give and to please, but the revenge life takes on those who

217

please and give too much was far beyond her understanding. Now that she was finding a way out of limbo, with Aunt Tossie to cherish, and the resurrection of Deer Forest to control, she must not be thwarted by any kind of subtle interference. Sitting up in bed, drinking scalding tea, she brought wilfully to mind cheerful and sensible ideas: as she invented them, her eyes filled and flooded.

An hour later, and with her dogs on their leads, Nicandra was at the foot of the stairs, when she heard Silly-Willie's voice sounding almost exuberant, on the telephone. "Oh, a grand breakfast . . . four rashers with fried toast and a good slice of black pudding," was what she heard. Then: "Yes. I'd say I have the situation in control. I wouldn't say we'd be needing you at all today."

"Who was that?" she asked when they met in the hall, both on their way to Aunt Tossie. She guessed who it was. This was clearly a matter for discipline.

"Dr Tynan, Mrs Bland, to enquire for Madarm."

"Yes, I'll speak to him."

"Oh, a pity! He's rung off."

"I'll ring back – what's his number?"

"I couldn't say. He's away on a difficult confinement. I wouldn't know where she lives, poor woman! She'd hardly have the telephone."

"I see. Well, please remember, in future, when the doctor or anybody else rings, let me know and I shall come to the telephone."

"Excuse me and pardon. I'm so used to speaking for Mrs Fox-Collier I wasn't able to delay him. He was on about his patient – having a baby is horrible don't you agree, if you thought about it you'd go mad."

"Mrs Fox-Collier is his patient too – and you do realize, Willie, don't you, that I'm going to look after her now. That will give you time to get on with your own work, won't it?"

Looking around her at the dust and grime, thick over everything, she felt herself an austere head-housemaid

– Lizzie, perhaps, rebuking some underling from the bogs. She remembered how frightened the underlings were of Lizzie.

Silly-Willie's eyes crossed and squinted up at her: "Do you wish me to bring Madarm her morning coffee? I was just on my way to making it."

It was not a query. It sounded more like a veiled refusal of obedience.

"Of course, for the present." Nicandra had a further answer ready. "In future, please leave the Cona in the morning room. And, that reminds me, the place must have a really good hoovering before Mrs Fox-Collier moves in."

For the first time he looked at her appalled, and spoke like a human being, not a pseudo-butler. "That'll be the day." The venom in his utterance was plain.

"You do realize, Willie, that changes really are necessary ... and, are Sir Dermot's dogs in? I'm going to let mine out now."

"Yes, Madarm. Don't you hear them yourself? It's quite pitiful the way they're crying in the pantry."

She watched him listening intently and could feel their crying went to his heart. A dog worshipper, she could understand his pain. She was hurting him – once, in loss and aimless loneliness, he had been her victim too. She had slashed at his legs with nettles obliging him to eat a snail. .... Ring-a-do-aday, Ring-a-do-a-Dandy-o, she had hummed while he ate his snail and did a few dancing steps to her order. Rather nasty, but only childish fun. Afterwards she had given him a slice of chocolate cake. She shied away from the thought of that other day, when his mother had found them.

This morning she nodded a kind but definite dismissal and went into the morning room where sunless light spread dull and coldly on yesterday's tea tray, with its unwashed cups and plates; on the dead fire where raindrops blackened the wood-ash; and on Aunt Tossie's aviary of tapestry parrots, blazing their colours against the faded, tattered covers of very old chintzes; mended and cleaned, Nicandra saw that they could be distinctive and pretty – in gentle accord with the sun-faded carpet, its many roses dissolved together through the years, its solid worth undiminished. Her sense of possession startled her: the decision that this room must never suffer a vulgar change would be the start of her purposes for the rest of the house. A spark of true interest was alive, and glowing purposefully towards Aunt Tossie's well-being. If only – Nicandra sighed at the thought – humans could be more like dogs: adorable, sensible and agreeably faithful. "Poor loves, you're bursting," she murmured as she loosed them from their leads outside the window, and watched them tear away round the corner of the house. At least she had made things safe for them. They could take their pleasures and fulfil their necessities unobstructed by her watchful anxieties. Between her and Silly-Willie that much was clearly understood. She shut the window behind her and walked out into the rain that was falling like a curtain between the present day and yesterday's brilliance and light – her hair was straight as wet straw, its points sticking to her face, as she tried to open the door of the caravan, swollen from the rain. "Push, push," Aunt Tossie's voice sounded strong, even formidable, as if beyond patience with some fumbling idiot. Nicandra pushed her way in, determined on the long talk she was going to have. It would be tactful, loving and firm.

Inside Aunt Tossie's dwelling place, everything was repulsively utilitarian; all was in total contradiction to the wild beauty of a proper gipsy caravan, horse-drawn and with walls and furnishings decorated by coloured stripes and strange, bright monograms, mugs hanging on hooks and one great teapot, a person in its proper right. Aunt Tossie's caravan was totally and hideously a mobile home, and not a very sound one either – as she struggled to shut the strained and swollen door, a heavy drip from the ceiling fell on Nicandra's bent shoulders. This pleased her, providing as it did a peremptory and visible reason for Aunt Tossie's return to the house.

Serene in her restoration, Aunt Tossie sat up, straight and strong against the pillows and cushions of her couchette or bunk. Tapestry parrots spread their feathers and opened their crooked black beaks in dumb squawks at her back. In her cage, Gigi was linked, curiously lifelike, to her swing. Some green feathers, fallen on the clean sanded bottom of her cage, lent an effect of reality. Another parrot, a green one, flying in another jungle, was coming to life under Aunt Tossie's expert needle. She felt that a show of vitality, of healthy busy-ness, ought to convince Nicandra that all was well with her; the regimen of her life re-established and secure beyond the power of the dearest and kindest interference. Here she was, toes in the foot muff from the Bentley, a blue hand-woven rug on her knees, biscuits and the bottle of whisky waiting in the po cupboard until William brought her morning cup of coffee – of course, in her refusal of change, she would be loving and grateful to Nicandra. Tactful too. She foresaw a competition in kindness to be fought out between them. But, in the end, by this evening, her darling child would see sense in the matter. Now or never, as Nicandra had decided earlier in the day, was the time to establish her rights. For Aunt Tossie the caravan stood for the same importances as those of a child's house in the woods: daring, independent of authority, a retreat from common cares. She put her tapestry work down in order to re-light the torch of lavender stalks, waving it about, an incense to dispel any hint of fugginess that might displease Nicandra. For herself and William she had no such anxieties.

Nicandra bent her knees as she advanced towards a morning kiss. Although it was not really necessary to subdue her height, the posture, unrecognized within herself, was taken to make the caravan appear a more lowly and meaner place.

"Darling, you *are* naughty," was all she said in reproof of Aunt Tossie's morning flight.

Aunt Tossie put her censer down, leaving it to smoulder on a saucer by her bedhead. "I know I am," she held up her cheek for the kiss.

Nicandra bent down and kissed through the fog of lavender smoke. "I do love you," she said, "but you *are* naughty."

"I'm better here – comfier – all my little toe pads and things like that round me. You do understand."

"Fancy jumping out of bed so early – the doctor did tell you to keep quiet."

"That young saw-bones! And so I am. Look at me."

"He was really worried about you. I hope he'll be back this afternoon."

"Shan't see him – don't need him."

"You can't hurt his feelings – you can't be rude."

"Oh, well. . . ." Aunt Tossie let the matter drop.

"You looked so ravishing in that super bed." There was cajolery in Nicandra's fanciful remark. Actually, Aunt Tossie had looked a distraught child in her white nightgown, small fat hands coming through tucked cuffs – star-fishes in distress. This morning, her sumptuous quality restored, she was an empress in her purples. Nicandra was not entirely pleased to see her looking so comfortable and so well. Last night there had been every reason for insistence on her acceptance of proper care. Today her early escapade and her healthy looks lessened the sense and strength of that side of the argument between them.

"Do agree, please," she pointed up at the heavy drip falling from the greened ceiling. "Only look! The whole place is pouring water."

Aunt Tossie looked the other way. "William always puts a po there if it's raining."

"It's raining now. Torrents. Where is the po?"

"Don't touch it, please," Aunt Tossie's arm shot out to defend the po cupboard – that sanctuary for biscuits and whisky; in doing so she knocked over the saucer of red-tipped lavender stalks, most of which fell to the floor, setting fire to a paper handkerchief and a fragment of cotton wool. Others scattered, still smoking, in all directions.

"Now you see," Nicandra said with entire satisfaction as she stamped out the flames, "why I worry."

"It hardly ever happens," Aunt Tossie kept a cool profile on the disaster, "and I can always ring my bell for William."

"And what about now? This very morning? Suppose I wasn't here? And Willie . . . ."

"Darling, I must ask you again. Do remember to call him William. He does rather like it."

"William. All right. I'll remember. William was off on his bicycle – what happens then? He comes back to find you in ashes."

"Oh well, we're used to that sort of thing in our family. Think of Great Aunt Emily – she was *boiled*. In her bath." Aunt Tossie laughed merrily. She went on laughing, delighted at the opportune interruption.

Nicandra felt suddenly overtaken by annoyance and impatience. "Look darling, I must ask you – if you don't like Dada's dished-up expensive tarty bedroom – and I *do* see the point – what room shall I get ready for you?"

"Oh, my dearest child, don't give it a thought. Please don't."

"Last night you did rather promise to move."

"I didn't say yes and I didn't say no. I said, well, yes, perhaps. For one night, I said."

"Oh, the misery of it! Can't you see, if you're not burnt to death in here, you'll drown in your bed."

"Don't worry about that – I'm a strong swimmer."

"Oh, be serious. Which room? The Blue Room? The White Room? The West Room? The Lady Room? Which do you want?"

"What I *don't* want are all those stairs for William, and trays and fires."

"Very well. All right. We could convert the morning room. What about that?"

"Pure desecration. Pos and Elsans in there. How could you? Think of Dada. The very idea of it would constipate me silly."

"There's the downstairs loo."

"Miles away."

"I could take you there in a wheelchair."

"What an indecent idea – and where do you plan to sit, if you ever do sit? Tell me that."

"Perhaps the drawing room."

"Cold as the graveyard, and two fires for William."

"Do take William off your worry list. When I'm looking after you there'll be less excuse for the filthy state of the house."

"What's the point of dusting and polishing while the whole house is being torn to bits? Thinking about it really hurts me. I'm far better away from it all."

"Darling, couldn't you . . . for my sake?"

Desperate and blatantly, Nicandra pulled out the softest organ-stop of all, and waited.

"Please, please, don't be such a tease," was Aunt Tossie's light response.

Past patience or understanding, Nicandra drew a deep breath, looking for strength to make her final statement on the matter. Before she could put her decision into words, Willie came knocking and pushing effortlessly at the door.

Aunt Tossie was loud in her welcome, "Come in, come in," she shouted, "it's my coffee – elevenses are really common, I know, and I do love them."

Nimble and adroit, Willie threaded his way between them; a hand spread out with a waiter's confidence beneath a silver tray and a silver coffee-pot.

"I'll have to disturb you, Mrs Bland," he said to Nicandra, "we use your chair as a bedside table. And the orders for the lunch, Madarm?" He handed a pad and pencil to Aunt Tossie.

Refusing to accept the agility of her dismissal, Nicandra sat down again on a sharpish corner of Aunt Tossie's bunk, waiting for Silly-Willie to take his orders and disappear. She watched as Aunt Tossie, barren of inspiration, pondered over the scribbling-block, obviously without an idea in her head.

"We have our pork chops we didn't eat last night," Willie suggested. "What would you think of that?" The enquiry took the edge off any presumption on his part.

"Wonderful idea," Aunt Tossie scribbled and handed back the writing-block. Still Willie lingered. "What a wicked day, we'll have to get out our Receptacle." He was on his hands and knees, fumbling beneath the bunk, always coming a little closer to where Nicandra sat. There was an impatience, a yearning in Aunt Tossie's waiting silence, and in Willie's delaying until they could be alone. Nicandra sensed how comfortable they were together in a collusion and in a place where she was as much a spectator as in the Gate Lodge days when he had danced to his mother's tune. Now, when he danced attendance on Aunt Tossie, she knew the same senseless, nearly sexual, dissatisfaction that had filled her when she saw him lolling, a cherished baby, on his mother's knee. Now he was Aunt Tossie's baby.

When, after a minute, he rose from his scrabbling under the bed, he held a vast enamel po in his hand. "Excuse me again, Mrs Bland," he said, "if it's to catch the drip, we have to place the Receptacle just where you are sitting." And, as Nicandra moved nearer to Aunt Tossie, he added, "I left you a coffee in the morning room."

"And do drink it, darlin', before it gets too cold." Aunt Tossie was quick to second the dismissal.

A giantess in the confined spaces of the caravan, where three made an absurd crowd, Nicandra, when she stood up, hit into and almost overturned the great birdcage that made a formidable fourth in the congestion. The impact threw Gigi off her perch. The feathered body fell on to the sanded floor. The legs, now bodiless, remained, still tied to and swinging lightly from the perch.

Aunt Tossie screamed. Willie, standing po in hand, appeared for the first time to be slightly disconcerted. Nicandra, without a further thought beyond finding a purpose for outstaying Silly-Willie, opened the wire door of the cage and pulled Gigi gently out, loosened feathers clouding around her hands; as she looked closer, she saw bald patches and, round them, terrible white mites squirming at the roots of the feathers which remained. With a yell of disgust and revulsion, she dropped Gigi on Aunt Tossie's gros point, a bright winding-sheet.

"She's crawling with lice – just look!"

"Oh *no*. Poor love ... my Gigi." Aunt Tossie put her little hands over her eyes.

"Don't upset yourself, Madarm, don't give it a thought. A dash of the Mothproof will soon settle that."

"How can you talk such nonsense? Open the door and throw that horrible thing out. The whole place must be infested." Nicandra's panic was well justified.

"I'll speak to the Post Mistress," Willie said, calmly. "She'll get after that Taxiderly fellow in Cork. It'll be O.K. Madarm. We'll have her back in two-twos and you won't know there was ever a thing wrong with her."

He had picked Gigi up, and Nicandra thought she could see the bird heave in his gentle hold. "Out, throw her out," she ordered. "Did you hear me?" As he still delayed, the unquestionable authority of her family spoke coldly: "At once," she said. She didn't wait to ask for Aunt Tossie's agreement. Delay was out of the question. The matter was vitally urgent.

"Oh no, don't. She'll get so wet." Aunt Tossie's voice was small and anxious, as though Gigi were alive with more than vermin.

"But you must see, darling, *now* you must see," Nicandra mislaid any tenderness, "why you can't possibly stay here?"

"Oh, Nicandra, please. Don't ask me to decide. I'm too upset. It will be all right, won't it William, just try the Mothproof." When she put her hands down from her face, Nicandra could see that she was turning a very queer colour. She recognized that, for the moment, she must accept defeat: a heart attack would be the next calamity.

"I'll see you in the morning room," she said to Willie.

"Yes, Madarm. The minute I know how do Madarm react to her tablet." He looked up from fumbling in the pockets of an enormous striped house jacket. Their depths swallowed his arm and seemed beyond the reach of his groping hand. When he straightened to his proper height, he was holding a pill bottle and spilled a tablet into the palm of his hand.

"Just the one," he spoke to Aunt Tossie, as a mother might coax a child. "Take it easy, pet, don't upset yourself, Madarm." Here, the small endearment was more than out of place: or was it? Nicandra, shocked and frightened by the tears and snivel on Aunt Tossie's face, and alarmed by her colour, felt herself to be the well-meaning District Visitor, interfering fatally in a family affair. To stay any longer in the caravan was suddenly beyond endurance: she would be crying too, or screaming, or scolding if she did not get out. As her foot slipped and she almost fell off the worn rubber-coated step of the caravan, she saw another cogent reason to overrule Aunt Tossie's absurd determination to defend (with Silly-Willie's entire co-operation) that horrid fortress.

In the morning room, Nicandra shook rain from her hair and stupid tears from her eyes, as she looked out at the hideous bulk of caravan, a monster nudging against the house, in its unsoftened glory of bathroom-white paint. Now it sheltered conspiracy. As Willie's absence stretched from minute to minute, anger grew beyond her control. Her rights to defend and comfort had been stolen from her with frightening slyness and – most bitter – the theft condoned and accepted by the one who was now the sole object for the love and care which could redeem her loneliness. She knew she must part them. She no longer saw any reason to maintain a false ambience of tact and conciliation.

When Silly-Willie came quietly in, he put down the coffee tray and the cardboard box he was carrying, shut the window with a sort of quiet insistence before, smiling and smug, he faced her, waiting politely for her orders, the tray balanced again and the box swinging from a loop of string round his finger.

How to begin? How to place her reproofs so that they might sting home? The question of Gigi's disposal hovered, hideously unsolved, between them. "What have you done with that stinking bird?" she asked.

"I was only very lucky to drop on this neat little shoe-box – Madarm's new felt slippers, I got a great bargain with them, only fifteen and sixpence in Keneally's Sale – I'll cycle away now before I miss the Post Mistress, it's her day for the bus to Cork."

"You don't seem to understand. That bird must be destroyed. Today." Gigi might have fluttered out of her box and risen on wings between them, her presence was so real.

"I think I might say we have the matter in hand, and Madarm is getting over the fuss now. She's taking a nice little doze after her tablet, and yourself saw, Mrs Bland, she was very, very upset. The heart isn't up to any annoyance."

"And when she finds these awful creepers in her hair, or in her bed, don't you think that's going to annoy her?"

"Yes, indeed. Wouldn't the thought of that sicken you?" Willie spoke in his most refined voice.

"Yes – it does sicken me, and it's not going to happen. Please believe that I know what is best for my aunt. That bird must be burnt, burnt UP."

"I couldn't do that, Mrs Bland, I couldn't annoy Madarm like that – if even there was a mouse in the place I'd catch it in my teeth before I'd upset her."

They stared at each other. Nicandra's eyes were big with anger. Silly-Willie's leaden-blue peep-holes in his head flared up at her, a light in them she had seen before. That was when Anderson held a lamb's head down between his boots. Helpless in her necessity to hurt, she lashed out at him: "And this very day," she said, "Mrs Fox-Collier is leaving that filthy bug-house."

"Don't do that – that's dirty."

When had he said it before? "Don't do that, that's dirty." The butler's voice was gone. They both remembered. It was on the morning when he had clung to his navy-blue shorts as, curiosity and cruelty the panaceas for the loss of love, in her loneliness, she held the tiny creature by the back of his jersey and whipped round his bare knees until he obeyed and stood, stripped to his school boots and stockings, so that she might see what it was that girls didn't have. She laughed at what she saw and switched round his legs again until he showed her how he made a trickle . . . that was when his mother found them. She pulled him into the house, still crying and trickling, and banged the door shut without a word to either of them. There was a silence before Nicandra heard him screaming. A word from her would have spared him the beating, but she did not say it. She turned and ran, back up the long avenue to her approved playthings: the pony, the bantams, the dogs, proper friends and companions for the little girl in the Big House.

Now the obscenity was alive again between them, freed from the impenetrable reserves of childhood, those silences that have no confidante. For who could understand such a strange caper? Or explain away the horror of kittens drowning in a bucket? Or the light in Anderson's green eyes? All were dark places, staying powerful with their hoards intact. Now, insanely returned to the levels of childhood, adult dignity and proper use of authority gone, her height dwarfing him as it had when he was six years old, she bent forward and snatched at the box in his hand. Regardless of servility, he dropped the tray he was holding, clutching Gigi to his stomach as once he had held on to his shorts. In fitting accompaniment to the scandalous mêlée, china and silver crunched and clattered under their feet as they fought for possession.

The contest between them was still undecided when the telephone rang, imperative, insistent for attention, demanding its answer. It would be the doctor; and this time, whatever it cost her, she was not going to be cheated out of her consultation with him. She let go her hold on the shoe-box, well aware that Silly-Willie would be off on his bicycle, pedalling as fast as he could go to deliver Gigi to the post mistress. But, as she hurried across the hall to the gun room, the idea that she would, of course, ring and countermand his instructions as soon as the doctor was off the telephone, came to her in a flash of relief. Angry and ashamed, her beauty fragmented away, and panting still from the ugly stress of the past minutes, she snatched the telephone from the wall bracket as its tenth bell importuned uncertainly. She was only just in time.

"Yes, Nicandra Bland speaking – Doctor Tynan? ... Oh, Doctor Tynan, how wonderful, I've got on to you ... Not? ... Who? ... Who is speaking? ... It's a hopeless line ... I'm so sorry ... could you say your name again? ... Oh........" She held the telephone away from her for a moment, then very close as though she must not miss a word that was spoken. When she answered her voice was formal, even businesslike, although the telephone was shaking in her hand. "Hadn't you better talk to my lawyer? Not? Why not? . . ."

A small cry choked its way back into silence as she listened.

Then she said: "No. You're so right. No, I don't. I don't believe you. You'll go back to her . . . of course you will – first chance."

She had put the telephone halfway on to its hooks when her mind changed and she went on listening. It was like reading a forbidden book – a book that seduced, proving all time well lost until its climax was reached.

Once she said: "No. I couldn't. You've hurt me too much!"

Soon, as she listened on, her fragmented beauty began to be joined again – there was delight even in her breathing. Mistrust and grievance were turning back into rapture. A surrender, coarse and true in its yielding, was changing her from cold laurel into eager nymph, feet on the floors of Paradise. . . .

"Where shall I meet you? Where? The boat train? I'll be there. . . . Yes, of course I mean it. And you'll be in time for lunch." She was giggling like a happy housemaid. "You won't believe it, but I've still got some of Robert's foie gras." Her mind was spinning fatally towards cooking and cosseting.

She listened again. "No. I hadn't heard . . ." Only for a moment something darkened the radiance that enclosed her . . . "Robert? *Dead*? No. Dropped over *France*? Are you sure? It's not very like him. . . . Useful – how? . . . Oh, the wine – yes, I see – all those contacts . . . Yes . . . Such a good grocer too, poor love. . . ."

She put the thought of Robert aside, and her voice, which had thinned, dropped again, heavier and sweeter, into the volume of her delight. In this blessed hour the air round her, shuddering and fully possessed by her happiness, could only be compared in its opposite intensity with the dark unease revisiting a haunted place. A great rush of energy, strong as a morning in spring, swept through her: her heart moved. She could feel the change.

Distraught in happiness, an idiot trust restored, she was hurrying on her way to the wine and the pâté and the car, when she heard once again, dreadful and unmistakable, the noise of dogs fighting. Slaughter was going on in the dining room. In a moment, pity and remorse seized on her. How had she forgotten them? Why had she trusted Silly-Willie to obey any order? She screamed for him as she ran across the hall, veering like a bird in flight down the winding lanes of stacked furniture. She screamed, remembering that the door would be locked and he had the key. Hopelessly, she tore at the handle and thrust against the door with her shoulder. It opened into the dark, shuttered room, quietly as though still dignified in service. When she called out to the distant dogs something of the rhapsody and exuberance in her voice reached and quelled them. Lifted back by their silence into her unearthly flight of happiness, she called again, her loving voice echoing sweet as honey down the empty room. She ran, almost waltzing forwards across the boards, bared as for dancing, until – blind and unknowing – she plunged down through the gap where rotten boards were torn away and the empty drop was left unprotected. She knew no terror, no cry came back as her head hit the flagstones of the wide basement passage. Her body, heaped together on the stones, jerked once or twice before she stayed still, coffined and certain in her happiness.

In the kitchen Silly-Willie crossed himself and said a little prayer before he ran upstairs to let out the dogs.

Abacus offers an exciting range of quality fiction
by both established and new authors.
All of the books in this series are available from good
bookshops, or can be ordered from the following
address:

Sphere Books
Cash Sales Department
P.O. Box 11
Falmouth
Cornwall TR10 9EN.

Please send cheque or postal order (no currency), and
allow 60p for postage and packing for the first book plus
25p for the second book and 15p for each additional
book ordered up to a maximum charge of £1.90 in U.K.

B.F.P.O. customers please allow 60p for the first book,
25p for the second book plus 15p per copy for the next
7 books, thereafter 9p per book.

Overseas customers including Eire please allow £1.25
for postage and packing for the first book, 75p for the
second book and 28p for each subsequent title ordered.